A LAUGHING MATTER OF PAIN

By Cynthia Hilston

© 2018 Cynthia Hilston

Published by Cynthia Hilston
No part of this work may be reproduced without written permission from Cynthia Hilston, except brief passages for review purposes.
This is a work of fiction. Any resemblance to real people or events is completely coincidental.
Cover design by Cynthia Hilston
Cover art from Jens Lindner at Unsplash

To Cole and Catherine

CHAPTER 1

Damp. Dank. Dusty. Dirty.
It's become a kind of game. I'm good at games. How many words that begin with the letter *D* can I come up with to describe this place?

Disgusting.

There's another point for me. 1-0, Hank, old boy.

Of course, you never talk much. I'm lucky to get the occasional grunt from you, Hank.

I roll onto my side, the lumpy mattress beneath me protesting as it pushes back in all the wrong places. Hank's sleeping, if you can call whimpering and moaning while he pisses himself sleeping. Nightmares, of course. Not that Hank ever has much to say about that.

But back to my game. It's not like I'm going anywhere.

Dank. Yep, that smell of musty, rusty mold growing on mold has attached itself to my nose like a cold that doesn't leave. It's my constant companion, whether I want it or not. I suppose it's like the games I'm so good at. So good, in fact, that when I lost one, boy, did I ever lose.

I don't know what nightmares plague Hank. Maybe it's what landed him here that's got him all caught up in nightly visions of Hell. Rumors say he killed a man in cold blood, but a man who wets himself like that ain't a cold-blooded killer in my book. Whatever his problems, I've got enough of my own.

I damn near laughed when the guard who swung by last week said Prohibition ended. Fourteen years of outlawing alcohol, and now part of the reason I'm here's legal again? How's that for justice?

Alcohol's my problem. Yeah, I admit that, but that's not my nightmare. Green accusing eyes, cruel laughter falling from a red-lipsticked mouth that kissed me silly too many times to count, and the red hair to match...like flames that burn my insides every time I close my eyes. I don't have to be sleeping to see her. Red everywhere, from the smashed in windshield, to her smashed in face, decorated with shards of glass as her stunned expression stares back at me with those eyes. Always those damn eyes. Even empty, they accuse.

* * *

Eight years earlier...

It's late, but the dusk is still dimly lighting the western sky. Overhead, the stars poke out from the black. Most wouldn't believe I have the calm inside me to stop and notice. When the others aren't looking, I sneak away into the back yard, that dewy grass tickling my neck as I lie in it and watch the stars.

Footsteps disturb my concentration. I bolt up, my eyes adjusting until a man's silhouette rests against the freshly painted white siding of our house.

"What're you doing, Harry?"

"What's it matter? Is Ma looking for me? Tell her I already put the delivery away."

"Ma said Mr. Morris was here hours ago and that you didn't touch the stuff till after dinner."

I try not to roll my eyes. "Then what's the problem, Erik?"

My brother plants himself in the grass beside me and sighs. Even in the near darkness, he's the pretty boy every girl wants. He got all of Pa's charm and looks: the blond hair, the blue eyes, the smooth-talking way with the girls.

"It's tomorrow," Erik says. "Graduation."

"Yeah? And? You haven't shut up about it for weeks, even months. What, you scared you won't be the center of everyone's attention anymore? No more calls from girls? Hell–"

"Harry, if Ma heard you–"

"Well, Ma's not here, is she? Virginia Williams called again, didn't she? I heard you," I say lightly, jabbing him in the side. "'Oh, Ginny, honey...'" I raise my voice an octave, but Erik cuffs me roughly. "Jeez, what's that for?"

"Can you be serious for a second, Harry?"

I raise my hands and eyebrows at the same time. "All right, I surrender. You wanna wrestle it out for old times' sake? This grass has our names written all over it."

Erik glares. "This was a mistake. Goodnight, Harry."

As he retreats, he kitchen light goes off once he clicks the back door shut.

"What's got his undies in a twist?" I mutter to the stars.

Erik and I were always scrapping in this yard as boys, always inseparable. In a few months, I'm gonna start tenth grade, and he's off to college. Not only does he have the looks and the ways with girls all right, but he's got smarts and talent on the field. Star pitcher of Benny Frankie High in Cleveland, Ohio.

Sighing, I stand and brush the grass from my pants. I head inside and find my annoying little sister standing on the landing of the stairs. It's Hannah, the older little sister. Irma's the other one, who's still so young that she really is little.

"Hey, Hannah-panna," I say, smirking.

"Oh, stop it, Harry. You think you're so funny."

"Actually, yeah."

"Ma was looking for you."

"Wow, I'm a popular guy. I almost feel like Erik, I'm so popular. Did a pretty doll give me a call?"

Hannah places her hands on her hips in a manner that's suited her well for years and sticks her tongue out. I laugh as she turns and stomps up the stairs.

"You know, for a young lady, you're pretty immature," I call up after her.

I quietly chuckle to myself. Hannah's always easy to get a rise out of. Sobering, I climb the stairs, and when the third step from the top creaks, I tip my imaginary hat at it.

"Goodnight, old friend."

I turn for the second door on the right, ready to see my esteemed brother. The door to my parents' room opens and Ma steps out.

"There you are."

I stare back at my twin—well, except that Ma is a good thirty-five years older than me and female, but the mousy-brown hair, the square jawline, and the plain face, yeah...thanks, Ma. I got Pa's baby blues, at least, but I ain't complaining, I swear.

I pretend to yawn. It's a convincing act, my mouth all wide and my eyes screwed shut, but Ma doesn't buy into my cheap acts.

"Tomorrow is an early day. I trust you're on your way to bed."

I smile. "Righto. Erik's big day. 'Night, Ma."

I kiss her gently on the top of the head. I'm taller than her now, so she tilts her head up.

"What was that for?" she asks.

The question's so simple, but it's not. Deep down, just like the times I seek out the stars by myself, some part of me reaches for my mother. I laugh instead.

"Can't a son give his old ma a kiss? Maybe I'll lay it on sloppy next time, like Flossie."

Ma isn't buying this, either. She doesn't seem interested in anything I'm selling these days, but maybe what she's buying into is more than just cheap tricks and one-liners.

"Harry, are you all right?" Her glistening eyes search me.

This look unnerves me. All the times Ma's glared at me don't probe me the way those hazel eyes see me now, like stripping me bare to my soul.

I shrug and smile. That's what she expects. What they all expect. Why give her anything else? "I'm fine."

CHAPTER 2

"You knew today was going to be an early day."

With a groan, I open my eyes, expecting to find Erik hovering over me like one of those strange alien space-things you read about in pulp magazines. Instead, sunlight blasts me straight in the eyes. I squint and manage to sit.

"Hey, good morning, brother," I say, my voice scratchy. "I don't suppose you brought some milk up with you?"

"You know Ma won't let us eat anywhere but the kitchen. C'mon, Harry. If we're late because of you—"

"No need to get all in a pickle. I'm up."

I smirk, half-annoyed, half-amused. Lately, Erik's sense of humor seems to have taken a detour out his backside. Maybe if he pulled out the stick he's got shoved up there, his sense of humor would find its way back in.

"What's so funny?" he asks.

I realize I've been smiling to myself. "Nothing you'd appreciate. Okay, let's get you graduated and moving on to higher edu-ma-cation."

Erik leaves, and I scratch at the poison ivy rash on my leg. I blame Pa for that one—making me clear out the weeds in the garden before planting a couple of weeks ago. By the time I'm downstairs, I find the kitchen table empty of people, my place setting left alone. Ma bustles about the place like a confused bee who can't decide which flower to pick.

"It's cold," she says, her back to me, indicating the food with a wave of the arm.

I'm already shoveling the eggs and bacon into my mouth like I haven't eaten in a week as she finishes talking. When I shrug and gulp down the milk, Ma turns and frowns. Hannah chooses that moment to walk in and wrinkles her nose at me.

"You're disgusting, Harry."

She's already dressed for this momentous occasion, her dark-blond, bobbed hair combed and held in place with a clip.

When I belch, Irma giggles as she prances into the kitchen and lands on my lap.

"Hello, itty-bitty Irma," I say. Like me, she's got Ma's brown hair and Pa's blue eyes. She's much cuter than me, though.

Irma beams and hugs me, but Ma shoos me out. As I stand, I stop to whisper in Hannah's ear, "At least Irma's happy to see me."

I leave her with those words of wisdom and run upstairs to throw together something that's presentable. When I return downstairs, I'm not surprised when Ma finds something to criticize me for.

"Did you even brush your hair, Harry? When's the last time you had a haircut? If we had the time now—"

"Pa's waiting!" my older sister, Amy, calls from the back door.

Amy is the eldest at twenty-three and is basically a more mature version of Hannah in terms of looks. In personality, she and Ma could be two peas in a pod. I've never been close to her. I think the words I've said the most to her over the years have been "I already have a mother, thanks."

Ma ushers me out the door. My sisters are crammed into the very back seat of our seven passenger Caddy. Pa is behind the wheel. I hope Ma and Pa don't get any ideas of springing another kid on us because I don't know where they'd sit. When Ma told us about being pregnant with Irma three years ago, I thought, for once, she was joking. You can imagine how well Ma took my remark at the time when I thought she was just putting on a bit of weight.

Ma takes the front passenger seat, leaving me my usual place next to Erik in the middle seat. Erik's already dressed in his navy-blue cap and gown, a medal around his neck for graduating Summa Cum Laude.

Pa starts the engine and pulls out of the driveway. As he drives, he doesn't remark on my tardiness, but that's Pa for you. He's Ma's polar opposite. In his easygoing manner, he says, "You know, Erik, I only went to school until third grade. I'm proud of you, son."

If Erik had any humility, he might've blushed, but he just smiles. "Thanks, Pa. Well, I worked hard. I won't let you down."

"Yeah, you're the first one in the family to go off to college," I say. "I guess the rest of us don't know much about working hard."

"Your grades could be better, Harry," Ma says. "Now, this is your brother's day. Don't ruin it."

Hannah sniggers in the back seat.

Eyeing Erik, whose gaze challenges me, I reply, "Wouldn't dream of it."

I lean back with exaggerated casualness, my arms raised and crossed behind my head. I close my eyes and try to imagine a house without Erik, a place where I might be noticed for something other than everything I do wrong.

Several hours later, after Erik has paraded himself across the stage and basked in the applause of hundreds, we're back home. My parents go out to eat about once a year, so we've met our quota for 1925 because Ma and Pa indulged Erik in his request for seafood. As I step out of the car, the fish doesn't sit well with me. Or maybe that's just an excuse.

"I'm going for a walk," I say.

"Be back in time for dinner," Ma replies.

"That's hours away, Lucy," Pa says, then looks at me. "We'll see you later, son."

"I don't think I could eat anything if I tried," I say. "If I'm not back for dinner, don't wait up."

Hannah purses her lips. "You mean, you're not hungry for once? Usually you eat like someone's going to take your food away."

I'm not in the mood for jabs as I turn and trudge down the sidewalk. I'm a good ten houses away when I hear a voice calling after me.

"Hey, Harry! Wait up, will you?"

I'm torn between stopping in shock and quickening my pace. Erik would probably outrun me, so I reluctantly halt and allow him to catch up.

"What?" I ask pointedly.

He raises his eyebrows. "Now who's in a bad mood?"

"Did you come to rub it in that you're moving up in the world?"

He holds out a basketball. "Actually, I was just gonna ask if you'd like to shoot some baskets, but if you don't–"

"I never said I didn't." My stomach settles.

My brother walks alongside me for a while in silence. We reach the park's courts and dribble the ball between us. The years fall away. The differences that have come between us seem to die as we become two boys playing a fun game again.

I laugh at the brother I used to know as he pretends to limp across the court and then shoots a perfect basket. Somewhere in the middle of all this, he says, "I wanted to tell you last night…"

I'm dribbling the ball as he speaks and lose my focus, the ball rolling away.

"What?" I ask.

Erik's eyes shift, as do his feet. Left to right. Right to left. He opens his mouth like a gaping fish outta water. Next thing I know, he darts off to the left, grabbing the ball and dribbling around me in circles.

"C'mon, Harry. Show me what you got!"

"Ha, I might not be as tall as you, but don't forget I'm not done growing. One day–"

"One day you'll be taller than me? I don't think so!" Erik taunts me as he lifts the ball just out of my reach, but I'm ruthless.

We go head-to-head like this for the next several minutes, teasing and laughing. I finally manage to snag the ball from him and make a basket. Stopping to catch my breath, I wipe my sweaty forehead with the back of my hand, my hair sticking to it. I wonder if Ma might've been right about the haircut thing.

"If we were smart, we would've brought some water and changed our clothes," Erik says.

"Oh? Brainy-boy Erik's admitting he's not as smart as he thinks? But yeah, Ma's gonna have a field day cleaning these. I can hear her now. It'll be just like old times."

"Old times," Erik murmurs. His grin droops, like someone painted a smile on an otherwise drawn face.

"This here, right now, is the most fun I've had in...I don't know how long," I tell him.

I've never been the sentimental type. I trip over my words like my feet trip over my laces as I step back.

Erik tosses the ball at me. "Rematch?"

I catch the ball, sure and steady in this sport. "Oh, you're writing your death sentence, old boy. I'm gonna wipe you out. You might be good on the ball field, but you got nothing on me in the court."

The time forgotten, we while away our afternoon like that. By the end of it all, we strip off our dress shirts and stroll home in damp undershirts, arguing over who really won and who smells worse.

I'm not sure who smells worse, but as far as winning goes, I'd say today was a winner for me.

CHAPTER 3

The moment I wake up, Ma's on my back like a heavy rock to do my chores. Erik and I pour sweat in buckets as we work in the garden. Every morning starts like this. Then Erik and I shovel vegetable soup into our mouths like we're starving at lunch. When done, we dart outta Ma's way before she smacks us for no manners.

"Honestly, you two," she says, her brow stern, "act your age. Don't forget that you have to spend the next hour either reading or sewing."

"Since when have we ever chosen sewing, Ma?" I ask. "Even Pa thinks it's ridiculous."

"C'mon, Harry," Erik whispers. "Best to just get it over with."

We go upstairs before Ma can say another word. Erik picks up a tattered copy of *Crime and Punishment* and lies on his bed, immersing himself in the novel, his nose practically buried between the yellowed pages.

I sigh and pick up *Huckleberry Finn*.

After five minutes, I say, "That book should be a crime and a punishment to read. It's certainly a punishment. Look how thick it is."

Erik lowers the book enough to look at me. "You know, Harry, some books are actually quite good. You never have the patience to give anything a chance. This story teaches us about the human condition."

"The human what?" I shake my head and reach between the mattress and the box spring and pull out my new pulp magazine. I slide it into my book and pretend that Huck Finn is as interesting as an alien invasion.

At the end of the hour, Erik remarks, "Don't think I didn't see that. What garbage are you reading now?"

"Nothing so enlightening as *Crime and Punishment*, I'm sure." I make to set the book aside, but Erik is too fast and snatches it from my grip.

"*Attack of the Killer Moonmen?*" He chuckles. "You don't really think men live on the moon, do you?"

I shrug. "Maybe, but who cares? Our time's up, so let's get outta here before Ma comes up with another list of chores."

Erik hands me the book back, and I stuff the magazine back under the mattress, placing the book on the night table.

Erik's already gone, and I wonder whether I should follow him. As I walk past the bathroom, I catch a glimpse of my reflection. There are three tiny hairs on my chin. I touch them almost reverently and smile. I'm becoming a man. I run my hands through my hair as I continue walking, feeling the botched job on top of my head. Ma was too enthusiastic with those scissors last week, so my hair sticks up in every direction.

When I reach the bottom of the stairs, I find Hannah practicing the piano in the living room. The music's been coming up through the floorboards for the past fifteen minutes, but I've learned to tune it out. I watch her move her hands over the keys in well-practiced fashion, a bit envious that she has such a talent. She stops playing and whirls around on the bench.

I lazily clap. She scowls.

"What are you doing, Harry?"

I smile to indulge my little sister. "You always think the worst of me, Hannah. It's like you don't trust me."

"I didn't say that, but you're usually looking for trouble."

"Yeah, well, you know what they say about trouble and middle names. I'm officially changing mine to 'Trouble' when I'm of age."

She smiles. "You're completely bananas."

"Mmm, bananas...sounds good to me. See ya later."

Ten minutes later, I walk down Madison Avenue with a half-eaten banana in my hand. There's no sign of Erik, so I check to see if Mitch Woods is home. I'm in luck as he comes to the door, and when my buddy sees the peel, he asks if I have any more food.

"Nah, sorry," I say as we walk along the sidewalk and toss the peel into a neighbor's trash can.

Mitch is two years older than me and has been friends with Erik and me since before I can remember. Plain's the word to describe us. We don't stand out with our brown hair and average builds.

"You haven't seen my brother around, have you?" I ask.

"Nope. Why?"

I shrug. "Just askin'."

"He's off to college, right?"

"Yeah, soon. We won't be seeing him for a while, but enough about my brother. So, what do you wanna do?"

Mitch eyes up Hatford Park across the street. "Remember?"

A LAUGHING MATTER OF PAIN

I share a devilish grin with him. "How could I forget?"

We dash across the street with the boldness of idiots. A few kids run around the picnic tables playing a game of tag, and off in the distance, a man is throwing a ball to his dog. Other than that, the place is empty. We approach a cluster of willow trees, the July breeze gently swaying the branches. Beyond the trees, the pond—what we called a lake when growing up—sits calm.

I chuck a rock into the water, creating ripples. As I throw another and then another, I don't know what's come over me, except that I want to disturb the peaceful water. "The girls were always trying to bust us when we were kids," I say.

"Yeah, but they thought it was funny to spy on us." Mitch chuckles.

"Ever think of doing it again?"

He looks at me like I've lost my marbles. "You crazy? We can't go skinny-dipping anymore."

I see the flush on his face. "Damn, you burn easy," I tease. "We can afford to live a little."

Mitch shakes his head. "In broad daylight?"

"Where's your sense of adventure, old boy?" I take off my shirt. "I won't let you live this down."

Mitch turns around as I strip down completely.

"What're you so worried about?"

I don't wait for his answer as I back up and get a running start, then dash toward the water. I cannonball into the pond, and as my body makes contact, I close my eyes in the thrill of the moment. After a brief stay underwater, I bob to the surface, laughing. I swim around the pond in large, exaggerated breast strokes and roll onto my back, gazing at the sun.

Then I hear the voice that seems to have a hobby of following me lately. "What the hell?"

I stop swimming and am not surprised to see Erik standing next to Mitch. I'm not sure whose face is more amusing, but I'm too caught up in having a good time to feel any shame. Erik's face changes from stunned to disappointed to downright disgusted.

"Get out and get your clothes on."

"Yeah, yeah," I grumble.

My good mood pops like an over-inflated balloon because of my brother's over-inflated ego. I swim until the bottom touches my legs, then stand and leave the water. While grabbing my clothes, I keep my gaze on an interesting patch of bark on one of the trees and dress.

"Where'd you go, anyway?" I glower at Erik.

"What's it matter?"

I turn toward Mitch, in the hopes that he might have grown a backbone in the past thirty seconds. I'm sorely disappointed to find him backing away with his hands held up in front of him.

"You know what, guys?" he says. "I just remembered...my mom wanted me to, uh, clean the toilet bowl before the day's done." With that parting remark, Mitch is gone.

"I don't wanna argue with you, Harry."

"Oh? That's news to me. Seems to have become a habit for you lately."

"Maybe I've grown up."

I hate that I want to punch my brother in the face, but I also want nothing more than to wipe off that smug look. "You say you don't wanna argue. Then what're we doin'?"

Erik steps closer. For a split-second, I think he's going to take a swing at me, but maybe that's because my hackles are up. "You're reckless. You don't take anything seriously."

I laugh bitterly. "You used to call it fun. Egging that cad Theodore Wilson's house was worth it. He picked on me all last year."

"What about when you tried smoking in eighth grade? I covered for you."

"So, what? It's called living a little. Ever think that maybe life isn't all about grades and books? Real life, Erik..."

"Ah, so it's experience you're looking for? That's your reason?"

"You say I'm never serious. Well, how's this for serious, brother?" I storm up to him, even though he's a good four inches taller than me, and shove him in the chest. He stumbles backward and falls hard on his ass. When I march off, he doesn't pursue me. I wonder if that stick he's got up his backside fell out when he hit the ground.

I don't return home for several hours. By the time I approach the back door, darkness has settled in. I stop, in no hurry to enter and receive an earful from Ma for being gone all day. While I wonder if she left any food for me, my gaze falls on the board that covers the window on the door. There used to be glass in that window, but I couldn't tell you how many times Erik and I broke it over the years from playing ball. Finally, Pa just put a plank of wood there and left it. I look up. No stars tonight. Only clouds. I grimace and make for the door.

Beyond the kitchen, light from the dining and living rooms spills through the doorway. The radio's on, the volume low. I expect to find my parents in their usual spots: Ma in the rocking chair with her knitting, glasses perched on the end of her nose, and Pa in the armchair, listening to the jazz music that Ma so dislikes. Before I can take another step, Ma is upon me, throwing the kitchen light on.

"Oh, thank the good Lord," she breathes, pulling me into a tight hug.

I awkwardly place my arms around her. "What's wrong?"

"We had no idea where you'd gone off to. Erik returned hours ago and said he hadn't seen you."

"Sorry, uh...I'm fine."

"Don't ever do that again, Harry."

Pa joins us and frowns. "You had your mother worried sick, son. I'd ask where you were, but I suppose we should just be glad you're home in one piece. Never again, you hear?"

"Yeah, Pa. Sorry. I didn't do anything, uh, bad if that's what you're thinking." Pa's disappointment stings worse than anything Ma could say.

Ma yawns and waves me off. The frown lines around her mouth are deeper than normal. Her puffy eyes are shadowed. "Eat something and be off to bed."

She's kept my plate covered. With nothing short of affection for Ma, I sit down and eat the chicken, potatoes, and vegetables. Despite the cold food, it sits well with me as a warmth at being missed settles inside.

The lights are out when I go through the living room and up the stairs to my bedroom. "Don't tell me you're still reading that garbage," I say in way of greeting when I find Erik still up.

Erik lowers *Crime and Punishment* and glares.

I drop onto my bed. "You didn't tell them about the skinny-dipping."

"No."

"Why?"

"And risk Ma having a heart attack?" Erik's tone is light, almost teasing.

Our gazes meet across the short distance, and even though Erik isn't quite smiling, I think he's trying hard not to.

"Thanks," I say.

CHAPTER 4

As the summer wears on, my brother continues to be an enigma. He used to be so easy to understand because he was just like me in many ways. If I'm honest with myself, I don't even understand why I do or say half the things I do anymore.

In August, Amy surprises us by saying she's dating someone.

"How did you meet this young man?" Ma asks over dinner one evening.

"I'd like it if you brought him by. I'd like to meet him," Pa says. The twinkle is out of his eyes, his mouth a firm line.

"We met through a mutual friend from work," Amy says. "I'm twenty-three, Pa. Really, don't you think I'm a bit old to be bringing my boyfriend around for my parents to meet? It might not even be anything serious." Her face flushes. She's probably twiddling her hands under the table like she always does when she gets agitated. I keep my eyes on her, taking a bit of pleasure in her discomfort, wondering how this conversation will go.

"You're still a young lady," Pa says.

"Erik gets tons of calls from girls," Amy says. "Why should this be any different? I'm five years older than him. Ma, you were my age when you met Pa."

"Hey, don't bring me into this," Erik says.

I smirk, trying not to chuckle at this free entertainment.

Ma sighs. "You're right. I was, but girls—women—were more mature back then than they are nowadays. The way they flaunt themselves—those flapper girls with their bobbed hair and too-short dresses. All that jazz nonsense, dancing, and illegal drinking. People are wilder than ever."

I try to imagine Amy dressed as a promiscuous young lady, smoking and drinking. It's damn near impossible.

"I'm hardly a flapper, Ma," Amy says. "How often have I told you times change? When will you realize that things aren't going to just go back to the way they were thirty or forty years ago?"

Ma harrumphs and digs into her food.

One point for Amy.

Pa shakes his head. "Can we please not argue at the table? Amelia Rose, despite your opinion on the matter, you still live under the roof of this house. Your mother and I wish to meet this young man because we want what's best for you. The matter is closed."

Oh, the full name. My gaze shifts from Pa to Amy.

"Father," she groans, removing the napkin from her lap and setting it on the table. "I'm suddenly not hungry." Amy walks away from the table and leaves through the back door.

"Enough," Ma says. "Let's eat before dinner gets cold."

"Well, I think it's awful that Amy has a boyfriend," Hannah states. "I agree with Ma and Pa that it just isn't right. Next thing you know, she'll be wanting to get married and moving out."

I chuckle. "Good one, Hannah-panna. You took the cake on that one."

"What?" Hannah asks, scrunching her face up at me. "It's the truth."

"I believe I already said that was enough," Ma said.

"But–"

I keep my mouth shut as Hannah's silenced, but I'm glad to see I'm not the only one who causes tension in this house. I don't bother Hannah the rest of the evening, although it's tempting. I'd love to see Amy have the gumption to keep dating this mystery man, but as the day gives way to the next, her bad mood doesn't lift. At breakfast, she hardly touches her food. She's out the door for work by the time Hannah comes down.

"You just missed Amy," I say to Hannah in between bites of oatmeal. "She was in a wonderful mood this morning."

Hannah rolls her eyes as Ma enters, Irma right behind her. "What did she say?"

"Not two words," Erik says. "No 'good morning.' Nothing."

I'm about to add my two cents when Ma says, "Amy went to work like she's supposed to. The rest of you would do well to finish up in here and be about your business. Your father has plenty of work for you boys outside with harvest time upon us and won't be too pleased if he comes home and it's not done. Hannah, you're going to help with the laundry."

Erik and I get done in the kitchen. I don't complain too much today about the chores. It's a nice day–not too hot. Besides, this story ain't over with Amy, and Hannah's disapproval of the whole situation adds another layer to it.

While Erik pulls weeds and I pluck lettuce and cabbages, I say, "What d'you think of all this?"

"What?" Erik keeps his back to me.

"Don't play dumb. C'mon, brother. You gotta admit–this is new for Amy."

"I say good for her. She's old enough. I kept wondering when she might marry and move out. She's well into her twenties, and if she waits too long, her prospects will be all dried up. No man wants to marry an old maid."

I laugh. "You planning on marrying young?"

"Marriage?" Erik asks incredulously. "I have college first, then find a job. By then, I'll be Amy's age. That's years away."

"Well, I never know with you, since you have at least a half dozen girls calling you at any given time. Who's the latest catch? Maybe you should bring her around."

"We're not talking about this anymore." Erik's neck reddens and I'm sure it's not from the sun.

I shake my head and return to picking vegetables.

By evening, Amy returns home with none other than her boyfriend. He's a good-looking guy who's easy to talk with. He introduces himself to Erik and me in the living room.

"Jack Banks," he says, his handshake strong.

"Hi, Jack. I'm Harry. So, my sister says she likes you. Lucky you."

Jack grins and wraps an arm around Amy. "I'd say I'm the lucky guy, but she is quite the doll, your sister."

Amy's practically glowing. If it were dark, she could light up the room.

Erik and Jack exchange introductions, and Großmutter, our grandmother who moved in with us a few months back, is saying something in German, but if her smile were any wider, the wrinkles on her face would crumble off.

Irma comes down the steps quietly and enters the room, and Jack gets down on one knee. "And who's this little sweetheart?"

"Irma," my littlest sister says shyly.

"What a beautiful name." Jack picks her up and tosses her up in the air. Irma giggles as he catches her.

Conversation flows naturally, and the lighthearted jokes are in full swing when Pa joins us. For a moment, I wonder if he's gonna kick this charmer out on his backside. Pa's taken with him the moment Jack approaches him. For Amy's sake, I'm relieved. Unlike Erik, I never imagined her as an old maid—not that I'd tell her that.

Before I know it, we sit down for dinner. Everyone seems to have taken a liking to Jack, except Hannah. All through the meal, my little sister sends little-concealed glares at Jack and strikes Amy like a question-firing squad. After dinner, she plays for us, and maybe she's a bit happier.

As I'm off to bed, I wonder what's been going on with Hannah and think of teasing her in the morning to get an answer out of her. It's not like I'd want her to think I'm really concerned or something.

A LAUGHING MATTER OF PAIN

* * *

Weeks pass, and Erik packs for Ohio State. It's September by now, and I've started tenth grade. I'm already being compared to my brother by many of my teachers, and I tell Erik that I have some big shoes to fill.

"It's true," I say the night before he's to leave for Columbus. "Do any of those girls you talk to know just how big your feet are?"

Probably in spite of himself, Erik stops in his tracks as he's about to put a stack of shirts in his suitcase and looks down at his feet. "You're exaggerating."

I roll my eyes. "Don't you get enough sweet talk from your admirers?"

Erik doesn't answer for a while. Instead, he resumes packing. When his suitcase is stuffed to the brim, he has a hard time shutting it and resorts to sitting hard on it to get it to close. "You might wanna start shaving, Harry, if you want a girl."

I smirk. "Maybe I'm trying to grow a beard."

Erik laughs. "That would be one pathetic beard."

I shrug. We fall silent and focus on everything in the room but each other. The sun is setting, casting an orange glow on the walls and furniture. The floor is well-worn from years of us tracking mud and sprinting across it to see who could make the most noise. On the dresser—Erik's stuff in the top two drawers and mine in the bottom two—we share a picture of us from probably ten years ago, our smiles reflecting our innocent mischief.

"Yeah, well...goodnight," Erik says.

"Goodnight, brother." I go for nonchalant, but my voice cracks a little at the end. How embarrassing.

The next day, Erik doesn't say much. Our sisters are crying, of course. Women. It's not like they'll never see him again. Ma's a mess. Pa's driving Erik down, and I'm still not clear on why Ma is staying home, other than her need to keep the house clean and the rest of us kids fed.

I stand out in the driveway, watching Erik load the last of his things into the trunk.

"Well, don't do anything too stupid," he says to me, a smirk on his lips but a plea in his eyes.

"Stupid? Me? Nah. You got the wrong guy."

Erik half-steps toward me like he's about to hug me, but he stops and nods. "See ya around."

"Yeah, see ya."

I keep my eyes on the back of his head as he gets into the car. As it pulls away, my head's filled with all the things I just couldn't say, and I ain't sure why.

CHAPTER 5

High school's been a notch up from junior high so far. I made the team for basketball and a bunch of new buddies.

Thanksgiving and Christmas came and went. Erik was home, and for a few days, it was like he'd never left.

Overall, I'd have to say I don't miss Erik that much. At least that's what I tell myself. But it's like I've got this freedom I never had before.

So, the guys from basketball and I are good. Good at winning. Good at flirting with all the right girls, the ones with the boobs and the looks, and damn, they know it. Good at having a good ol' time.

I've just finished another game on a frigid January evening, and the team gathers around school afterward. George Michaels, who's just turned sixteen, is boasting about being able to drive. My parents were at the game, along with my younger sisters, and they expect to drive me home, but the pressure's high to go out with my pals. Truth is, I ain't sure what I want to do.

"Hey," I tell George, "gimme a minute. I wanna check with my folks."

"Don't take too long. I'm not waitin' up."

I grin like a fool as I walk away. We won. Again. At this rate, we'll be going to states. I spot my parents waiting at the bottom of the bleachers, near the exit.

"Good game, Harry," Pa says with a wide grin. "You've really got some talent on the court."

"Thanks, Pa. Hey, listen—"

"Are you ready to get going?" Ma asks. "It's late, and Irma should have been in bed an hour ago."

I bend down and look my tiny sister in the eyes. "Ah, but you had fun, didn't you, Irma?"

Irma nods. "Yeah, you're the best, Harry!"

I stand and pat her on the head, then turn to my folks. "See? She's fine. Doesn't seem tired to me. Anyway, about that... I was hoping you'd let me go out with the team for a victory celebration of sorts."

"What does this involve?" Ma asks, her mouth a firm line.

I breathe a sigh of relief. "You know, just going to the malt shop nearby for some milkshakes for a couple of hours. George can drive now, so we're good."

"That seems awfully late, and for a bunch of underage boys to be driving, unsupervised... I don't like this," Ma states.

Hannah's strangely quiet through all this, but my eyes are on Pa now. Come on, Pa. Don't be a wet blanket.

"Well," Pa says, "you promise you'll be home by 11:00? You tell this George fellow that."

"Thanks, Pa!" I'd hug him if we weren't in public.

"Gus," Ma says, "do you really think this wise?"

Pa's eyes shine with mirth. "You're only young once, Lucy. Harry's been working hard this year. I'd say he's earned it."

"Working hard at basketball, yes, but his grades—"

I'm already walking away before they change their minds. When I join the gang, George raises his eyebrows. "Well?"

"I'm coming."

A few minutes later, we pile into George's car—well, probably his dad's car, but even then, it's a real jalopy. There's more of us than should ride in it, but we don't care.

"Sarah said she'd get the girls there," Willy Thompson, the tallest kid on the team, says. His feet are almost in my face as we ride in a mess of tangled limbs.

"You're havin' us on, pal," says Ed Miller.

"No, it's the Real McCoy," Willy insists.

"Ya might wanna get some foot powder, Willy, old boy," I say, trying to move my face a couple of inches away from his rank feet.

"Hey, guys. We're here," George says.

We all pile outta the car and into Jimmy's Malt Shop a minute later. The place is filled with the hustle and bustle of a young crowd out for a good time. As we find seats along the marble countertop, my reflection appears in the large mirror where the workers take orders at the other side. We spin on our seats, laughing raucously and competing to be heard over the noise in the small place.

We yell out our orders, pretending to ignore the scowls the owner's sending in our direction. I take the cue from Willy and lay it on thick with one of the girls who's working there as she asks me what I want. She's a real doll, with her red hair—probably not natural, but who cares?—and bright green peepers, the kind that seem to see right through me. I stare like a lovestruck fool at the cute freckles on her nose and look away only for a second to catch what's written on her nametag.

"Can I get you anything?" she asks.

Shaking myself out of my daze, I say, "That's a good question, Wilma. What d'you suggest?"

She doesn't seem taken by my act. "The chocolate is good. That's what everybody gets." Her voice is dull, bored, tired.

I drown out all the other voices around me and lean in, the cold counter pushing against my elbows. "Maybe I'm not interested in what everybody else wants."

There. That line was a winner.

"I didn't say 'wants.' I said 'gets.'"

"Well...just because someone gets something, that doesn't mean they want it, yeah?"

"Sir, are you going to order, or should I move on?"

Damn. This girl doesn't know the definition of the word "joke." I consider my options: risk further making a fool of myself or just place the stupid order. "Okay. No need to get your panties—"

Wilma gapes.

I sit up straight, done with the whole messy charade. "Sorry. Chocolate's just fine." The wind outta my sails, I lean back in my seat and turn, allowing the swivel chair to take direction. Then I spot them: the girls Willy had been going on about.

George sees them first and waves. "Sarah! Emily! Over here!"

The chairs are already filled, so there's a moment of awkwardness as the guys and girls try to work out the seating arrangement. I may not know much, but Ma raised me to give my seat to a girl. Seems some of these other guys could use a lesson or two on chivalry.

Emily Voss stands closest to me, so I stand and say, "Sit, please."

She's a cute little thing, the type of girl who looks like she could break if squeezed too hard. She runs a hand through her curly, dark brown hair and smiles shyly at me, those brown eyes looking down. "Thanks...uh..."

"Harry."

"Right, sorry, Harry. I'm terrible at names."

I wave her off. "It's okay. I don't expect to stand out in this crowd, unless it's maybe by my winning good looks." This earns a giggle from her. I know I'm being a ham, but dealing with girls is like entering a foreign country and not knowing the language, except maybe how to ask where the bathroom is. That's always handy to know.

"You played well tonight," she says. "What position do you play?"

"Point guard, and thanks."

"Sorry, I know nothing about basketball."

"I dribble a lot and pass the ball off to the guy who shoots it—usually George."

"He's the guy with the car, right?"

I glance over at George, who's got Sarah on his arm, but the moron's sitting as she stands and leans on him. "Yeah. Lucky stiff."

"Do you drive?"

This catches me off-guard. The truth would be the right thing to tell, but where's the fun in that? "I might."

Emily's eyes light up. "I'd love it if you'd drive me sometime."

"Yeah, sure."

My shake arrives, but before I can take a sip, Emily grabs it and drinks. Almost half is gone before she stops. "Sorry, I was thirsty. You don't mind?"

I might mind a little, but I shrug. This is the first time a girl's shown interest in me for something other than making her laugh. "It's yours. I can get another."

"You're sure?"

"Yeah. No problem."

We talk for the next few minutes, and the crowd starts to thin around us. I take the empty seat next to her and find I'm totally taken by this doll.

George stands. "C'mon, boys. Let's blow this joint."

"We were just getting started," I mutter, but no one hears me over the crowd.

"What about us?" Emily asks.

George eyes Sarah up and down. "Okay, you gals can come."

We pay and leave, but instead of piling into George's car, we walk around the back of the building. It's dark back here, and I'm freezing as the wind blows. I'm about to ask why he's brought us here, when he pulls something out of his coat pocket. After a few seconds, I see it's a flask.

"Lookee what I got here," George says with awe. "Nicked it off my old man."

Willy, Ed, and the other guys' eyes light up. Sarah laughs and claps her hands. Beside me, Emily seems tense.

"Well, ya gonna share or just stand there?" Ed asks.

"Whiskey...1899 or something," George says. He unscrews the cap and takes a swig, passing it off to Ed.

I watch as each boy knocks back the booze, screwing up his face at the taste. When it's my turn, I hold the flask a moment longer than everyone else. Emily tugs on my hand and whispers in my ear.

I raise the flask to my lips. The sensation goes straight to my stomach as the warm liquid burns on the way down. I pass the flask back to George, who grins.

"Good stuff, eh? Consider it a toast to another win. Who's up for more?"

I join the guys in their toast. Emily frowns and whispers to me, "You don't have to do this, Harry."

"What's the harm?"

"You could get drunk."

"Not off a coupla swigs." I laugh, grabbing the flask and taking part in our victory celebration.

We pass the booze around until it's gone. Every last drop. I feel slightly heady, but I'm much warmer in the winter air. George beckons us to his car, and the girls make to go their separate way.

Before Emily can go, I grab her hand and tug.

"Hey!" she protests. "A little rough, don't you think?"

I pull her toward me and chuckle. "I can be rough if that's your thing, doll." I lean in to kiss her, but her little hands shove me away.

"Ooo, so, you do like to play rough," I tease.

Emily wrinkles her nose at me in a very Hannah-esque manner and spits, "Clean up, Harry," and saunters off.

I turn to find the guys smirking, all grouped together.

"Tough luck, pal," Ed says.

They laugh, and I'm torn between joining them and taking offense. In the end, I join them. Can't mess up my reputation by being anything other than a clown. We cram into the jalopy Studebaker and scram, the engine roaring as George skids down the street.

* * *

Ma and Pa are none the wiser when I return home. As the weeks pass, I'm given more freedom than I know what to do with. The victory celebrations continue, although Emily's too much of a Mrs. Grundy to join the crowd again. There's no shortage of girls, though. George supplies the team with a flask every week, and I gotta admit—the alcohol takes the edge off. I'm not worried about a silly girl's rejection. Truth is, most girls are happy to be a part of the action.

There's a dance for Valentine's Day, and I snag a date with Mary Shermer. She's not quite the looker Emily is, but she'll do. I bet Erik never had this good a time. The gang heads out back after all's said and done, and George, good buddy that he is, has the booze. I taste Mary's sweet lips through the liquor, and all I can think is I've died and gone to Heaven.

"Damn, doll," I said, coming up for air. "You don't mess around."

Mary giggles, looking up at me through her lashes. She's the perfect height to rest her head on my chest. "Anyone ever tell you you're a good kisser, Harry?"

I smile. "All the time. Let's put that to the test, eh?"

Mary doesn't say a thing, because her lips are attacking mine again. I could get used to this, but then some killjoy chaperone yells, "Break it up! No necking on the premises allowed."

I reluctantly step away, but Mary winks at me. "There's always next time," she says.

* * *

After the Valentine weekend, it's back to school. That Monday night, I'm still up in the clouds. At dinner, I brag about my skill on the court, and Pa beams at me.

"You shoulda seen me at practice today," I say. "The coach said there isn't a better point guard on J.V. He says if I keep it up, I'll have no problem making varsity next year."

"Well done, son. I'm proud. Your school's got the best record in the county."

"Yep. Coach Davis says states are lookin' real good."

Ma sighs. "If only you had the same passion for your school work as you do for basketball, Harry."

But's Ma's remark doesn't get me down. Not tonight. Irma can't help but be happy whenever I am, sweet girl. Even Amy smiles at me. I eat a few bites and notice Hannah's been quiet through the whole conversation. I consider making a snide remark at the table, but Ma'd probably whack me.

After dinner, I follow Hannah up the steps and slap her playfully on the shoulder when we reach the top. "Did you see the look on Pa's face when I told him how well I've been doing at basketball?"

"Yeah," Hannah replies.

It's one word, but it's like all the fight has gone out of her. I stop and really look at her for a moment. Her back is tense, her shoulders drawn in. She's been in an off mood for weeks now, but tonight, something in her's finally broken.

"It's usually Erik and his sports abilities Pa notices. C'mon, little sis," I say more seriously. "You're a younger sister. I'm a younger brother. We can relate."

"What do you mean?"

"What I mean is, haven't you ever felt like you get overlooked?"

Hannah laughs bitterly. "All the time, lately." She pauses, then says, "It's nothing," and makes to walk away.

Her words could be mine, at least a few months ago. I get it. I really do. Deep inside, I grope for the right words, because I'm no good at this. But the feeling is there, that void looking to be filled. Yeah, I get that, even if I don't understand what I'm supposed to do about it.

"Hannah, come on. I'm mean it. With Erik gone, I finally feel like I'm free to shine in my own way and be noticed. When Amy's gone, you will, too."

"Maybe." Hannah doesn't seem convinced.

"You don't want her to leave."

"How do you know that?"

"You think I'm just jokes and good times, but I see the look on your face every time Jack comes over or Amy even mentions him. I can relate, little sister... All those times Erik got calls from girls when he was around, I hated him for it."

There. I've said it. I'm broken, too.

"But you and he were always together and goofing around, Harry. You seemed happy."

"A smiling face can hide a lot of pain, Hannah. Our time will come to shine. And you already do when you play the piano. Ma and Pa have loved that about you for years."

"Then that's why it's so important for you to be good at basketball." Hannah smiles. "Am I talking to a stranger? Who is this boy?"

"Maybe this boy is becoming a man, after all. Who would've guessed?"

A joke. After all, how else can I deal? I'll fill myself with endless jokes until I've convinced myself and the world that I'm happy.

CHAPTER 6

1930

I'm twenty, still living with my folks, and keeping plenty busy learning Pa's trade: making houseware deliveries and understanding the ins and outs of running his small company.

Erik's all moved out. In fact, he got himself hitched last year to a pretty little doll named Lily. They're down in Columbus, making their way in the world.

Amy's out, too. She married Jack a few years back and just had a baby girl, so Ma's happy as can be about that.

That leaves me as the oldest at home. High school seems like another lifetime. All those glory days of being a star player on the basketball team don't really measure up to much in the so-called real world. When I'm out on the town with Pa working hard, no one cares about Benny Frankie High's unbeatable record two of the three years I was there. Senior year, we messed up. Maybe got it in our heads too much that we were something special. No state champs that year.

I kept in touch with a few of the guys for a little while after high school, but they've all moved on. Mitch down the street got married earlier this year. Seems like everyone's getting on with their lives, and here I am, still trying to figure out mine.

Which leads me back to my family. It's funny, looking back a few years. I'd never have thought I'd be close friends with Hannah-panna. She gets me. I get her. I guess it's that simple. Once Amy left, it wasn't the end of the world for Hannah any more than it was for me when Erik got out.

I've dated here and there. Nothing serious. It seems like every girl I meet's just looking for a good time, and that's all good with me. Unlike Amy and Erik, I'm nowhere near ready to get held down by some old ball and chain.

It's September, and I've just finished up another hard day's work. The past year's been a rough one: the Crash, my grandma suddenly dying, and then our old dog right after that. But the Rechtharts keep plowing on.

After dinner, Hannah seeks me out. "I have something to ask you."

"What is it, Hannah-banana?" I flash an easy smile.

"Please don't call me that, Harry. We're not kids anymore."

"Sorry, sorry." I hold up my hands in mock-surrender. "Someone's a bit touchy, isn't she?"

"Harry, I'm being serious—"

"Something you're quite skilled at. All right. What's this about?" I can't help but smirk. Something's got her all in a tizzy, and I can't wait to hear what.

"I have an attractive friend at work named Kat."

"Meow!"

Hannah seems to smile in spite of herself. "Anyway, there's a party this weekend—some friend of hers. Kat's going to set me up with her brother, and she asked about you coming along as a sort of date for her."

"Some young doll wants me to go on a date? Sign me up!"

"I'll be telling her 'yes' tomorrow?"

"You'd better."

"All right, then."

* * *

I've been waiting for Friday night all week. It's funny how when you're anxious for something, the days seem to drag. "Just take your time, why don't ya?" I wanna ask.

The way Hannah's talked up this friend of hers, I don't wanna disappoint. I make an effort to look the part of a well-bred young man, so when I come downstairs with my hair combed and having shaved, I think Hannah might just faint from shock.

"I almost wouldn't recognize you, Harry."

I wave her off. "You look pretty spiffy yourself, little sister."

She blushes, and Pa walks into the room before either of us can say another embarrassing word.

"You kids have fun tonight, but don't stay out too late, okay?"

"Sure thing, Pa." I wink.

"I'll make sure we're home at a decent hour," Hannah says pointedly, challenging me with a look that rivals one of Ma's.

I raise my eyebrows and smile.

"Hit the road, you two," Pa says with a laugh.

We wave goodbye as we step out the door. The beams from the headlights of the jalopy pulling into our driveway are the only light we have to see by. The car screeches to a halt, and something bangs under the hood. The driver's side door opens and a man steps out, followed by the back door opening to reveal a woman.

The man holds out his hand to Hannah. "Hello, you must be Hannah. It's a pleasure to finally meet you."

Hannah giggles softly as they shake hands. "Hi there. And you must be Will."

"That's right. My sister has told me lots about you."

The woman who must be Kat steps next to Will. She hugs Hannah and whispers something in her ear. Hannah smiles and turns her attention to Will.

My sister and her new boyfriend seem to fade away as my eyes fall on Kat. The dark hides most of her features, but from what I can glean, she's a looker: full lips–good for kissing–and a small nose–again, good for kissing.

"Ah, you must be Kat." I grin as my hands dig in my pockets to keep my excitement down.

"Well, hello there, Harry." Her voice is like chocolate in my mouth. I could savor the sound of her words alone for days. She holds out her hand.

I take it and kiss it. No handshake for this dame. She giggles and takes hold of my hand, pulling me into the back seat.

Everyone's in the car in no time, but this old thing's cantankerous. It takes Will several tries to get the car to start, but luck's on our side once the engine roars to life. Will takes the wheel. Kat explains that we're going to a party at a house that belongs to her friend who married some big-wig doctor from the Cleveland Clinic. Damn. Millionaires Row. Everyone who lives in Cleveland has driven by those small palaces on Euclid Avenue, but how many have gotten the chance to go inside one, and to a party nonetheless?

I half-listen as Hannah goes on about our folks and Pa's job, but Kat doesn't seem to care about that. She turns to me and asks, "And what about you, big boy? I hear you're following in your father's footsteps."

"That's right. Even in these tough times, there's a need for deliveries."

Kat's practically sitting on my lap. Hannah focuses on Will. I take this moment to get a better look at Kat and see that she's got vibrant red hair. I can't tell the color of her eyes in the dark, but I'm banking on knowing by the end of the night. Her heart-shaped face is decorated with a pouty smile and lots of makeup.

"So, tell me more about yourself." Kat wraps her arms around my neck. She smells like vanilla and cigarettes. An intoxicating combination.

"What d'you wanna know?" I bring an arm around her lower back and draw her closer.

"Hmm, are you a good kisser?"

"Ah. I've been told so on a few occasions."

"Just a few?"

"Okay, more than a few."

Kat laughs. "So, you're an experienced man. Lots of heartbroken girls in the world because of you?"

"Something like that." I grin. "What about you? You a heartbreaker, Kat?"

"Why are you asking? You worried?"

"Nah." I wave her off.

Her smile widens, and she whispers in my ear, "I'm looking forward to a good time with you tonight, baby." Her breath tickles my lobe, the tingle going all the way down to my groin.

I'm about to respond when Kat turns her attention to what Hannah's saying. She must have one ear trained on my sister to have picked up on the front-seat conversation, because I thought we were in our own little world here in the back seat.

"I'll likely be married in a few years and then stay home," Kat mimics my sister. "Hannah, you sound so last generation! Why should every woman be expected to stay home and raise kids? Barefoot and pregnant, they joke, but it's true. You have a decent head on your shoulders. Why waste it when you could do anything you want?"

"You're older than me, and you're working as a secretary just like me," Hannah replies.

"I'm not old yet," Kat retorts.

Will pulls into the wrap-around driveway of an estate. As we step out of the car, we've entered a foreign world, the territory filled with orchestral music and butlers, guys toting trays of fancy-schmancy finger foods and wine, crazy-large chandeliers and winding staircases that make my head spin.

Kat and I follow Will and Hannah into a sitting room that's bursting with people. I exchange a look with Will that says, "I'm impressed." Will smirks back and wraps his arm around my sister's back. I make to do likewise with Kat and realize my arm's already in position. Kat is so close, she's breathing on me, my cheek warm—whether from her breath or the crowded room or my body's reaction—I don't know.

A bunch of introductions to what I guess are supposed to be famous people—or at least rich folks—begin. I make lazy conversation with these faces. One of the tray-guys is upon Kat and me, and I grab two glasses of wine, meaning to give one to Kat, but she's already snatched one for herself. Hannah shoots me a disapproving look, but what can I say? I'm here for a good time, and I've found over the years that a little booze can't do any harm—not that I'd tell Hannah that. She's too much of a goody two-shoes to drink a drop. I shrug and smile at her, and she turns her attention back to Will.

"You know," Kat purrs in my ear, "we don't have to hang out near your sister and my brother all evening. The night's young. We're here to live a little."

"I'm up for anything." I finish the first glass and set it on the nearest table.

"That's what I like to hear. Besides, Hannah's a great girl and all, but you have to admit, she's a bit uptight."

I laugh, already beginning to feel tipsy. I'm surprised to find my second glass empty. When did I grab that? "Looks like we'll need mora these." I hold up the glass to Kat.

"There's plenty more where that came from." Kat flashes her brilliant smile at me, and I notice the color of her eyes—a striking green. Hot damn.

She drags me by the arm into the dancing crowd, the music now in full-swing jazz instead of the earlier orchestral type. We lose Hannah and Will, but I'm too swept up in the moment to care. The alcohol's put me at Kat's mercy. She has me under her spell. This doll could ask me to drink poison and jump off the Brooklyn Bridge, and I'd do it just to see her smile.

I lose track of time as we dance the night away, everyone else fading into the background. We laugh, we drink, we eat, we smoke, and we dance some more. Sometimes we're with Hannah and Will, but most of the evening we're off by ourselves. Kat's laughter is like a drug, and by later, I'm not sure if I'm more drunk off her or the booze.

When the music slows, I expect her to lean into me and allow me to hold her close, but instead, she takes me out back into the gardens. Since the air is cool, goosebumps raise on my arms and neck. My legs aren't working right, all jiggly and wobbly. Kat leads me to a bench, and we sit. We haven't done much talking, but she doesn't seem interested in that right now. Her mouth finds mine and claims it. Our tongues mingle, the aftertaste of the wine still fresh. My hands busy themselves as they rub her back, then make their way lower, testing their luck by reaching under her blouse. I come to her bra and push further. My hand fondles her, my fingers working at her hard nipple. Our breathing grows heavier as our kiss deepens. Every part of me's on fire. This is living. I float into the closest thing to Heaven on Earth my foggy brain can imagine. Kat's hands glide down the front of my shirt and untuck it. She fumbles with my fly. I'm about to break entirely, to spill open my pent-up desire.

"There you are, Harry."

Hannah's voice is like a thousand trumpets waking me up in the morning, a bucket of ice poured over my head. With reflexes too quick for a guy who's had a few drinks, I draw away from Kat. "Yeah? Wha's goin' on?"

"Don't you think it's time we were leaving?"

Will stands beside her, looking uncomfortable. I half-wonder if he saw me groping his sister. Or vice-versa.

"Aw, don't be such a spoil sport," Kat shoots at Hannah. "The night's still young."

Hannah frowns. "We really ought to be getting home."

"We can always come back, dear sister," Will says to Kat.

Hannah goes quiet after that. The whole drive home is a blur. I might've passed out for part of it. Will pulls up to our house, and Hannah helps me out of the car. Kat blows a kiss at me and winks. I mean to smile, hoping it doesn't look more like a grimace.

After they leave, Hannah turns toward me, her brow creased. "Can you walk?"

I lean on her shoulder. "I'm fine." I sway, falling into the grass and laughing.

"Shh. If Ma and Pa find out, they'll have your head. Harry, what were you thinking?"

"I was thinkin' I'd have a good time. Kat certainly didn't mind."

"I'm not sure if Kat's company is good for you."

"She's your friend." My laughter dies. I bend over and puke in the grass. My head spins.

"Come on. Let's get you inside as quietly as possible. You're lucky it's Friday and not Saturday night, so no church in the morning. I'll make your excuses that you're sleeping in because you were out late, but never again, Harry."

I manage to stand and allow Hannah to lead me to my bedroom. We stand just outside the door.

"Take your clothes off and change. Give them to me. I'll...take care of them."

"Door closes first." I chuckle and enter my room.

Hannah frowns as she pulls the door shut.

I change into my nightclothes. I open the door and shove the smelly bundle of clothing at her.

"Go to bed," Hannah whispers. "You'd best hope you don't throw up again."

I smirk. "You worry too much, Hannah-panna. G'night."

CHAPTER 7

Next thing I know, my eyes open to a blast of sunlight. I groan, trying to sit up in bed, my head spinning, my throat parched, and my stomach in knots. I feel like someone ran me over with Pa's truck. For a moment, I wonder why I feel like crap, but then I remember.

A hotsy-totsy doll named Kat Jones. A wild party in a mansion. And booze. Lots and lots of booze.

Ma calls my name up the stairs, and I try not to cringe. A half-remembered memory that could've been a dream comes to mind of Hannah taking my clothes and saying she'd cover for me. Good ol' Hannah.

I manage to drag my sorry ass outta bed and trudge downstairs. Grateful to see my breakfast laid out, I eat, beginning to feel better as the food settles in my stomach.

"You certainly slept in," Ma remarks, her back to me as she kneads some dough.

It's Saturday, which means she'll be baking bread and kuchen all day long.

"Late night," I say in between bites. "Sorry."

Ma turns and surveys me in only the way my mother can. She wipes her forehead with the back of her hand.

"Your father will expect you out back when you're done, so you'd best hurry up and get dressed."

I smile. "Of course, Ma."

I find Pa a few minutes later. He's harvesting the last of the corn.

"Ah, good morning, son. I trust you had a good time last night?"

"Did I ever!"

Pa chuckles, adding a couple ears of corn to his basket. "What was your date like? Will you be seeing her again?"

"Her name's Kat, and she's something." A glimpse of fiery hair, a flash of green irises, the curve of her hips, the feel of her lips, the heat of our bodies...my mind won't stop replaying her memory. "I hope so. I'll have to talk to Hannah. She works with her, you know, so she's kinda my connection."

The crow's feet decorating Pa's eyes crinkle deeper as he grins. "You're about the age to start finding a good woman, Harry. Maybe she's the one."

"Maybe." I busy myself with the harvest. I haven't really thought about a future with Kat. Only the heat of the moment mattered when I was with her, but I find myself wanting to be with her again, before her vanilla scent and tantalizing voice fade away.

Hannah finds me that afternoon sitting on the glider in the backyard as I watch the clouds. She joins me and doesn't say anything for a long time. Finally, when she speaks, she sounds like a younger version of Ma. "I take it you're back to normal?"

I laugh. "If by 'normal,' you mean not drunk, then yeah. Otherwise, I don't know the definition of the word."

Hannah smiles, although her eyes sparkle with concern. "What I said last night, Harry–I meant that. I won't cover for you again."

"We've always had each other's backs. Remember the time you admitted to pulling the fire alarm at school? I never told a soul."

Hannah sighs. "I know, but, Harry, this is different. You could get in a lot of trouble. It's illegal."

"All right, I get it. Yeah, I overdid it a bit. It won't happen again. But you can't blame a guy for wanting to have one or two drinks when he's havin' a good time with his girl."

"Is that what Kat is? Your girl? It was only one date."

"Well, what about Will? You plannin' on seeing him again?"

Hannah blushes. "I had fun with him, so yes, I'd like to."

"Then it's settled. Why don't you ask Kat when you see her at work on Monday about us gettin' together this weekend?"

Hannah looks like she's considering this, then finally replies, "All right. I guess it can't hurt to go out again, but it would be nice to do something other than a wild party."

* * *

But another wild party, at least according to Hannah, is exactly where we find ourselves on Friday night. I gotta admit–Kat's sure got connections. I don't ask questions, but just roll along for the ride.

These weekends quickly become a trend. I don't hear Hannah complaining about the booze anymore, but so far, I've kept my promise. It's hard, but I don't go overboard with the drinks again. Kat gets me drunk enough with her body pressed into mine as she takes me for her own. Sometimes it's in some broom closet or servants' quarters. I've lost track of how many bedrooms we've danced horizontal in.

It's now December, and the first snow's covering the ground. Kat loves being the life of the party, but she also seeks out the gardens at these stately dwellings. As we stroll through the skeletal trees with their coating of white, Kat squeezes my hand.

"I like you, Harry," she says, swinging our arms. She lets out a long stream of smoke from her cigarette.

"I like you, too, Kat." I stop walking, taking in the scenery as I puff away on my own cigarette.

"What?"

"Just look. The stars."

Kat raises her eyes to the clear night sky. She releases a breath she'd been holding, the warm air visible in the cold. I stargaze, too, then I turn my eyes on Kat and enjoy watching her.

"It's funny... It's like seeing them for the first time when I stop and really look," she whispers. Her voice takes on a reverence I've never heard from her.

I give her hand a squeeze. "It's something I do sometimes," I confess, "go outside and just look at the stars."

Kat turns her eyes on me, her face more serious than I've ever seen it. "You do surprise me, Harry." She smiles, taking one final drag and putting out the smoke under her heel.

"I suppose I could say the same thing about you. I gotta ask, Kat... We've been seeing each other for a few months now, and I don't know much about you." I smash my cigarette underfoot on the pavement.

"What do you want to know?"

"Anything. Everything."

"Well, that's quite a tall order, Harry, my darling." She kisses my cheek and leans into me. I wrap my arms around her, keeping her warm. She sighs contentedly. "Well, there's not much to say about my life growing up. We're just an average family, but it's just me and Will. I think my dad always wanted his son to be the oldest. I really never got along well with my folks. They were always on my case about something. If isn't wasn't my grades, it was who my friends were."

I chuckle softly.

"What's so funny?" She turns and looks up at me, as if searching me.

"I get that more than you know. One difference is that I have an older brother. My ma was always goin' by his standard. 'Harry, why can't you be more like Erik?' 'Harry, your grades could be better.'"

"I don't like to talk about my family," Kat says, "but thanks for understanding. Working with your sister is okay, but it's not my dream. Anyone can be a secretary. My parents don't think it practical to be a hairdresser, even though I've made it clear for years that's what I really wanted. Even did my mom's hair since I was fifteen, and she was impressed. I guess that didn't matter much because she always harps on me about getting married and popping out a grandkid every year."

"So...marriage isn't something you're lookin' for?"

"Not right now. Don't tell me you are." Kat's voice takes on an edge, and she stiffens in my arms.

I release her, take a step back, and laugh it off. "Of course not, doll! Weren't we just talkin' about the expectations our folks have for us? Well, I'm too much a rebel to settle down."

Kat shoots me a wicked grin and launches into me, kissing me full and hard on the lips. When we catch our breath, she says, "Come on, Harry. There's a party in full swing inside, and I'm freezing out here. We're here to have a good time, so let's ankle!"

"I got no problem with that, doll," I say, allowing her to pull me along like a puppet. "About that havin' a good time part..."

But Kat's not listening. Tease that she is, we've lost ourselves in these gardens on warmer days, but something or someone always seems to ruin the grand moment. Now it's too damn cold outside. I try to think more with the head on my shoulders as we go back inside.

We dance like fools the rest of the evening, the earlier conversation trampled under our feet and lost in our minds in the haze. Hannah finds me and goes through her usual routine: It's late. We need to get home. Ma and Pa won't be happy if we get back after midnight.

Twenty minutes later, Hannah and I are shivering in our driveway as Will's tires squeal on the icy cobbled street.

"I'm thinking of bringing Will around to meet Ma and Pa," Hannah says as we walk toward the house.

We go around to the back door. It opens with a creak, and we step into a dark kitchen. Hannah throws on the light, and I wince for a second as my eyes adjust.

"Jeez, Hannah-panna, a warning would've been nice."

"You look done in. Your eyes are all red."

I blink and rub at them. "It's nothin'. But about Will...so, you're serious with him?"

"After what Amy went through with Jack all those years ago, I thought it best to be honest with our parents. What about Kat?"

"What about her?"

I yawn, moving into the dining room and then to the living room toward the stairs. Hannah turns off the kitchen light as she follows, and in the near darkness, I can barely make out the framed pictures Ma keeps on the mantel. Of course, I can't see the faces, but I know them like old friends. Our parents' wedding picture is in the middle, Amy and Jack's to the left of it. To the right, a casual photo of Erik and Lily sits, no official wedding one taken. I try to imagine pictures of Will and Hannah, Kat and me joining them. Kat and me. In a wedding photo.

Is that even possible?

Hannah's question could be a door that I'm trying to find in a blackened room, and even when I do, dare I open it? What lurks behind it?

"Well?"

I blink, but Hannah doesn't see that, any more than she sees that I'm falling for a woman who I think feels the same way about marriage that I do about lima beans.

I hate lima beans.

"I hate lima beans," I say.

"What?"

I laugh softly. "Gotcha, Hannah-banana. C'mon, let's hit the hay." I'm already heading up the steps before she can say otherwise. I close the door to any further questions.

CHAPTER 8

Christmastime brings the perfect opportunity, the perfect excuse, for Hannah to tell our folks that she's bringing Will around. I can already hear the question they wanna ask me, can see it in Ma's probing eyes and in Pa's twinkling ones.

"Yeah, I guess I'll ask Kat, too," I say at dinner a week before the holiday.

Kat doesn't fit into the Rechthart mold. She certainly ain't cookie-cutter. She's more like some exotic dish prepared by some fancy-schmancy chef in an overpriced restaurant.

When I ask Kat a couple of days later, she smirks, a gleam in her eye as she answers with a drawn-out "yes."

When the glorious day arrives, Ma still treats us like we're little kids, although Irma's still young enough at eight to get excited about gifts. Erik and Lily have driven up from Columbus, and Amy and Jack are there with their baby, Jean.

"So, I hear you've got someone special," Erik whispers to me after we finish dinner, like he's sharing some conspiratorial secret.

"Yeah." I shrug. Play it calm and collected.

"Tell me about her."

I gaze at my brother for a long, hard moment, wondering if he's just digging for something to criticize. "Oh, you'll meet her soon enough."

Erik raises his eyebrows and turns his attention back to his wife. I don't see much of them, but whenever they visit, they're usually huddled together. Lily's a nice enough girl, definitely pretty, but she hardly says two words to me most of the time.

As if on cue, the doorbell rings, and it's a race between Hannah and me to get there first. We reach the door simultaneously as my brother chuckles behind us. Since Hannah's closer to the knob, I give her the honors.

Sure enough, Will and Kat are standing there. Kat's hair is a new shade of red. Women might accuse men of never noticing stuff like that, but with Kat, nothing about her goes unnoticed.

"Well, merry Christmas!" I say in an over-the-top voice. "Do come in."

Hannah half-smiles at me and beckons them inside. "Don't mind him. You know he's crazy by now."

"Just by now?" I ask.

Hannah shakes her head as they enter. Kat kisses me on the cheek, and I wonder if everyone's watching, not sure why I should care.

Pa, kind as ever, approaches first. "Ah, this must be the elusive Kat," he says, holding out his hand.

Kat shakes it and grins. "That's me, Mr. Rechthart. And you're right about the elusive part."

Pa seems to like her, but he likes most everybody. You'd have to be a real downer to not like Pa in return. He moves on to Will.

I glance at Kat, and she whispers in my ear, "I like your dad. I can tell where you got your personality from."

I half-smile, about to reply, when Ma's upon us. "Thank you for joining us today, Miss Jones. I'm Harry's mother, of course. I do hope we aren't keeping you from any important family time."

"No, nothing important in my family, Mrs. Rechthart. My parents aren't big on holidays."

Ma's eyes enlarge, like she's just heard a foul word. "Well, I trust they went to church last night, at least?"

I want to pull Kat away as quickly as possible, knowing this conversation isn't headed anywhere pleasant. Luckily, Erik intervenes. "I'm Harry's brother, Erik. Maybe he's told you about me?"

Kat seems to indulge him. "Oh, plenty, but he said you were off doing some successful job far away."

Erik and Kat continue talking. That's my brother for you. He can charm any woman in a tenth of a second and then have her eating outta his hand by the time the second's up. Maybe this ain't the lucky break I thought it was.

"And this is my brother's wife, Lily," I say.

Lily's been standing next to Erik the whole time. Erik turns, as if stunned, and introduces his wife to Kat. I'm not sure why he should be at all surprised to find her there. Glad to have thrown him off his game, as that's what this feels like, I wrap my arm around Kat and draw her away from the rest of my family. Everyone else is wrapped up in conversation in the living room as we sneak through the dining room and toward the kitchen for some privacy.

"What's for dessert?" Kat asks. "Smells great in here."

"You can be my dessert, doll." I kiss her.

"Mmm, I like how you taste." Kat's eyes shift toward the door. "You know any place a little more, well, away from everyone else?" Her eyes turn back to me briefly, before focusing on the back staircase. She grins and nods her head toward it.

Before I can make up my muddled mind either way, Kat pulls me by the hand up the rickety stairs. Once we reach the short hallway, she asks, "Which one's your room?"

"That door." I point to the one closest to the stairs. "'Course, I shared it with my brother for most of my life." Funny how I don't bother telling Kat that those stairs could've given out under us. We don't use them unless necessary. I guess this occasion counts as necessary.

Kat doesn't seem interested in talking, as she's already down the hall and entering my room. I follow, my stomach in knots as the voices from downstairs travel up the steps. "Kat, what're you doin'?"

She flops onto my bed and laughs. "Aw, come on, big boy. Don't tell me you're choosing now to play coy?"

I close the door. "Of course not."

She eyes up the room. I wonder if she's expecting to find some sort of big secret, like I keep a collection of eyeballs in a glass jar or something. There's nothing remarkable about this room, however. A few of my brother's old baseball trophies linger on our dresser, and there are my basketball ones as well. Kat sits up and approaches the trophies. Maybe she saw the way I was scrutinizing them.

She picks up the largest—a behemoth from Erik's senior year, recognizing his years of excellence on the field. "Jeez, you could use this thing for weightlifting," Kat jokes, placing it back. She studies the trophies for a few moments and then asks, her eyes still on them, "Does it bother you?" Her voice has turned soft, gentle, like she's talking to a kid.

"What?" I ask, the sunlight coming through the window gleaming off the trophies, uncomfortable on my eyes.

"That all these, I mean the ones that belong to your brother, are still here. It's like, I dunno, it's like he's still hanging around, not giving you your space. Look, his trophies are all bigger than yours."

My eyebrows draw down and inward. "Do we hafta talk about this? Ain't it enough that Erik had you under his spell downstairs? Yeah, maybe I oughta just throw the damn things out."

I pick up the biggest trophy and open the window, making to toss it.

Kat stops me by placing her smaller hand on top of mine. "Sorry. I didn't mean to upset you."

I return the trophy to its place, rightful or not. Its shadow hovers over the smaller trophies, making sure they all know who's boss around here. "I'm gonna ask Erik to take them with him before he leaves. This hasn't been his room in years."

Kat doesn't reply, but instead she guides me toward my bed. I'm like a rag doll as she pins me down and claims my mouth with hers. I don't think as I return the kiss hungrily. Our hands are all over each other. We can't seem to stop. Breathing doesn't seem important anymore. All I want is her, the girl who gets me.

And she can get me all she wants. Kat undoes her blouse. I push the bra away, but she's already unfastening it. I may have just gone to Heaven, because damn, this right here is better than any gift under the tree. She's unwrapping herself just for me in the privacy of my own bedroom.

As Kat runs her hands under my shirt, I fumble with the buttons. She yanks the shirt open, losing a couple of buttons in the process, and smiles deviously at me. She runs her hands through my hair and kisses me again. My eyes close as I spark with elation at her touch.

I'm a firecracker ready to go off. As I tug at my fly, our little party on the bed is interrupted by a knock from the door.

"You gotta be kiddin' me," I hiss as I bolt up from the bed, making to fasten my shirt. I feel like someone simultaneously punched me in the gut and hit me over the head with a frying pan. "Just a sec." I glance at a frazzled Kat and find her tugging on her blouse, her bra already on.

"Harry, Ma's about to serve dessert. We wondered where you'd gone off to," Erik's muffled voice says behind the door.

I can't help but smile at Kat. Trying to contain my laughter, I say, "We'll be down in a minute."

There's a pause. If I'd heard footsteps retreating down the hall, I'd've thought Erik left. Finally, he says, "What are you doing in there?"

"Can't a guy show a girl his room? Jeez, brother."

"I'll see you downstairs, Harry."

Finally, the footsteps. I let out a sigh of relief, and Kat begins giggling. "Oh, you should've seen the look on your face," she says.

"My face? What about yours?"

"Think they'll notice your shirt?"

I smooth the fabric down and remember the missing buttons. Luckily, one is from the very top and the other from the very bottom.

"Nah, I'll be fine. You good?"

"Ha, I was more than good a minute ago. Your brother couldn't have chosen a worse time to knock."

"We'll just hafta pick up from where we left off next time." I walk over to Kat and pull her to me, kissing her until she's breathless.

By Cynthia Hilston

When I pull back, she whispers, "Next time."

CHAPTER 9

Kat's every bit the well-behaved girl during dessert, at least she plays the role well. Ma even warms to her when Kat compliments her on her chocolate cake, a family recipe that means practically the world and the moon to Ma. So, yeah, Ma's happy and keeps trying to force more cake down Kat's throat after that.

After dessert, I walk Kat to the door, and we go outside while she waits for Will.

"What's keepin' them?" I ask, picturing Hannah and Will in their own necking session. I stuff the thought away, not wanting to imagine my sister like that.

"Does it matter?" Kat asks, swinging my arm as we hold hands.

Although we saunter toward Will's beat-up old car, it's clear Kat's in no hurry. She stops and gazes at the sky, frowning. "No stars tonight."

"I have my star right here," I say.

"You're quite the poet, aren't you?"

I smile and shrug. "Call it cheesy, but it's true. Anyway, you wanna pick up from where we left off, at least a little?"

"Well, if you insist, but my shirt stays on. It's too cold."

Kat leans into me, but just as we're about to kiss, Will and Hannah step outside. Hannah remarks how chilly it is. I settle for giving Kat a peck on the lips, but Kat doesn't seem put off. Instead, she wraps an arm around my neck, pulling me down to her level, and kisses me full on the lips, a long smacker–and loud, too.

"Have a little decency, Kat," Will says with a sneer. "Don't suck the poor guy's face off."

Kat laughs derisively at her brother. "Oh, don't tell me you never kissed a girl like that before. Well, Hannah, you'd know firsthand. Tell me, how's my brother measure up in your experience?"

Hannah's quiet for a moment, then says, "I don't think this is something we ought to be discussing, Kat. Harry, are you ready to go in?"

I can tell the conversation is headed in a bad direction, so I say goodnight to Kat and kiss her, gently, one more time. Will and I briefly shake hands, and after he kisses my sister on the cheek, the Joneses hop into their car and are gone.

As we walk back toward the house, Hannah remarks, "I sometimes wonder about her."

"Who? Kat?"

"Yes...maybe I'm just worrying about nothing here, Harry, but something about her doesn't sit right with me."

"You always worry too much, sister. If there's nothin' to worry about, you make something up."

"I hope so."

I playfully slap her on the back and say, "C'mon, even Ma liked Kat well enough, and that's a tough test to pass. Let's go in."

Hannah smiles. "You're right. Don't listen to silly me."

We go back in and start helping with the cleanup. Amy and Jack left over an hour ago to get their daughter home and in bed, and Erik and Lily will be staying overnight. I thought they might spend the night at a hotel, so they could sleep in the same bed and have some privacy, but it looks like Erik will be in his old bed and poor Lily on the cot downstairs.

After everything is taken care of, I trudge upstairs and find Erik's already there. Having him back in my—our—room feels wrong, a recipe for disaster overcooked.

"Don't think I don't know what you were doing up here before," Erik says in way of greeting.

Deny. Deny. Deny. I'm a master liar. At least I like to believe I am. "I don't know what you're talking about." I walk to my bed, my back to my brother. "Hey, d'you think you could clean out some of your junk?" I point toward the trophies and a few other odds and ends on the dresser.

Erik, however, ain't buying my distraction. "Are you nuts? Right in our parents' house? Harry, I'm just sayin' you oughta be more careful." Erik's voice slips into that easygoing way of speaking we used when we were younger.

"Nothing happened. Not really."

"Really, old boy?" Erik holds up the two missing buttons like they're pieces of evidence from a murder scene.

I snatch the buttons from Erik and bury them in my pockets. "Why aren't you with your wife, eh, *old boy*?"

Erik chuckles. "I've got you all hot under the collar, brother. It's funny seein' you squirm."

I relax, sitting on my bed as my shoulders release their tension. "I never know what game you're playin' anymore, Erik. I expected you to, I dunno, come in here all preachy and talking like the educated fool you are."

"C'mon, Harry. I just wanna talk. What's she like? All I know from what Hannah told me is that you met at a party a few months ago. When's the last time we just shot the bull? We can talk man-to-man now. You'll be of age soon."

I smile. "Kat's like...looking at the stars. She's a million possibilities to keep me guessing what's gonna come next. Erik, I think I love her."

"I hope it works out for you, then. Lily is like that to me. It's like...seeing everything through a new pair of eyes. She makes me better."

I wonder if the same can be said about Kat. Does she make me better? She encourages me to be free, but free of what? In the dark parts of my mind, I bury every glass of booze I've consumed and every time I've made whoopee with Kat, wondering if I'm burying myself as well. "That's the bee's knees, brother. I'm done in, though. Think I'm gonna hit the sack."

"Well, goodnight...and, Harry, don't do anything—"

"Stupid. Yeah, I know." Thanks for the vote of confidence, brother. Sure would be nice if we could've ended this conversion on a positive note. Then I realize why Kat means so much to me—because she frees me from doubting myself. What I'm burying is nothing more than the ugly parts of me that no one wants or deserves to see.

* * *

"C,mon, baby. We don't always hafta spend our time at big, flashy parties."

It's Valentine's Day weekend, and I'm borrowing the family Caddy to take Kat out on a night on the town. Cleveland may not be New York, but it's got its own charms.

"Harry, I know you mean well, darling, but it's not like... Well, you aren't the richest fellow in town."

I laugh. "Ain't that the truth? But seriously, doll, I wanna do this. I may not make much money yet, but one day, Pa'll retire and I'll take over the family biz. I do get the occasional tip from a grateful patron. I've saved up for a while now, so let me do this for you. It's nothin' fancy, but—"

Kat mock-pouts. "Aw, is it your pride, big boy?"

"You could say that." My tone is casual, but inside, I'm anything but. I'm nervous as hell, hoping this whole charade doesn't blow up in my face.

"Well, okay. This oughta be interesting."

I drive to a local automat and park. The place is hopping, but for nickels, people are happy to eat out. I step outta the car and go around to get the door for Kat. When she sets her high-heeled shoe on the slush-covered concrete, she frowns.

"I see I overdressed." Her eyes are on me. "Harry, you aren't serious."

"What's wrong with the automat? My dad took us here for special treats. It was always fun."

"Boy, you sure know how to romance a girl," Kat says sarcastically, sighing. "All right, let's get this over with."

"Hey, we don't have to if you're so against it." My hackles rise.

"I didn't say—"

"You've already got your mind made up. Just forget the whole damn thing." I make to go back in the car, feeling like the kid who's wearing the dunce cap on the stool in the corner of the classroom.

Kat grabs my upper arm and stops me. "I'm sorry. It's just…this reminds me of the truth."

I turn and gaze deeply into her eyes. "What's so wrong with the truth?"

She laughs humorlessly. Snowflakes are gently falling, collecting in her hair, dusting her eyelashes. I notice the tiny freckles on her pale nose standing out in the dim light of the streetlamp. I want nothing more than to kiss her silly. "The truth is… Okay, maybe it's not so bad."

"Not so bad?" I ask softly, slightly teasing.

Rather than kiss her silly, I'm tender as my lips search hers, like a boy kissing a girl for the first time behind the school, half-afraid she's gonna reject him and half-elated he's man enough to try his luck.

When the kiss ends, Kat whispers, "Let's go in."

I smile and hold her hand, and we enter. We make our selections by putting our nickels in the slots and then lift the windows to get our delicacies—mac 'n' cheese and beans. We take our waxed paper-wrapped gifts to an empty table and sit.

Despite the setting, the noise from the crowd's just like that at any of those extravagant parties we've gone to—boisterous and all around. We settle into the atmosphere, and if I'm honest with myself, I'm more at home here than in any mansion.

After our simple supper and easy conversation over cigarettes and coffee, Kat and I go outside. As we climb back into the car, she says, "I'm sorry about earlier. It was great. Thanks, Harry."

"I'm happy to hear it, but I gathered from the way you'd been smilin' in there and the way your eyes lit up as you talked that you were just fine, more than fine."

"Like your dad, mine took Will and me to the automat a lot when I was a kid. It used to be a real adventure to go somewhere to eat, and we'd dress in our best sometimes. It was kind of silly, but when I was a little girl, it was like magic getting food from one of the vending machines. I thought little people somehow put it in there. By the time I was twelve or thirteen, the magic wore off. I haven't been to an automat in years, and now I get it, Harry. I mean it—thank you."

I kiss her. "I'm glad, doll, but just wait until you see what's next." I don't know how to tell her what I really think, what's in my heart right now, because I'm no good at this. What I feel, I know it's real. Tonight wasn't about trying to show off. It was wanting to do something nice for her, something from me, something that showed her who I am without the bells and whistles, without the booze and the sex and the jokes and the games. Why, if Kat can love me as just plain old Harry, I'd kiss every star I see in the sky.

"I can't wait!"

I'm king of the world tonight, and I know that sounds cheesy, but give a guy a minute to bask in his moment of glory. "God, I love you, Kat."

The words are outta my mouth before I know I've said them. Kat stares at me, her little tulip mouth slightly open. She closes it, purses her lips, and giggles. "Aw, you don't know what you're talking about." She jabs me in the ribs. "Let's blow this joint, Harry. Where to?"

"How d'you feel about a jazz club? Val's in the Alley's not far."

Kat claps in delight. "Sounds like a ball!"

I start the car up and nod, smile painted in place, suddenly not so much a king, or even a prince, but more like the court jester. "Art Tatum's not playin' tonight, but I'm sure it'll still be a good time," I say, every word a note to the song whose tune I don't know.

CHAPTER 10

After our simple date on Valentine's Day, Kat seems happy to do more casual things together. While we still go to those hopping parties most weekends, as the weather warms, we go off by ourselves on walks. We walk everywhere—the boardwalk at Euclid Beach Park with the smell of popcorn and taffy filling our noses, the well-worn trails in Hatford Park near my house with the smell of spring everywhere, and down Madison Avenue with the smells of too many things to pick just one. All this time, Kat never invites me over, never introduces me to her folks, and never speaks about them, unless it's to complain. I don't know what smells might be on her street. We don't walk there. I've only ever driven down Wheeler Avenue to pick her up and only seen the light blue house that's so like mine from the outside.

It's late April now. While Hannah and Will are off having their own fun, Kat and I are taking another walk in gardens filled with daffodils behind her friend's estate—the one married to the doctor.

"A walk's nice, but with the warmer weather, Harry, I was thinking..." Kat smiles suggestively.

"What'd you have in mind?" I ask with a lopsided grin, finishing my glass of wine. I think this was number five...or six, but I can't be sure. But I know what she has in mind.

Kat motions toward a shed on the edge of the property. "The sun's getting low. We'd never be missed. Everyone's inside or near the house."

"Doesn't seem very comfy," I joke.

"You want to try our luck somewhere else?"

"Maybe the host's bedroom?" I laugh. "Oh, you oughta see your face! I'm not that crazy, a little drunk or not."

Kat giggles. "I can never be entirely sure with you, big boy. Other rooms, sure, but not where my friend and her hubby sleep."

"Funny, I could say that same about you, doll—the not being sure part." I pause, then add, "But I love it that way."

Kat leads me along like she always does. The shed's door creaks as she opens it, and for just a second, she stops, looking around to make sure no one's around. "Come on." She waves me in.

I enter and find nothing remarkable in the nearly dark interior. "You tease me about not bein' very romantic," I say, "but shovels, rakes, axes? What're you suggesting, doll?"

Kat shakes her head. "You're nuts, Harry."

"Right about that."

I take Kat in my arms, and we waste not another moment waxing poetic about yard tools as our lips and hands set to work of a very different kind. I'm going mostly by touch, as it's too dark to see. My hands work themselves under Kat's blouse and find their home there. She breathes heavily as she removes her top and her bra in one fluid motion. I rip my shirt off as well, and our bare chests touch, our skin hot on each other. Kat's hands are all over me, running up and down my body like she can't decide where she wants them to be. If she's like me, her brain ain't doing much of anything but sitting in her skull like a useless rock. We kiss any exposed bit of flesh we can find, as the booze intensifies my hunger for her.

Her hands fumble with my fly, and I impatiently pull it down. My pants fall to the wooden floor, and then her skirt joins them. With our clothing as our mattress, we work our way down, and I lie on top of Kat. In the haze of the booze and our hormones, I remove the final piece of clothing that's keeping me from making love to her.

* * *

When I wake, I'm not sure how late it is. All I know is my head's pounding, and my body's stiff and uncomfortable. For a second, I forget where I am, but then I realize I'm lying naked on a pile of clothes in a shed. I push away the physical pain and grin.

I reach beside me. My hand makes contact with Kat's smooth arm. She's still with me. Still naked. She's beautiful. Every square inch of her's beautiful. Her breathing is steady for a moment, then changes.

Kat shifts beside me and sits up. "Mmm, Harry, you were amazing."

I chuckle. "I'm glad you think so, doll."

Kat laughs and throws her arms around me. "Oh, I love you, Harry!" She kisses me.

I smile like the fool I am, too taken by Kat to even think. My mouth moves on its own with "I love you, too" and kisses her back.

Kat's still giggling as she stands and hands my clothes to me, one at a time. I can just make out her silhouette as she dresses. "As much as I'd love to stay in here with you, we'd better see what's going on out there. Can't have your sister worrying about getting home too late."

I finish buttoning my shirt. "Nah, can't have that. Hannah'll have kittens lookin' for me."

We step out into the cool night air after we're done making ourselves decent. My head spins, my hangover in effect. I'm relieved to see the party's still in full swing. So, it ain't too late. We walk back to the house, my footsteps dragging. When we arrive, I'm happy to see Hannah dancing with Will.

"There you are!" Hannah exclaims. "We were beginning to wonder if you'd ditched us for a better party."

Kat laughs. "No way, Hannah. It looks like you and Will have been dancing the night away. Mind if we join you?"

I marvel at the way Kat can insert herself in any situation like she's always belonged there. "Just a sec." I grab two glasses of wine and pass one to Kat. If I can take the edge off, maybe we'll be good to go.

After two quick glasses, I pull myself together, the unpleasant feeling of the hangover passing. I'm heady again with pleasure. I pull Kat into my arms, and we begin the foxtrot.

Will and Hannah seem to be competing with us, so we each dance faster and faster, laughing. I'm still floating, remembering Kat's words to me in that musty, old shed. She loves me!

By the end of the night, Will leans into me and mutters, "You look like you're completely under my sister's spell, buddy." He elbows me playfully in the side and winks.

"I ain't complainin'," I say.

"You aren't the first, ya know."

"Heh, probably won't be the last, either. Gals like her are special." I only half-pay attention to Will's words.

Kat interrupts by slipping between her brother and me. "What are you filling dear Harry's head with, esteemed brother?" she asks Will with a mock-pout.

"Nothing that isn't true, dear sister of mine."

Hannah comes to Will's side and takes his hand. Her face lights up around him, as does his when he's with her. "You ready to go home?" she asks the group.

We pile into Will's car. I keep one arm around Kat in the back seat and close my eyes, replaying the night.

One thing is sure. Kat loves me.

CHAPTER 11

I haven't come down from my personal cloud. As May comes, I begin to wonder if I should propose to Kat. Several months ago, I would've thought myself nuts to even entertain the thought, but now that's all changed. If we love each other, ain't that enough?

I toy with the ring in my pocket that Friday all evening at another party. My fingers become best buds with the brass. It's not much, but it's all I can afford.

I don't know when the right moment will come, but just as I'm about to ask Kat to come with me outside, she says, "Where do you suppose Will and Hannah have gone off to?"

I shrug. "Does it matter?"

Kat leads us outside. Instead of time alone with her, we walk onto a scene we probably shouldn't.

"I don't have a ring yet, but soon. I promise." Will grins like a lovestruck fool.

"Did we miss something?" asks Kat.

Hannah and Will turn toward us.

"Well?" Kat insists.

"Only that we're now engaged," Will says.

I chuckle, thinking how crazy it is that we're all of the same mind here, and clap Will on the back. "You dog! You got my little sister. Best be careful."

Hannah smiles at me. I hug her close and whisper, "Congratulations." I've already had a few drinks, and all this happiness is adding to my dream of a future with Kat. Everything seems to be falling into place. I look at Kat as I pull her into a half-hug.

"Ain't it somethin'?" I ask, watching Hannah and Will walk away to maybe share their news with others.

"Yeah, it's something, all right," she says in a voice that's hard to discern.

"Ah, your time'll come, doll." I kiss her on the cheek, in too drunk a stupor to know what I'm really doing.

By Cynthia Hilston

* * *

On Monday, I fight to contain my excitement. I can just imagine the looks on Ma and Pa's faces when they find out not one, but two, of their kids are engaged. Hannah's already shared her news with the family, but I'm keeping quiet about my big plans.

On Tuesday, Hannah seeks me out. "I just wanted to let you know, Harry, that Kat and I aren't friends anymore, at least I don't think we are."

"Well, that's a shame, sister. What happened?"

"We fought at work yesterday. She doesn't approve of my engagement to Will."

"Hey, chin up, Hannah-panna. She's just jealous. Don't let her ruin your happiness. I'm sure she'll come around."

"I don't know." Hannah isn't looking at me, and it seems on purpose. "Harry, just be careful with her."

"There you go, worrying too much again. I'm a big boy. I think I can handle Kat."

Hannah gazes at me, and it's like she's looking right through me, seeing past the jokes and half-truths.

"All right. I'm sorry, Harry. If you're really happy with her, then be with her. I just don't want to see you hurt."

For a second, worry twists my heart. "Kat said she loves me. She meant it. And I love her."

"Okay, that's good to hear. But this Saturday Will and I are going on our own date. You and Kat should, too."

Thanks for the permission, Hannah-banana. "Righto. I'll think of something."

* * *

On Saturday, I'm a right mess. Hannah's talk about Kat and the ring in my pocket are fighting, and as I pull into Kat's driveway with my parents' Caddy, I'm not sure who's gonna win.

Love wins, I tell myself. But that's sorta some fairytale I was told as a boy. Besides, Hannah can be a real fuddy-duddy sometimes.

When Kat gets in the car, I push my conflicted thoughts away. Damn, she's gorgeous. I kiss her and say, "Did I ever tell you how good you look, doll?"

"All the time, big boy. You're not too shabby yourself."

Kat's her usual playful self. If she's upset about her argument with my sister, she doesn't say. I half-wonder if she's as good as me at gluing on a smile and forcing a laugh to hide the stuff we don't wanna share.

"I was thinkin'—" I say.

"There's a huge party tonight," she interrupts. "Remember that house just a few down from my friend's?"

"Oh, that dump, you mean?"

Kat laughs. "If that's a dump, I hate to think what you'd call our houses."

"Cardboard boxes. A regular Hooverville." My joke's probably in poor taste, but Kat's already talking up "this party to end all parties."

I make the drive. After parking on the street some distance away to get outta paying the valet, we walk to another mansion.

After months of parties, they all start to feel the same. Only difference is this time Hannah and Will aren't with us, and even though we don't spend all our time together, it's still strange. Almost feels like I'm missing part of myself.

The good times come easy. The dancing is sweet. Kat's lips and breath are the easiest and sweetest of all.

A couple of hours in, I'm convinced I've got this doll wrapped around my pinkie finger. She's certainly got me wrapped around hers. Wrapped around her whole fist.

The ring's still in my pocket, that steady reminder that I've got a question to pop before the night's through. Like many warm nights, we eventually make our way outside to look at the stars and maybe dream. Dream about a life together. Kat and me. Taking on the world. Kat as my wife. Me as her husband. That's the kinda dream I've got in mind tonight.

It's time.

I find a spot surrounded by trees, cut off from the rest of the hubbub going on everywhere else. All that matters is right here, right now, this girl with me, her eyes shining in our shared starlight.

"Kat." Damn. My voice trembles. I clear my throat and start over, taking her hands. "Kat, I've really had the time of my life with you these last several months."

"I've had a good time, too, Harry."

"What I'm tryin' to say—and probably failing something awful—is that...Kat, will you marry me?" I hold out the ring like I'm holding out my heart to her.

For what feels like forever, Kat stares, first at the ring, then at my face. Her mouth is open like a fish outta water. Then she laughs.

I smile, not sure what to make of this. "Well?" I ask, hopeful.

"Harry, what—?"

"It's a simple question. Will you marry me?"

Kat stops laughing, and her face scrunches into a frown, her brow creased. "I must've misled you if you thought this was what I wanted." She takes a step back.

Every word's like a dagger to my heart, driving itself deeper. "What are you sayin'?" My face heats.

"I was never interested in marrying you, Harry. I thought I'd made that clear months ago when I said I wasn't the marrying type." Kat crosses her arms over her chest. I'm not sure if it's suddenly cold or she's putting up defenses. Probably both.

"But—" I search for something, anything. The right words. "You said you loved me." Even as I speak, hope drains from me like someone's pulled the plug, all the water going down, down, down. Hope falling down. Drowning me.

Kat frowns. "My God, Harry. You're really serious."

"Of course, I am. I'm not all jokes, you know. Why the hell would I joke about something like this?" I storm away, tossing the ring into the bushes. Worthless.

I enter the house and grab the closest glass of wine and down it in a couple of gulps. People are too busy dancing and chatting to notice me. Until now, I'd had one glass of wine tonight. My head was clear. My heart was full of love for the girl who I thought loved me.

But it's all a joke. This is a big game for Kat. My heart. My love. Nothing but a laughing matter of pain.

I lose myself. In the crowd. In the chatter. In the dance.

I just lose myself. Lose all track of who I am anymore.

My hands seem to be moving on their own, my mind completely dead. No control. The drinks take over, and I'm more lost than I've ever been.

Somewhere in all this mess, Kat finds me. "I want you to take me home, Harry."

"Wha—?"

"Home. I'm done here for tonight."

"Aw, c'mon, doll. We're just gettin' started. Ya wanna go out back and—"

Kat drags me outta the house and takes me to the Caddy. I laugh 'cause this is all so damn funny.

"Don't wanna marry me, but I'm all good, honey. All good times, sweets."

We fall into the car, and when I lean over to give Kat a big ol' smacker, she recoils. "Just drive, Harry. We're done."

"Whatever ya say. No need ta get all in a tizzy, doll."

I drive and Kat's silent. I keep shooting sidelong glances at her, smirking at her, looking for that smile of hers. She finally looks at me, but there's no smile. When she turns her face back to the front, she screams.

All I see is black.

CHAPTER 12

Not sure how long I was out, but when I open my eyes, everything's blurry. My head feels like someone took an axe to it and split it like an overripe watermelon. There's pain going all up and down my body, coursing through me like blood.

Blood. I feel it on my forehead. I touch the wound. My face. More blood. My hand comes away. Even more blood.

Somewhere in all this I ask, "Kat?" I turn toward her if see if she's okay, but she stares at me without blinking. Those eyes. The green looks right through me. "Kat?" My voice breaks.

I reach for her, but her face is like a shattered mirror, mirrored by the shattered windshield. I touch her. She slumps back toward the seat. Doesn't move.

Panic sets in. Fear such as I've never felt grips my guts and twists. It can't be... No.

Tears burn in my eyes as I reach with my left arm for Kat and shake her. My right arm isn't moving. Neither is she.

"Kat, please, wake up. Wake up, Kat."

But as the truth of what's happened settles in and on me like a boulder, I stop shaking her. Now I'm shaking. My head spins.

Those eyes. Those damn eyes. Those damning eyes.

I can't stop myself as I stare. They stare. Accusing me. Always.

My injuries are too bad to try to get outta the car and walk. Even if I could, how could I just leave her like this?

Kat's... God, it can't be!

DEAD!

I fall into her and wrap my good arm around her already cooling body. I sob into the crook of her neck, her hair tickling my cheek with false comfort. Somewhere in the middle of all this, the cops arrive.

By Cynthia Hilston

An ambulance comes within a minute. Before I know what's happening, I'm loaded onto a gurney and into the ambulance. Cops are asking questions, and I'm trying to answer, but I don't know what happened...

On the drive to the hospital, my head begins to clear some. With the haze of the booze lifting, I know full well what happened. I drank too much. I drove. Like an idiot.

I killed Kat.

Once I'm in a hospital bed, two cops, a nurse, and a doctor surround me. While the doctor starts examining my injuries, the one cop asks, "Who should I call, son?"

"My– my parents." I give him the number and try to breathe.

But the other cop's upon me, ruthless. "Were you drinking, young man?"

I stare at him, hearing the words, but not understanding. Nothing makes sense anymore. Everything I thought made sense–me and Kat, how we felt about each other, our love–all was and is a damning lie. "What's gonna happen to her?"

"Answer the question. Were you drinking?"

"What about Kat?"

"Is that the name of the young woman? I know you were drinking. I can smell it on your breath. You should have never stepped into that car. Do you realize the implications of what you've done?"

I wanna scream at this asshole. You think I don't know what I've done? You think I need you throwing it in my face?

But any accusations I might toss at that bad cop are cut off as the good cop comes back and says, "Your parents are on their way." He looks at his evil buddy and says, "That's enough, Davis. Son, we'll talk more tomorrow when you're in a better state of mind." He aims this last bit at me and nods.

Before I can thank him for this small mercy, the cops leave. I know I won't be in a better place tomorrow. Of all the lies I've told myself the past few months, the biggest lie is that I'm ever gonna be happy again.

While the doctor and nurse take care of my physical wounds, my mental wounds bleed like a festering half-severed limb. I laugh weakly when they tell me I have a broken arm.

"Is something funny?" the nurse asks.

"I just remembered–today's my birthday."

Happy twenty-first birthday, Harry. Welcome to the rest of your damn life.

CHAPTER 13

It's a new day, a bright morning that I can't appreciate. Everything's different.
Pa and Ma came by really late last night to see me. I only half-remember it. Ma's tears and the disappointment in Pa's dead eyes are as clear as if they were still sitting next to me. Of everything that's happened in the past day, it's their eyes and Kat's eyes that plague me. Can't get them outta my head if I tried.

I don't try.

I tell myself I deserve it, every bit of guilt, self-hatred, shame, and bitterness that've made their homes in my broken heart. A heart broken by a girl who I broke in return. Broke beyond repair.

On the outside, I'm all bandaged up. I've been told I've got some bruised ribs and a concussion, on top of the broken right arm. I don't even wanna look at my ugly face, the bruises and swelling more reminders of how I messed up big time.

I played the game of love. I lost. I lost it all.

The cops come back after breakfast. The firing squad of questions begins, but it's like I'm standing naked as a real firing squad shoots me down, already charged guilty. There's no denying the truth. Why try?

As the day wears on and no one visits, I wonder if my parents are so ashamed of me that they're staying away, telling the rest of the family to stay away, too.

But I'm wrong. In spite of it all, I don't know what's worse: facing them or them never coming.

They come that evening. Ma and Pa are the first ones to enter my room.

Ma makes to hug me, but I wince from her weight on my chest, and she withdraws, the tears starting all over again.

"Ma, please don't cry."

She chokes back a sob and pulls out a handkerchief, dabbing at her eyes and blowing her nose. She looks like she's aged ten years overnight. My God, what've I done to her?

"How are you holding up?" Pa asks.

I know he's trying to be kind, to pretend everything's all hunky-dory. I shrug and then wish I hadn't. Damn ribs are gonna be the death of me.

"The rest of the family's here to see you, too, if that's all right with you," Pa says.

"That's fine," I mutter.

"Harry, my boy—" Ma starts, but can't finish.

We spend the next several minutes not saying all the things that need to be said. Or maybe they don't need to be said so much as understood. Yeah, that's more it—an unspoken understanding between us that somehow, all's gonna be right with the world again. But that's a lie, like everything else. Ma and Pa won't lie to me, but it seems they don't know what to do with me anymore.

I don't blame them.

When the nurse says their time's up, Ma's tears begin all over again. She can't even look at me as Pa wraps an arm around her and draws her toward the exit. He looks back at me one last time and tries to smile. It's a pained grimace.

Amy and Irma are next. When I see my baby sister, I smile for the first time since this whole damn ordeal began. I can't help it—Irma brings out the best in me, whatever little kid's left hiding behind all the jokes, games, and booze.

"Hi, Irma," I say. "Can I get a hug? Be careful, though, 'cause I'm pretty beat up here."

Irma smiles shyly and comes to me, gentle and unafraid. I'd expect her to be more scared of me than anyone in my family, but her quiet acceptance is like a balm to my wounds. After her light touch, she asks, "Are you gonna be okay, Harry?"

"Sure, kid. Don't worry about me." Another lie. But I don't have the heart to break hers.

Amy watches this exchange, her lips pursed in a firm line like Ma's. Only Ma's been crying too much to do likewise right now. "Well, I'm glad you're going to be fine, but, Harry, what's next?"

The full question goes unasked, so it can go mostly unanswered. "Dunno. How's Jack? Little Jean?"

"They're fine. Irma, are you ready to go?"

So, this is it. Irma looks at me with her big, blue eyes, begging not to go. Not yet.

"Why the hurry?" I shoot at Amy. Irma starts crying. Damn it. "Hey, hey," I say softly to my little sister, "none of that. I'm sorry—"

"Yes, we know you are," Amy says coldly.

While I reach for Irma, Amy takes her by the hand and pulls her toward the door.

There's no time for goodbyes. There's no place for them. My sisters are gone, that empty doorway speaking more truth about my plight than anything anyone can say. I wonder if that's it. Maybe Amy's told them all that they just oughta hightail it outta there.

But then Erik shows up with Lily. Outta the frying pan and into the fire.

Lily, being a nurse, is at my side in an instant, asking, "Harry, how are you feeling? Are you being taken care of well?"

"Yes, Lily, I'm okay. Thanks."

Lily smiles. Besides Irma's childlike innocence, Lily's face is the first I've seen that's happy. At least she puts up a good front.

Erik stands next to her, his arm wrapped around her shoulders, like he's afraid I might harm her. As my eyes fall on my only brother, I wonder what kinda monster he thinks I am. Of course, maybe he's right. I've already killed one sweet girl. Still, the way he looks at me, it's like I'm a squashed bug on the bottom of his Sunday best shoe.

"Well, brother, are you gonna just stand there lookin' pretty, or are you gonna say something?" I ask.

Erik's brow darkens, my weak attempt at a joke falling, crashing on the white hospital floor. "You've looked better before."

Lily scowls at him. "Erik, honey–"

He steps away from his wife and comes closer to the bed. "You're lucky you weren't killed. Harry, what the hell were you thinking?" He scoffs. "It's obvious that you weren't thinking. I told you–"

"Erik, I really don't think–" Lily starts to say.

"No, Lily," I interrupt. "Don't try to defend me to him." I gaze at her with pleading eyes and shake my head. Looking back at Erik, I continue, "You've made your point clear, big brother. No need to rub it in."

Erik sighs and steps back. His shoulders slump, like all the fight's gone outta him. "You've always been reckless, taken too many risks, Harry. Now it's gone too far."

"Ya think I don't know that?" I ask, growing irritated. I lift my left hand and rub at my face, wincing from the pain and wishing I hadn't done so.

"You could've died."

I frown, gazing at Erik. Deep in his eyes I think there's concern, but like everything else, too many lies cover the truth. I don't know what the hell's supposed to be truth anymore. All I know is my life's a joke. Always been. Always will be. "Yeah, well, I killed someone instead," I say flatly.

The moment the words are outta my mouth, I wish I could grab them and stuff them back in. Too late. It's always been too late.

Erik shakes his head. He returns his arm to its spot around Lily's shoulder and draws her to him. "I'd hoped you'd grow up eventually." Erik turns for the door. Lily glances sideways at me, nothing but pity written on her pretty face.

"We can't all be like you, Erik," I say as they leave. I glare at the empty door, writing my own death sentence with every word I say. I'm burying myself here.

Then Hannah enters.

My insides are about to drop out, but for my sister's sake, I push on and try to smile. She doesn't need to see me like this...this ugly monster version of myself I've become.

"Hi, Hannah-panna."

"Oh, Harry," Hannah says, sounding like she's about to cry. "Look at you."

"I'm a right mess, sis," I weakly joke, but she ain't buying it.

"How are you feeling?"

I shrug like nothing's amiss, then wince again. "Ow, probably shouldn't have done that. Ribs."

"Is the pain that bad?"

"Let's just say I've felt better, but these bruises and broken bones will heal. Some things don't heal so easily, Hannah. I know what happened. Everything. The jokes are my way of dealing with it, like always. That's Harry, just one big joke. Always the one for a good time, a laugh. One big screw up, so why shouldn't I live up to my reputation and be a drunk, too, hmm? A law-breaker. A murderer."

I can't seem to stop myself once I get going. I hate myself right now, and maybe I'm trying to convince Hannah to hate me, too. Tears fill my sister's eyes, but it's like I don't care. No, that's not true. I care too damn much about her. About my family. And I've hurt them. Beyond repair. Now all I can hope for is to drive them away, to save them any further pain.

I'm not worth it, I wanna yell at Hannah. Just stop. Just go. Go away. Far away and never come back if you know what's good for you.

But Hannah's always been stubborn to a fault. So damn stubborn.

"Stop it; just stop it," Hannah says when she can find her words. She pushes the tears away. Or at least tries. "This isn't funny, Harry."

"I never said it was. Do I sound like I'm joking now, Hannah?"

Nothing's ever been further from a joke. I don't know if I even know how to laugh anymore. Not a true laugh. Lost in a mountain of lies, a pile of crap. Laughter's only meaning is mockery now.

But Hannah pushes on.

"You sound...like a man at the end of his rope, and I'm worried for you, Harry, very worried."

"I am a man at the end of his rope, or at least the end of hope. I'll go to the slammer for this, Hannah. What's the sense in worryin' when we both know what's gonna happen?"

"But you don't know that for sure. Harry, why are you being so callous?"

"Who're we kiddin' here? We both know that it's illegal to drink, period. And then to have killed someone on top of it—"

"Your actions were compromised by the alcohol. You didn't kill her willingly, Harry. You're not a murderer."

"Murder or manslaughter, I still killed her, Hannah, and I *loved* her. Don't you see? I *loved* her. I asked Kat to marry me that night, and d'you know what she did? She only laughed, thinking it a joke. When I grew serious, we began to argue. Rather than deal with the fallout, I drowned my rejection in drink, and by the end of the night, Kat demanded I drive her home. She said she was done with me, with us." I stop speaking, feeling my throat closing up. Tears come. I don't try to hide them. "Well, there you have it. You're the only one who knows the whole truth, Hannah. You must think me a complete loser."

Please just go, Hannah. There's nothing left to see here. Nothing worth talking about.

"I think nothing of the sort," Hannah says instead in that damned gentle voice of hers. "I think you've been dealt a horrible blow. Even though she's dead, Kat should've had more sense than to ask you to drive her home when you'd had so much to drink, and, Harry, I wish I'd told you that Kat was never the marrying type. Will told me that she'd been married and divorced at a young age and that was why she was bitter on men. She told me herself that her relationship with you was nothing serious. That was on Monday, when we argued at work. She hated that Will and I were engaged. Our friendship was already at an end. Oh, God, I shouldn't have kept this from you, but trying to tell you... I knew how you felt about her. I could see it in your eyes every time you looked at her. Harry, you were head-over-heels for that girl, but you deserved better."

Oh, I knew she wasn't the marrying type. At least I did months ago. Idiot me thought that'd changed.

"Don't speak like that about Kat," I say bitterly. "She's dead because of me, and whatever her shortcomings, she didn't deserve to die because of them. So, you fought. But you didn't kill her. Nothing you could've told me would've changed my mind, so don't you dare go blaming yourself. The only one here who's to blame for all this mess is *me*."

Now, please, for the love of God, Hannah, go. Just go. Go.

The nurse chooses that moment to enter and announce that visiting time's up, saving us both further agony. Hannah stands. She sighs and bites her lip, then leans down and kisses me on top of the head.

"Good night, Harry. I hope you forgive yourself."

Before I can say a thing, she's gone.

CHAPTER 14

In the next few weeks, Ma and Pa are the only ones who visit me, first in the hospital and then in prison as I wait for my trial. I'm not surprised by Amy and Erik's silence, and I'm sure that Irma would come if she were older. But Hannah's a real shocker. I'd've thought she'd be here daily, trying to be my own personal cheerleader.

Ma can't look at me without crying, and Pa's eyes have lost their long-held sparkle. It's like in killing Kat, I also killed my family.

I wanted them to go away. I got my wish.

When the trial comes, I don't deny my guilt. I somehow manage to meet the eyes of Kat's parents and Will, and all I find is condemnation. Charge me for Kat's death. I know what I've done.

What's worse than their stares is my own family being in the courtroom. I lock eyes with Hannah once and just as quickly look away, keeping my gaze on my hands, bound in cuffs. A constant reminder of where I'm headed.

I get three years as my sentence. Guilty of manslaughter and illegal drinking. Guilty of falling madly in love with a girl who didn't love me. Guilty of being fool enough to think anyone could ever love me for me, instead of some rag doll version who's held together by jokes and laughs. He's tattered and torn, that rag doll Harry. The final string was pulled, and he fell apart.

Three years. It's no less than I deserve. Maybe three years I won't ever get back, but it's better this way. As the cops haul me off to the county slammer, I accept my fate. I give up the clothes on my back on this sultry July trial day and don prison garb. I'm thrown into a ten-by-ten cell that smells of piss and mold with a guy who grunts for conversation.

My arm, ribs, and head are healed, but that's about it. Everything that ever mattered is broken.

For the first few weeks, I go through the motions of sleeping, eating, pissing, and walking in circles outside during our hour of exercise. I manage to figure out my cellmate's name—Hank. Trying to sleep's the worst part. The mattress is lumpy and stained under its thin sheet. I lie there for hours, hoping sleep might come and listening to Hank as he groans in his half-sleep. Nightmares, I guess. The smell of piss overwhelms right after midnight every damn day when he finally loses control of himself.

When I do fall asleep, I have my own nightmares. But that's not something I wanna think about.

I thrash on that small mattress one late summer night, just like every other damn night. My ill-fitting grey clothes scratch my front and back every time I switch sides.

Unsure why it's taken this long to hit me, I bolt up on the cot and stare out the high-barred window. I run my hand over my stubble on my face and sigh. The dim glow of the moonlight comes in and settles on the ceiling. I crash to my knees, not caring that I'll have bruises in the morning. I've known for weeks what happened to get me here, but seeing that moonlight beyond the bars, it's like hope teasing me that maybe I still got a fighting chance.

I'm not really the praying type. It's not that I don't believe, but I guess I haven't really thought about God in years. Maybe I thought I was doing fine on my own, that I didn't need Him, but, God, I'm on my knees like I'm five damn years old again. I'm begging and crying and baring my heart to you. I don't even know where to start, how I got here, how any of this happened, how I could've been so...stupid, irresponsible, reckless, blind...a drunken fool, zozzled by love, hammered by booze. Thinking I had my life all figured out, and then, bam! Damn! Everything...gone.

I'd scream until my throat hurt if I could, but silence, silence, and more silence is the rule around here. Most of the guards just smirk and chuckle whenever they walk by and hear Hank moaning in his sleep. So, I keep quiet, tears coursing down my unshaven cheeks.

When I'm done with my pathetic plea to the Good Lord, I stand and wipe at my face.

"What're you doin' outta bed?"

I turn and meet eyes with Officer Riley, the bad copper. Beyond him, almost blackness, but I know it's rows and rows of identical cells, three stories high. He's standing right under the dim light outside my cell. That light ain't doing him any favors, making that long, nasty scar on the side of his face stand out even more. There are plenty of rumors about how he got it. If I were just a guy walking by him on the street, I might have the balls to ask him about it. Instead, I return to my bed like a good boy and make to lie down.

"What's that look for, boy?"

My eyes enlarge and I shrug.

"Don't get smart with me, Rechthart." He steps closer to the bars and leers at me. "You're lookin' at my scar, ain't ya?"

I nod like an idiot.

He runs his finger down it slowly, smiling at me without any sort of kindness or happiness behind it. "Maybe one day I'll tell ya. Got it from a smart-aleck kid like you. What's more entertainin' is what I did to him. Some of the men've told me about you. You were a real joker, huh? Think you're funny?"

"Something like that," I whisper, growing agitated.

"What was that, boy?" Riley growls.

Another guard joins him and says, "That's enough, Riley. We've got a whole cell block to watch. C'mon." The other guard—I think Evans is his name—nods in my direction and says, "Get some sleep, Rechthart."

They leave, but I'm not at peace. What the hell's that guy's problem? It's one thing to serve time, but all we do in here is rot, left alone for hours with our thoughts and told to shut up. Maybe if I had something to do, some sort of work, I'd at least feel a small sense of usefulness. Stupid laws've ruined that much for prisoners. Anything made by us lowly scumbags ain't worth a lick to anyone living outside the state, so with no money to be made, they stopped putting us to work. Instead, they let us go crazy and then wonder why we do stuff like give ol' Riley a nice slice down the cheek? The bastard probably deserved it.

I look at the bricks and sigh. What's happening to me? I'm wishing for bad things to happen to another man. Bad cop or not, Ma'd be ashamed of me for not respecting authority. Tears prickle at the corners of my eyes when I picture Ma baking in the kitchen, her hair sticking out of her messy bun and the sweat on her brow as she wipes it with the back of her flour-covered hand.

God, what I'd give to taste one of Ma's breakfasts or even, at my age, have her wish me goodnight. I'd never be embarrassed about you again, Ma, if you hugged me in public. Hell, I'd hug you back and never let go.

Because what they say is true. You don't know what you've got till it's gone.

Thoughts of Ma draw me back to my lousy bed. I lift the mattress and retrieve one of her letters. I can't read it in the dark, but every word is memorized.

Dear Harry,

I wish I could say things are going well here, but the times are hard on us. Your father isn't bringing in what he used to, so Hannah has had to start helping us pay the bills and keep food on the table by giving the family most of what she earns. I told her she didn't need to give so much, but that it was appreciated nonetheless. I want for her to be able to save some for the day she is married.

Amy and Jack stopped by the other day. It was lovely to see Jean again. That little angel brightens my day on the darkest of them. I do wonder when we will have more grandchildren. The house has gotten so quiet. Even Irma doesn't run around like she used to.

I do hope you are as well as you can be, dear. We love you, your father and I. He sends his best, although you understand that he's not really one for writing letters.

Love,

Ma

I let the smoothness of the paper rest in my fingers for a while, a small piece of home. Ma touched this paper. Then I fold it, kiss it, and return it to its hiding place, telling myself I'll have the guts to write back tomorrow.

* * *

The next day at breakfast, I stare at gruel. Tastes like sawdust, but it's food. As I shovel it into my mouth, I gaze around the mess hall. Mealtimes are one of the few occasions where we're allowed to talk. In the distance, I spot Riley by the door, doing his best to be intimidating.

Across from me sits O'Malley, a guy a little older than me who's serving time for stealing cars and selling them.

"That was before the Crash," he explained to me last week. "You know, when things were goin' good and people had the dough."

"A lot was goin' well before I was put in here," I remarked.

O'Malley and I struck up a kind of friendship, if you could call it that in a prison. In some ways, living here's like walking the halls of high school again. There's a very real sense of a hierarchy. There are those who rule and those who are ruled. You don't go messing with the wrong sort if you know what's good for you. So, I keep my head down and mind my business.

But seeing Riley again makes my blood boil. Leaning across the table, I ask O'Malley, "What's his story?" I jerk my head in the guard's direction.

O'Malley's face pales. "Riley?"

"Yeah, him."

"There was a guy here on death row years ago. Don't know his name, but Riley had it in for him."

"His name was George Peters," a middle-aged man next to O'Malley says. "Peters raped and killed at least a dozen young girls. One of them was Riley's daughter."

My eyes bulge as a sick feeling rises in my stomach. "That's awful."

"Awful don't begin to describe it, friend," the older man continues. "As the date of execution drew nearer for Peters, Riley grew increasingly restless. He attacked inmates without provocation. He went nuts one day when he saw Peters and started clubbing him, probably hopin' he'd get his own justice and kill the guy. Peters fought back, bein' six and a half foot tall with the hands of a beast. Cut into Riley's cheek with a piece of glass he got, 'though don't know from where."

I push the remainder of my breakfast away, my appetite gone. Before I can ask how accurate this man's information is, Riley announces the end of the meal and orders us to file out. When I reach my humble abode, I lie on my cot, cross my arms behind my head, and stare at the ceiling.

When Hank joins me a couple of minutes later, I turn toward him and whisper, "Hey, Hank."

Hank doesn't seem to hear me. Nothing new there.

"C'mon, buddy. Give a guy a break here and talk to me."

Hank glares at me and shakes his head. This is more than he's given me since my arrival. I glance toward the bars to make sure there's no guard in sight. Most wouldn't care if we keep our voices low, but there are others besides Riley who are hard asses.

"What d'you know about ol' Riley?"

But Hank's now lying on his own cot in much the same manner I am. I'm going outta my mind here, and this bit of gossip is the first thing that's sparked my interest.

"Yeah, I thought as much," I mutter.

My mind drifts to better times when I shared a room with my brother. I wonder what Erik's up to these days. Is he ever gonna be a dad?

Dad. Father. Pa.

I'd love to see my folks, but they haven't visited yet. Maybe I really have gone too far.

With nothing better to do, I close my eyes and try to sleep. It's the only escape I'll have for a long time.

By the end of the day, I still haven't written back to Ma.

CHAPTER 15

No one gives me a straight answer about Riley in the following weeks, and since I don't wanna stir the pot too much, I shut up. What's my fascination with this guard? I guess I spent too many years fooling around, thinking life was a joke, to completely turn off that part of me.

As the weeks pass, the cooling wind stirs around us whenever we walk in circles outside during exercise time. I try to keep track of the days, but they all blur together. The number of dreary days outside increases until being outside ain't much better than being inside. Everything's grey and lifeless. Since there aren't any trees in the courtyard where we walk, I miss seeing the leaves change for the first time in my life.

How crazy that something so common could mean so much to a guy. I'm not usually that sentimental, but since I have all the time in the world to think, my mind doesn't stop. My childhood street was lined with dozens of old trees, so we had the time of our lives as kids romping and rolling through the leaves. If I try hard, I can still hear them crunch under my feet. Erik and I are laughing and chasing each other, much younger and a hell-of-a-lot more innocent than we are now.

I sit up on the bed. The only book I have is the Bible, so I open it to some random page and read. It's the familiar words of Philippians that Pastor Jones read more times than I can count: "Be careful for nothing; but in every thing by prayer and supplication with thanksgiving let your requests be made known unto God. And the peace of God, which passeth all understanding, shall keep your hearts and minds through Christ Jesus." I close the holy book and set it aside.

What does that even mean, "the peace of God, which passeth all understanding?" I'd love nothing more than to feel this peace, but I ain't got the first clue how to find it. Where's peace when Hank whimpers in his sleep? Where is it when I'm taking a shower with fifty other guys and they're making jokes about shoving it up yours and some are serious about it? How the hell do I look for this supposed peace when screams fill my head, both outside and inside? No, there's no peace to be found in

Hell. I glare at the Bible for a moment, but my anger is short-lived. Then the tears start. Peace was lost with my innocence. My laughter from days of rolling in leaves surrenders to the piercing cries, then dies.

God, if I could do it all over again, I swear to You I wouldn't be such a clown, the family screw up. I'd made Ma smile more by giving her the grades she wanted. I'd help Pa more instead of being lazy. I'd know to leave Kat be and find a girl who loves me like I love her. I'd stop drinking myself stupid.

I end my silent prayer, looking toward Hank. I ain't sure what I'm expecting from a guy who grunts for conversation, but my own company's getting old. Tucking a scrap of hope into my heart, I close my eyes and try to dream of better times.

* * *

There's little joy around here. It's not like the guards put up greenery along the hallways and wind garland around the bars. There aren't any Christmas lights hanging from the ceiling. It's just the same dull, dim overhead lights, the kind that make a guy look even more like death than he already does in here. It's a week before Christmas, give or take.

So, when I'm told I have a visitor, my heart leaps with the first joy I've felt in a long time. A guard brings me into the meeting room, where I'm seated on one side of a long table with bars separating the prisoners from the visitors. I sit and stare into Ma's concerned hazel eyes.

"Hi, Ma," I say, although it sounds more like a croak. "Uh, sorry I haven't written."

Ma's mouth moves, but nothing comes out. Instead, she starts sobbing. She keeps wiping at her eyes with a handkerchief, sniffling, and shaking her head. Finally, she sets the handkerchief in her lap and pulls something outta her purse. It's bright red. She shoves it toward me through the bars.

"I made it for you."

Picking the item up, it's soft. I realize it's a hat. I glance toward the guard, who's got his eyes on me, and pull the hat down over my ears, hiding my messy hair. Heart-gutting gratitude stabs at me. God, Ma, why'd you have to make me something?

"I don't have anything for you, but thanks, Ma."

She shakes her head. "Nonsense, Harry. Why would I expect you to have something for me? The best gift I can ask for this Christmas is to see you. I just w-wish–"

My eyes drop to my hands. The hat feels warm on my head, a piece of home, like her letters. "I know, Ma. So do I. I'm sorry."

"I'm sorry we haven't come sooner. I just– I just couldn't bear that thought of seeing you here."

"I'm sorry." I don't know what else to say. It's pathetic but true. Somehow, two little words do next to nothing to explain how much I wish I could undo the past. I wanna tell Ma that she'll one day be proud of me, that when I get outta here, I won't let her down. It's not a promise I can make.

Ma starts sobbing all over again, and before I can say another wretched "I'm sorry," the guard says our time's up and ushers her out. I'm about to stand and leave, because if I need to blubber like a little kid, at least let it be in my cell instead of here, but the guard tells me I have another visitor. I plant myself back in the seat. I'm on the edge, my legs shaking.

Pa comes in and sits. He tries to smile, but the grimace doesn't reach his dull eyes. "Hi, son."

"Hi, Pa. How're things at home?"

Pa shrugs. "Quiet. It's just us, Hannah, and Irma now."

"How's work?"

"I manage. Not as much business as I used to get, but I'm holding it together fine. Hannah is helping pay the bills with her money from her job."

"Yeah, Ma said so in her letter. That's Hannah for you. Always lookin' out for others." I try to smile.

"Yeah..."

"So, uh... Any plans for Christmas?" I wanna kick myself for speaking to my father like I'm making small talk with a stranger in a food line.

"Amy, Jack, and Jean will be there. Don't know about Erik and Lily yet. We don't really hear much from your brother anymore."

My insides churn as my thoughts darken. What's Erik's problem? He's got all the freedom in the world, yet he can't pick up the phone or be bothered to visit his family? "He's lucky he's not in my shoes. You know what I'd give to be there?"

Pa sighs. "Don't be too hard on Erik, Harry. We all have our own battles to fight."

I cross my arms over my chest. "Yeah, well..."

"It won't be forever, son. I hate seeing you in here, but just give it time."

"Time's all I've got, Pa. I'm losin' my mind here."

Again, Pa tries to smile. It's who he is, what he's always done: give that smile to fill us with hope, to cheer us on, to make us believe in ourselves when we couldn't on our own.

"I wish I'd have known you had that problem, Harry."

His words are soft, but a firm undertone holds them up. He won't even acknowledge what "that problem" is in words. Go ahead, Pa. Tell me I'm a drunk. Instead, I nod and am man enough to look my old man in the eyes when I reply, "I know. Truth is, Pa, I never thought it was a problem."

"Until it was too late."

"Yeah, until then." You must be ashamed of me. That's the real reason why you and Ma haven't come to this hell-hole till now. I don't blame you, Pa. If I were you, I'd stay away from me, too, but I'm kinda stuck with myself.

"Time's up," the guard says without feeling, and he waits for Pa to join him at the door to see him out.

As Pa stands, he says, "Ma and I will be back soon, son. I promise."

"Yeah, see you around, Pa."

And then he's gone. I stand and walk toward the door on my side, looking through the bars one last time, maybe expecting to see the other side without that barrier that tells me exactly where my place is.

"What's that you've got there, boy?"

I frown at Riley. He hadn't been here earlier, but the guards must've changed shifts while I was busy trying to keep it together in front of my folks.

I'd also forgotten that I'm wearing Ma's hat. "It's from my mother."

Riley smirks, an ugly sneer that doesn't do his scarred face any favors. "Aw, your mama got ya a gift, did she?"

I pull the hat off and hold it close.

"Give it here."

"Why?"

"Prisoners ain't supposed to have stuff."

"But others have gotten things from visitors. It ain't like it's a knife or somethin'." I try to keep my voice even.

"Other guards might be soft, but I ain't. You rotten lot don't deserve special gifts. Give it." Riley roughly yanks the hat, and while I try to keep my grip on it, it tears.

In one motion, I lose my hold completely. "What did you do?" I ask, aghast.

Riley laughs, holding the ruined token of Ma's love for me in his nasty hand.

"Give it back."

Riley acts like he's about to hand the hat back, but then snatches his hand away at the last second, erupting in laughter.

"Maybe I shoulda had a piece of glass instead," I say before I realize what's come outta my mouth.

Riley stops laughing. "What's that, boy?"

I'm on a roll now, so why stop? "You heard me. A piece of glass, so I could give you a nice cut on the other cheek to match the one you've already got."

Riley drops the hat and lunges at me, all animal-wild, teeth bared and hands out like talons. A couple of other guards come to his sides, holding him back.

"Enough," the older one says. "Jorgenson, take Rechthart back to his cell."

The younger one, Jorgenson, replies, "Yes, sir," and takes my arm.

I go without comment or fight, but as I walk away, I glance back at Riley. He's glaring at me with the hatred of a man who wants to squash the bee that's stung him. I've stung, and now he's ready to smash me for good.

What have I gone and done now?

CHAPTER 16

"I still can't believe you did it," O'Malley says at dinner that evening. His voice barely carries over the din of the crowded room. The voices of inmates echo off the high ceiling and concrete walls.

"....., well, too late now," I say. I force a spoonful of what resembles a cross between oatmeal and grits into my mouth and swallow.

"You're off your rocker," says Dawson, an inmate in his fifties who's across from us. "Riley ain't one ta mess with, son."

"You've signed your death sentence, old boy," O'Malley says.

I scoff. "I'm not here for that. I'll be outta here in two and a half more years."

"Two and a half years where Riley can make your life a livin' hell," O'Malley says.

"What provoked ya?" asks Dawson.

I shrug, but my blood boils from hours ago when Riley stole Ma's gift. "He deserved it. Who's he think he is? Big, bad guard? We might be in the slammer, but we're still people, ain't we?" My words are tough, but my insides churn, knowing the truth about ol' Riley.

"Well, some of us are," Dawson remarks. "That's ta say, somma us're decent enough folk for criminals." He chuckles.

I can't help but grin. "You're a decent guy, Dawson?"

He laughs louder, and a guard yells, "Keep it down."

Recovering himself, Dawson says softly, "Depends on your criteria, son. Ya wanna make a life for yourself one day, when you're outta here?"

"Why?" I ask.

"Don't blame ya for bein' suspicious o' me, son, but I wasn't always a crook. Damn Depression made a lot o' decent folks do stuff they wouldn'ta done otherwise."

"Okay. Maybe..."

"We'll talk later." Dawson goes quiet, and I'm glad to get my mind off Riley.

"Where's your head now?" O'Malley cuts in.

I snap outta my thoughts and shrug. "Dunno. Don't you ever wish you could do somethin' useful 'round here?"

"Yeah." O'Malley sighs. "I used to be lazy before I was here, lettin' other guys do the work, unless it benefited me, ya know? Funny how that changes."

"Yeah." I sigh as well. "I used to help my pa for his business, deliverin' stuff. Before that, it was chores around the house. My older brother was always gettin' on me about not working hard enough. Same with my ma." I smile sadly.

"That's a mother for ya. Mine was the same way, but I'm glad I didn't have an older brother tellin' me what to do. Must've been quite an ass, your brother."

"Me and him used to be really close as kids, but as we got older, things changed. I guess he felt like he had to prove himself or somethin'. But know what the funny thing is?"

"What's that?" O'Malley shoves the remainder of his dinner away, wrinkling his nose.

The guards are starting to dismiss us, table by table, so I don't have long as I reply, "I need to prove myself when I get outta here. My folks visited for the first time today, and I could see their disappointment in their eyes."

O'Malley and I stand, and we're forced into silence once more. He half-smiles at me, like he gets what I'm saying. When we reach the exit, I go one way and he goes the other. I return to my cell and lie down like a good boy.

* * *

Christmas and New Year's come and go without any further visits from my parents. No one else in my esteemed family drops by, either. The extent of celebrating Christmas in jail amounts to an extra half-hour at dinner and red and green gelatin for dessert. Some of the guys get visitors and gifts, of course, and there are letters and cards delivered. When no gift or even a simple letter arrives for me, I can't help the deep-seated sadness that pokes at me like a needle to the chest. As the days pass, it keeps working its way deeper, until resentment begins to make its home in my once open heart. Then again, I had my gift, and Riley took it away.

I steer clear of ol' Riley. Whenever we're in passing, he glares at me like he wants to grind me into mincemeat, but I'm not having it. Some days, the dark part of me wishes him ill, like he'd just fall over dead and do us all a favor. Then I just as soon turn on myself, wondering how the hell I became this monster. Other days, I pity Riley. I see the way he curses and spits, the twisted look on his face with its ugly scar. But his scar goes deeper, like mine.

On the worst days, the cries of a fellow inmate carrying across the prison hit me in the gut. In those moments, I almost understand why Hank pisses himself.

Sometimes the guards beat a sorry ass for talking back. Their club strikes me in the stomach every time someone else screams. My body trembles. Usually Riley is the first to bring his club out. But other times some Fred or Joe or Tom just loses his shit and cries for his mother because he can't do nothing else. We all carry our scars. Some bleed and never heal. The bludgeoning only raises them to the surface.

On the worst nights, I just lie on my side, the lumpy mattress offering no comfort, and try to block everything out. Better to go crazy by the tormented voices clawing inside than the ones outside.

* * *

On a frigid January day while walking outside in circles and shivering to the bone, Dawson approaches me and mutters, "Hey, ya got a minute?"

"Uh, sure, but...now?" I glance toward the guards. "We ain't supposed to be talkin' now, Dawson."

"'Course not. Just wanted ta catch ya, so we'd sit near enough at supper."

"All right."

Before we're reprimanded, Dawson falls back in line behind me. My legs are about to completely freeze off by the time we go back inside. It ain't warm inside, but it's better than outside. If it weren't for seeing the sky, I'd rather stay in on days like this. Still, it's just daytime clouds. I miss the stars.

While I waste away another day, I wonder what Dawson wants to talk about. Suppertime finally comes.

"Ya look like you're starvin'," he says with a laugh as he takes a seat across from me and O'Malley. "Slow down, son."

Realizing my plate is nearly empty, I nod and ask, "What d'you wanna talk about?"

"Ya know how I told ya I was thrown in here for cheatin' others? Well, truth is, until a coupla years ago, I was an honest man. Fixed people's cars, ya see. Business picked up somethin' nice last decade with all those cars bein' made. I had a family to feed like anyone, so when things got bad, I got, well, desp'rate. Started chargin' people more than was honest and tellin' 'em things was wrong with their cars when it weren't. Got too many people too worked up and couldn't hide my lies forever. So, here I am, servin' my time for lyin' and cheatin'. Thing is, I'll be out in a few months. Gettin' business goin' again ain't gonna be no easy thing, but I'm willin' ta try by the Good Lord's name. Young guy like you seems like he's gonna need all the help he can get when he's outta here."

"What're you sayin'?"

"If you'd like, you'd have a job lined up for ya, Rechthart, son. I've learned the error of my ways and'd be a good 'n fair boss. Ya ever thought o' fixin' cars?"

"I, uh, dunno. I mean, I helped my pa here and there growing up, tinkerin' in his garage, but I'd have lots to learn."

"I'm willin' if you are."

I smile. "Yeah, that'd be, wow... Are you sure?"

"Sure as the day's long, son."

"Gee, thanks, Dawson. I don't know what to say." For the first time in a long time, there's a bit of hope in my future.

"Lucky stiff," O'Malley says next to me. He looks at Dawson. "Hey, what about me?"

"Sure, son. Ya think ya could do it?"

"I know a thing or two about cars, Dawson. I stole a few in my lifetime." O'Malley grins and chuckles.

"Well, so long's ya don't steal any o' the cars you're workin' on, I don't see why not. I'm hopin' ta get my garage up and runnin' again within a few months' time, so by the time you're outta here, things oughta be goin' good...I hope. When're you two boys due out? Wait, ain't you said somethin' 'bout two years 'n such, Rechthart?"

"Yeah, try two years and some months," I say, trying not to grumble.

"Hey, it ain't forever," Dawson says.

"That's what my pa said when he visited."

"Hey, Rechthart, chin up," O'Malley puts in. "I've still got over a year."

These guys know why I'm here. While they're serving time for stealing, they don't seem bothered by the fact that I killed someone. I can't even say her name anymore, 'cause it's too much. I see her face every time I close my eyes, and no amount of trying to rebuild my life one day is ever gonna change that.

I shake myself outta my thoughts and force a smile. A few others sitting nearby have been listening in, but no one seems to care what we're talking about. Most of these guys are just trying to get by, one lousy day at a time. I smile because that's what I can do.

"Hey, thanks again, Dawson," I say.

"Anytime, son. Just passin' along some kindness. Need ta prove ta my fam'ly that I'm a good man again."

As the guards announce the end of the meal and begin filing us outta the mess hall like a bunch of mostly obedient dogs-in-training, I fall into silence. Not only is that silence enforced, but what could I say to Dawson? I understand all too well how he feels about having to show the world, especially those closest to him, that he ain't such a bad guy after all.

By Cynthia Hilston

* * *

Several months later, Dawson gets out like he said he would. Before he steps outta jail and into the world again, he tells me, "Trust me, Rechthart, son. Two more years 'n you'll have a place. Promise."

I hold fast to that promise. Also to the hope that I'll be a better man. I'm sure by now that my family views me as the black sheep. Only Pa and Ma have come by these past several months, and it's only been a handful of times. The amount of time between visits and letters has stretched more and more as well, and I'm beginning to wonder how much longer that rubber band can go before it breaks.

As for Riley, because I've kept my head down, I've given him no reason to come at me with his club or mouth. The punishment of others is punishment enough for me. Whenever we pass, I turn my eyes to the ground.

"Hey, look at me when I talk to you, Rechthart," he says with a growl one fall afternoon.

Surprised it's taken this long to try to provoke me, I say, "I'm just goin' back to my cell, sir."

"Then hurry the hell up, smartass."

I meet his eyes and tell myself there's only tormented sadness reflected back at me. Forcing myself not to even nod, my eyes fall back to the worn concrete floor. They follow the dirty path many have trod.

* * *

When the weather grows cold again, I'm called to the visitor's room. I'm ready to tell my folks not to bother coming by anymore. As I step into the room, my eyes fall on Hannah. She looks nervous as the guard who brings me in seats me on the other side of the bars.

"You have twenty minutes," the guard says dully as he leaves. This is nothing new to me. Twenty minutes is all I ever get. It used to seem like not enough time. Now it's too much time. All the damned time in my small world.

Hannah looks at me like she doesn't recognize me. She's dressed like she just came from work in a tidy blouse and skirt, a long coat over it all. Her dark blond hair is longer than last time I saw her, just past her shoulders. She seems to carry herself with the same grace she always has–chin held high, shoulders back–like she's trying to convince the world she's strong. She is strong. Determined. I see that spark in her eyes, yet something else shines there. I fear it's unshed tears.

If she's expecting my trademark grin or the mischievous gleam in my eyes, she's got another thing coming. I suppose my unshaven face and messy hair aren't doing me any favors, but vanity around here ain't my priority.

I stare right back at this young woman. That's what Hannah's become. The girl who was my sister has died to me, just like the rest of my family.

Finally, Hannah grimaces, though I suspect she's aiming for a smile. "Hi, Harry."

"Hannah," I say after a long time. "Fancy seeing you here of all places."

"Harry, I'm sorry for not visiting sooner."

"Don't be."

"I wanted to see how you're doing. Not a day goes by that I don't think of you."

"I see. So, I'm in your thoughts, but that's not enough to make you come and see me? It's been over a year."

Hannah keeps blinking, like she's trying not to cry. For a sec, I almost give in and break. But I can't. What good would more tears do? Better to give her good reason not to return to this hell-hole and me, one of the demons who lives in its rot and stink.

"I know, and all I can say is I'm sorry. I've been a horrible sister. Do– do you have other visitors?"

I push regret away and lean my chair back, balancing it on the rear legs, and cross my arms over my chest. "Things must've really changed on the homestead if you don't know. Yeah, Pa and Ma, they've stopped by a few times, but it's been a long stretch. I think it took them a good few months after my incarceration before they swung by for the first time. Of course, all Ma ever does is look at me and cry, and then Pa comes in after her time's up and tries to act like everything's fine. No one talks about what got me here. It's like some big secret we're all keeping, just trying to see who can keep quiet the longest. I'd say it's a fun game, but I'm not sure if that's how you'd see it."

That's not completely true–that no one talks about my drinking. Pa tried at first, but even he's given up. So, as far as Hannah's concerned, she doesn't need to know any more. Her words interrupt my dismal thoughts as she says, "I don't think it's a game at all. It's your life."

I laugh without humor. "Ah, but there's the rub, Hannah-panna. My life is a game, a joke. Those are easy to put away when you have no use for them. This old game isn't so much fun anymore."

There's the punch in the gut, the last straw, the sure-fire way to drive home the point to Hannah. As the words exit my mouth like vomit, I can't believe what I'm saying.

"You won't be in here forever. What about when you get out?"

My face hardens. "It's obvious my problem has burdened my family enough, Hannah. Trust me when I say that it's easier this way. You shouldn't have come today."

Tears fall all over Hannah's crumbling face as she glances at the clock. I hide my tears like so much else, but if Hannah could crack me open, she'd drown in my sorrow. Five minutes left.

She stands before our time's up, but if she's like me, there ain't any words to fill five minutes. Let the damning silence descend like it always does and grab those five minutes and add them to the next year and a half I have left in the slammer. What do five minutes matter?

Five minutes might've made a difference on a day a couple of years ago if I would've just told Kat Jones that I wasn't interested in her. Five minutes could've mattered before getting into the car that night she'd rejected my love and my proposal when I'd drunk myself silly. Five minutes might've saved Kat's life and mine. Hannah's and my family's relationship.

Instead, Hannah says in a voice so broken, it's clear I'm beyond repair, "Officer, I'm ready to go."

I stare at my lap as I hear her footsteps retreat.

"Officer," I call. "Take me back to my cell."

CHAPTER 17

Another year passes. O'Malley's out now. Here I am, alone.
When 1933 draws near its end, I laugh humorlessly when I hear the news—alcohol's now legal. What a damn and damning joke.

"What d'you think of that, Hank, old boy?" I whisper to my cellmate on Christmas Eve. "You wanna raise a glass with me?"

Hank glares, grumbles, and rolls onto his other side, turning away from me as he lies on his bed. I smirk at his back for a minute and then sigh as the nasty smile drops from my face like an overused one-liner. With nothing better to do, I stretch out on my own bed, the uneven mattress molding somewhat to my body by now. I shift and a piece of paper hangs out from under the mattress. I snatch it, hoping for an old reminder from home. Although the letters between Ma and me stopped long ago, I keep every one.

As my eyes adjust to the low light, I realize it's Dawson's latest letter. I smile as I read:

Rechthart

As you no I got the garage up and running again. Wasnt sure how it'd go but business is stedy maybe even good. Had to hire a guy last week on acount of how many cars are comming here.

I'd ask how life is for you but I no. Make any new friends? You can prolly do better then an old fuddy duddy like me.

Ok. Chin up son. Like I told you it aint forever. You got a job waiting for you when your out. Dont forget. (Dont think this new guys going to work out anyway.)

Dawson

I fold the letter and stow it away like a precious gem in a treasure chest. I owe him a letter soon. Right now, he's my connection to the outside world. My eyes grow heavy, maybe from trying to read in the near dark, maybe because I think too much. I let them drop, and I fall asleep.

The next morning, Jorgenson, one of the nicest guards, comes by. "Hey, Rechthart. Up and at 'em. You've got someone here to see you."

I sit up in bed. "What? Don't visiting hours start later?"

Jorgenson smiles, a genuine sort that reaches his eyes. "I made an exception for Christmas Day. Besides, he says he hasn't seen you in years."

"I, uh, I don't really wanna see anyone if that's okay with you."

"You may want to make an exception, Rechthart."

I stand and stretch. "Oh, all right, since it's Christmas and all."

Jorgenson leads me to the visiting room and says, "Hey, I'll give you an extra ten minutes, pal."

I nod, murmuring my thanks. Among the guests, I finally spot him: dark blond, slicked-back hair, cold blue eyes, and that look about him that tells me he's still got a stick up his ass. I glower and sit. I cross my arms as my face heats. "What d'you want?"

"Merry Christmas to you, too, Harry."

I lean back into my chair, dropping my arms to my sides. "Merry Christmas, esteemed brother, but is it really? Merry, I mean?"

"Harry, I didn't come here to argue."

"No? Why show your face after years, then?"

"I'm in town to visit our parents, so I thought I'd stop by to see you. Is that a crime?"

I bark a short laugh. "Funny you should talk about crimes. You wanna trade places? What's your worth these days?"

"Harry, would you please—"

"Face it, Erik. You always thought you were better than me, and now that's a fact. I'm surprised you gave the dirt you hide under the rug a second thought."

"You've changed."

"So have you."

"Harry, look, I didn't come here to dig up old hurts."

"Just seein' you is reason enough to open old scars and bleed them dry." I lean toward him with my hands on the table.

"That's your problem. You made your own choices, and so did I."

"Yeah, but I was never an asshole about it."

Erik's eyebrows raise. "Excuse me?"

"Listen to you—talkin' all fancy-schmancy with your education and high-payin' job."

"You're jealous. You've always been—"

"Don't you dare. Why would I wanna be some pretty boy?"

"You're not the only one with problems, Harry."

"I never said I was."

"For your information, ever since Pa broke his leg last year in a trucking accident, he hasn't been the same. He walks with a cane now. He can't manage the business. If you were free, you could've taken over for him."

Pa was in an accident? My insides churn. If only I'd written back to Ma and Pa, maybe they'd still be writing to me. When I manage to speak, it's laced with shame. "My God, Erik, you think I don't know that I was supposed to follow in Pa's footsteps? So, Pa's in a bad way. You want me to cry my bleedin' heart out for you, confess my guilt to you like you're some damn priest?"

"No, I–"

"You should go."

"Harry, wait... I just wanted to tell you that–" Erik looks torn between staying and leaving. He finally stands. "Lily and I have tried for years to have a kid. We're beginning to wonder if we'll ever know the joy of being parents. In the meantime, Amy's had another daughter."

It's like someone's punched all the wind outta me. I blink, staring at my lap. When I look at my brother, I swallow and say thickly, "I'm sorry to hear it. You'd make a great dad."

Erik sits back down. His face is all screwed up. "So would you, Harry. That's why, seeing you in here like this, I hate it. You're better than this. I know you are. You've always sold yourself short."

A second punch to the gut. I look down, shaking my head. "Why didn't you tell me that years ago?"

"Maybe I was too full of myself. You were right. I'm sorry, Harry."

"Yeah, I'm sorry, too...but what good'll it do now? I've written my sentence in stone."

"You have six, seven more months?"

"Yeah."

"Then start over. You think I care if you have a record?"

"I dunno. I'm never gonna be like you, Erik. It's not that simple."

"You shouldn't try to be like me. Be yourself. Do what you've always done when the goin' gets tough. Make a joke out of life. It's not that serious, is it?"

I smile a bit. "I didn't usually think so, but look where it got me. You know, a guy can smile and goof around all he wants, but it doesn't change reality."

"But it changes how you see the world. I mean, if you really believed all those light-hearted, crazy things you used to say, I don't think you'd be so bitter."

"No, probably not. Truth is..." I lean forward, lowering my voice. "Yeah, I hated bein' in your shadow. I wanted our parents to be proud of me. I lied to myself for years, Erik, thinkin' I was happy when I wasn't. Thinkin' some girl loved me who didn't. People were along for the good ride and nothin' more."

"You don't honestly think Ma and Pa were just along for the ride, do you? That I was? Hannah? The rest of the family?"

I sigh. "No, I guess not, but the damage's been done. I can't look at Ma and Pa straight in the face anymore. I haven't seen them in about a year."

"What? They haven't visited?"

"They have, I'm sure, but I've refused any visitors...until you today."

"Well, I'm glad you decided to see me, Harry."

"I didn't want to. I had a feeling it was you when the guard said my visitor hadn't seen me in years, but this talk's gotten too mushy for my tastes." I try to laugh it off.

Erik smiles. "There's the Harry I know. Look, I'll tell the rest of the family I stopped by to see you. Is there anything you'd like me to pass along?"

"No. I don't think I'm ready to face everyone yet, even if it's through you."

Erik stands. "I understand. I'll see you soon, Harry. Merry Christmas."

"Merry Christmas, Erik."

After he leaves, I stand and look to the guard, expecting to find Jorgenson. Instead, Riley's ugly mug glares at me.

"C'mon, boy, back to your cell," he growls.

"Merry Christmas, Officer Riley," I say, walking next to him, surprised he hasn't grabbed my upper arm.

He stops mid-step and turns toward me. "What's that?"

"I just said—"

"You playin' games, boy?"

I hold up my hands. "No, sir. Just thought you'd appreciate bein' told as much as the next guy."

"Don't celebrate Christmas, not that it's any business of yours."

I meet his eyes. "I know a thing or two about bein' miserable."

"Shut up."

"Sorry. I just thought I'd say I'm sorry for sayin' what I did to you two years ago."

"Don't know what you're talkin' 'bout. That's enough, Rechthart."

We arrive at my cell. Riley leans in close and mutters, "You're lucky it's Christmas and I'm goin' easy on ya. Now get back in there before I have reason to change my mind."

I keep the smile off my face as I enter my cell. As Riley leaves, I wonder what this one small mercy cost him.

There's nothing different about this day from any other, except for Erik's visit. That's made all the difference. If my brother can see something good in me still, maybe I'm not through trying to make something of myself.

"The Good Lord finds a way of bringing good from the bad," old Pastor Jones used to say.

I'm starting to believe that.

CHAPTER 18

The months count down. I pray silently every night before bed. Hank never says a word to me, but I sometimes find him watching me. I wonder if he's saying his own prayers, what they might be. Even Officer Riley leaves me alone. I think he knows I have no fight with him.

Despite trying to keep the faith, I got demons—one with red hair and green eyes visits me nightly.

"Oh, c'mon, big boy. Don't you have a kiss for me?" she taunts.

I try to tell her I can't drive her home, but she gets into the car. I drive, the wheel sliding under my fingers. I panic and try to stop the car. She kisses my cheek. Then she straddles me, runs her claws through my hair, draws blood. Her kisses tear into my skin with her fangs. More blood. Her legs are like a steel vice on my body. I'm paralyzed. She screams, shrieks.

She's sprawled out on the seat next to me. Blood everywhere.

And those eyes. Always those green eyes.

Then I wake up, sweat on my brow, my breathing fast. Like every night, I look into the darkness for an answer.

When will you stop haunting me, Kat Jones? There, I've said your name. It's like your ghost is beside me in this cell.

I pray again for peace. My breathing calms, and I fall back asleep. In the morning, I jump outta bed. This earns a glare from Hank.

"Sorry, old boy," I say with a grin.

"Don't be."

I stop, stunned. "Did you just speak?"

But Hank just stares at me with haunted eyes. The corner of his mouth twitches like he might smile or speak. Then he turns away.

"Hope you find your peace one day, Hank."

It's all the hope I can offer.

I'm a restless mess as I wait for the cell door to open. On the way to breakfast, my feet want to run, not walk. At the table, I devour the sawdust like it's Ma's finest cooking. My legs dance under the table. My fingers twitch at my sides. I can't seem to find a place for my hands.

After breakfast, Riley approaches me. "Wipe that stupid grin off your face."

"Can't help it, sir. It's my last day here."

"Follow me."

He escorts me to the exit and hands me the clothes I wore the day I entered prison. I keep quiet. After changing into my regular clothes, I almost don't recognize myself in the mirror. I've been so used to the grey prison garb for so long that the young man in jeans and a worn blue shirt simply can't be Harry Rechthart. My hair's a disaster, and a good shave would be just the thing. I can't help but think I look older than twenty-four. It's like prison's aged me a decade.

I leave the bathroom and pass my prison garb off to Riley. He takes it without comment and ushers me outside beyond the fence. I step into the humid July sun and see the trees again for the first time in three years. I smile, breathe in the fresh air. God, I can breathe again, really breathe!

"I don't wanna see ya back here," Riley says.

"I don't wanna be back here, either." My grin widens.

"Hmph. Lots of luck to ya, smartass." With those words of wisdom, Riley's gone.

I step out onto the street with not a penny and only the clothes on my back and start walking, taking several turns. After a while, I check the sign. Good, old Euclid Avenue. I'm just another guy here among these folks. They don't know me from Tom, Dick, or, well, Harry. The Terminal Tower stands tall and proud not far off. I spend the next hour or so just walking in the sunshine as a free man. The noise of the city—the cars, the people, the busses, the streetcars—is like listening to jazz again. My feet half-dance, half-walk at times. I receive more than a few startled looks.

I consider going to a bus stop and checking the routes for the bus that'll take me back to my childhood neighborhood. But then the thought occurs to me: Do I have to go home? Is it still home for me? Sure, my family knows I'm due outta the slammer around this time, but no one's paid me a visit since Erik back at Christmas. I disappear into the city's framework. My mood sours at the idea of seeing my folks and siblings too soon. This much I know—I ain't ready to face them.

I remember Dawson and his promise. He gave me an address before he got out.

It's not a long walk to what's left of the Haymarket area. It's a rundown neighborhood, certainly different from what I've been used to—not that growing up on Madison Avenue meant we were rich. Still, it's a real eye-opener to see the slums. This is where Dawson lives and works. This is where he's offering to help me. This is where I'm thinking of starting over.

I remember Pa talking about how there were three families living in some of the houses here. Dockworkers crowd the Cuyahoga River. The air is heavy with smoke from trains and factories. Bits of different languages hit my ears as I pass people. And there are bars everywhere. Not a good sign for a guy like me. Still, maybe I need the challenge. I've already been in jail, been brought lower than a fly on a cow's backside. How much lower can a guy go than that? This around me now ain't rock bottom. It's a chance to be a new man.

I arrive at the address I've pinned to my memory like a note tacked on a board. Just as I'm wondering whether I oughta knock, a man walks outta the garage toward me, with a yellow-toothed smile standing out among the grime on his face.

"Well, I'll be damned! Harry Rechthart! It's really you, ain't it?"

His smile warms my face more than the sun as I hold out my hand and Dawson shakes it. He's fatter than the last time I saw him. A cap covers his bald spot. Still, Dawson's face is like a beacon of hope.

"Business goin' well?" I ask.

"Oh, damn, ya wouldn't believe it, young man!" Dawson extends an arm and gestures toward the half-condemned buildings around us. "It ain't exactly paradise city here, but people from all over Cleveland are comin' here 'cause I keep my prices low. Don't care 'bout bein' rich, so long's I have enough to support the family, ya know? Crazy thing is, Rechthart, I realize I coulda made more money bein' honest and chargin' less afore I was thrown in the slammer, if ya know what I mean, 'stead of cheatin' good, honest folk."

"That's great. So, uh, does your offer still stand, 'cause I understand if–"

Dawson waves me off and wraps a thick arm around my shoulders like a father as he leads me into his garage. It only holds one car at a time, but behind the building is a small lot filled with broken down jalopies.

"O'Malley never showed his face. I know ya two were pals, but ain't much I can do 'bout that. I offered, but he ain't here. But you are. Now, how's about you and me sit down and have a bite and talk shop, eh?"

My stomach growls, and I chuckle. "I guess that answers it for you."

Dawson laughs heartily and invites me into his home, which is in front and to the right of the garage. Once inside, he says, "Better take off your shoes if ya know what's good for ya. The wife'll never let me live it down. Betty keeps a clean place, so spic-'n-span ya can almost eat off the damn floor."

"I heard that," a woman's voice calls from the back of the house.

"That'll be Betty now," Dawson says, his voice turning warm and his face softening.

A middle-aged woman with curly, orange hair and a friendly face enters the room. She smiles. "You must be Harry Rechthart," she says with a slight Irish accent.

I smile, knowing Ma would have a few things to say about me spending time with someone who's probably Catholic. "Yep, in the flesh. Your, uh, husband was kind enough to give me a job."

"That's my Ernie for you, bless him. We'll be married thirty years next month."

Seeing these two, it's hard to believe Dawson ever served time, that he was the kinda guy who'd lie and cheat. Before I can think further, a younger woman steps into the living room. She's her mom's twin, only a good twenty-five years younger.

"Kathy, my youngest," Dawson explains. "Never had a son. Only daughters. She's the only one left at home."

Kathy blushes when she sees me.

I smile at her. "Nice to meet you, Kathy."

"Hello," Kathy replies quietly.

Dawson grins at me.

I nod and let my smile do the talking.

"Yes, well, lunch is ready." Mrs. Dawson raises her eyebrows. "Best you two wash up, and then we'll eat. Nothing fancy, but then again, who expects anything fancy these days?"

I follow the Dawsons into the kitchen, where Dawson and I run our hands under the warm water until they're clean. I awkwardly join them at the table. Whatever Mrs. Dawson's thrown together, it smells a hundred times better than any of that sludge we ate in prison. She sets a large pot in the middle of the table and begins ladling some sort of vegetable soup into our bowls.

A little while later, not realizing I was this hungry, I try not to blush when Mrs. Dawson remarks, "An empty bowl already, young man? Don't they feed you in jail?"

I blush more. "'If it's good enough for the pigs, it's good enough for us' we used to say." I laugh weakly.

Kathy giggles as she holds her hand up to her mouth.

"I'll take that as a compliment," Mrs. Dawson says. "You want more?"

"That'd be great. Thanks."

Dawson leans back in his chair and pats his belly. "Careful, son, or she'll try ta fatten you up, too. She's done good with me."

Mrs. Dawson shakes her head as she fills my bowl. "Don't go layin' blame with me, Ernie. That's all your doing."

Dawson chuckles. "Can ya blame a guy for likin' his wife's cookin'?"

"Is that your way of saying you want more?"

"Yes, ma'am."

I can't help but feel at home here. It's only been a half hour, and it's like I've known the Dawsons for years. After Dawson and I are done with our second bowls, I say, "That was delicious, Mrs. Dawson. Thanks."

"You still hungry, young man?"

"Nah, I'm good, ma'am, even if I could stand to gain a few pounds."

"All right, then. Off with you two. Kathy and I will do the clean-up."

Dawson stands. "A man knows when he ain't wanted." He winks at me. "Best we'd get back into the garage, and I start 'splainin' things to ya, son."

Once we're back in the sweltering heat, he opens the hood to the Ford he's working on. "Know anything 'bout an engine?"

"Not much, but I can learn."

"Okay. Let's see. This here's the exhaust manifold, and right under's the intake manifold. Exhaust manifold's job is ta collect exhaust gas from the cylinders, see, and d'liver it to the exhaust pipe. Intake manifold's job's to make sure the combustion mix is gettin' to the intake ports o' the cylinder heads. This's important to keep the engine runnin' smooth-like."

My head spins. "Uh, right. And what's this thing here?"

Dawson chuckles. "That's the motor valve cover, son. One thing at a time, eh? Let's stick ta what I talked 'bout. You're lookin' at a completely diff'rent part o' the engine."

"Sorry, it's just...a lot."

"Well, I'm gonna teach ya your way 'round these here engines like nobody's business. This beauty's in here ta fix the exhaust, so let's start there. Ya learn that, and then we'll go to the next thing."

"Righto, sir. What d'you want me to do?"

Dawson points toward a shelf filled with car parts. "Get me that there exhaust pipe on top."

I walk to the shelf and stare like an idiot. The top shelf's overflowing with pipes of all sizes. "Uh, which one?"

Dawson shakes his head, laughs a bit, and joins me. "Okay, see, the thing ya need t'know 'bout pipes is..."

He goes on to explain the intricate details of exhaust pipes. I never gave much thought to the thing that spouted out smelly fumes from the back of Pa's truck or the family car. I cringe, thinking about the old Caddy. I glance out the back door at the lot filled with old clunkers and wonder if maybe I can fix one up and give it to my family one day.

One day, maybe. For now, I listen to Dawson and try to understand what the hell he's talking about. It's like hearing the German my old grandma used to speak when I was growing up.

After a couple of hours, I'm sweating something fierce. Dawson takes pity on me.

"Take a break, son. I'd say ya earned it."

I step back from the car and wipe at my forehead, annoyed at the hair hanging in my eyes. A haircut's in the near future. I imagine my face's as dirty as my hands. My arms are up to my elbows in black.

Dawson steps out for a sec and returns with two beers. He offers me one. "Here, take a load off, son."

"Uh..." I hold up my hands and shake my head as I take a step back. "Sorry, sir, but I probably shouldn't."

"Oh, damn." Dawson's face scrunches up as he sets the bottles aside. "Sorry 'bout that. I forgot."

"It's okay. Really. D'you have a smoke? Can't tell you the last time I had one. Guards hardly ever let us light up."

"Don't remind me." Dawson pulls out a pack from his shirt pocket and passes a cigarette off to me. We light up.

I relax as the smoke works its way into my body. "You know, don't worry about the beer. I appreciate it...and everything."

Dawson waves me off. "Should I get ridda the stuff? I mean, not wantin' ta tempt ya and all."

"Well, I'm here to work, right? Not drink on the job."

"True, son, but we haven't talked 'bout 'rangements for livin'."

"Oh, well...I'm sure I'll figure somethin' out." Standing there, I have no idea where I'll be laying my head tonight.

"How 'bout this? We've an extra room from when the older girls lived at home. Can I trust ya?" He gives me a look, and there's not a question in my mind what he means. I've seen Pa flash the same look at guys who've dated my sisters.

I hold my hands up. "Honest to God, Dawson. You ain't got nothin' to worry about with me. Hell, you've been like some saint to me, sir. The last thing I'd do–"

Dawson's face melts into a smile as he chuckles. "All right, all right, son. I get it! Just wanted ta see ya squirm a bit, I did."

"Well, it worked." I laugh and take one last drag from my cigarette, then smash it underfoot. In the back of my mind, I remember the stuff Kat and I did.

"As for your lodgin', I know a fella down the street a ways who's lookin' for a roommate, someone ta help pay the rent. I reckon we can work somethin' out wit' him tomorrow."

"Sounds great."

"Okay, son. Let's get back ta workin', eh?"

I follow Dawson back to the car. He spends the rest of the afternoon teaching me all about exhaust systems. I'm mostly clueless by the end of the day, but as I kick my feet up in a real bed, nothing but gratitude fills me. To know there're people in the world who are decent and willing to give a guy like me a second chance is nothing short of a miracle.

CHAPTER 19

Two weeks in, I'm used to my new routine. I hardly see the guy I share a place with. His name's Hank—a strange coincidence. He's nothing like my old buddy from the slammer. This Hank's about my age, a friendly, outgoing kinda guy. He works third shift at a factory, so when I'm working, he's sleeping. Then we flip-flop roles.

At work, I've gotten my first paycheck. Dawson is the role model of patience. I've yet to see him annoyed or angry when I mess up. When he sees I'm getting stressed, he stops what we're doing and offers to share a cigarette.

A guy could get used to this.

Besides my job and housing, I can't help but get Kathy's eye from time to time. The most she's said to me is "hello," "bye," and "how are you?"

As August starts, I step outta the bathroom in the Dawsons' house and nearly run her over. "Uh, gee, sorry about that." I feel the blush on the back of my neck.

Kathy blushes, too. "No, it's my fault. I should've watched where I was going."

I wave her off. "Don't be silly. Here, you need this?" I step aside and motion toward the bathroom.

"Um...yes."

I move outta the way and turn away as I hear the door shut. I make to head back to the garage, but decide to hold up a minute. I wait downstairs in the living room. A few minutes later, she comes down the stairs and stops on the last step. Her eyes grow large when she sees me, and I realize I'm pacing.

"Um, hi again." I stop in my tracks and almost trip over my two left feet.

"Hi, Harry." She says my name for the first time, like she's testing it on her tongue to see how it feels. "So, did you need something?"

"Just wanted to talk...if that's okay with you."

"Sure, but won't my dad be looking for you?"

"He can wait a minute."

Kathy takes the last step and stops at the bottom of the stairs. She smiles. "Yeah, my dad's pretty patient. You've never seen him when dinner's running behind, though."

We share a quick laugh. "I'm sure. What guy doesn't love to eat?"

Kathy giggles. "My dad met you in jail, huh?"

It's a simple statement, no accusation in her voice. Even though I know Kathy's aware of my past in the slammer, I'm not sure how much she knows about what got me there.

"Yeah, not one of my finer moments, uh, years."

"My dad says the same thing. It was awful when he was in jail, being just my mom and me. My sisters' husbands kinda looked out for us, but I don't think they wanted to. My dad's a good guy. He was just–"

"It's okay. I know. He told me about it, and I believe you both. Anyone'd have to be a damn fool to think your dad's anything other than kind."

Kathy's smile reaches her eyes. "That's the nicest thing anyone's said about him in a long time, besides my mom. I mean, he gets customers, but it's not the same. They don't really know him."

"Still, I'm sure his customers have nothin' but good things to say, right? I've never heard any different. Then again, I haven't been here long."

Kathy drops into an armchair and sighs. "Most of them are nice enough, but there are some who... They whisper about him when they think we won't hear. I can be out running an errand and overhear talk on the street, you know?"

"Then they're fools. Your dad believes in second chances, and so do I."

"Thank you."

I begin to smile. Dawson enters through the front door. He doesn't look too pleased–probably due to my long break. His eyes shift from his daughter to me, and he smiles. "Ah, so my girl's holdin' you up, eh?"

"Oh, no, sir. It's my fault. Sorry."

"Go find your mother, Kathy." Dawson waves her off good-naturedly.

Kathy gives me one last smile and leaves.

"Got your peepers on my girl, huh?" Dawson raises his eyebrows.

"She's a nice girl."

"Yeah, she is. Special one, too." He heads out the door, leaving me unsure what the hell to think.

I shake my head and follow Dawson out. When I join him in the garage, it's back to business as he picks up a wrench and beckons me over. "Okay, look here..." He points toward the intake manifold.

"Right, sir." I try to screw my head on straight and concentrate.

Dawson spends the rest of the afternoon completing my training on exhausts. I'm exhausted by the end of it. Like always, he invites me to stay for dinner. Part of me wants to tell him I'm good, that he doesn't have to keep giving me so much, but I know it'd be an insult to his hospitality. Besides, Mrs. Dawson's cooking rivals Ma's, and that's the highest compliment I could give.

After dinner, I gaze at the phone hanging on the kitchen wall.

"You wanna call your folks?" asks Dawson.

"What? No, that's okay, sir." I tear my eyes away from the phone.

"Ya sure?"

I try to smile as I look at Kathy clear the table and bring the dirty dishes to her mom at the sink. For a moment, it's like I step outta time. The kitchen changes into the one in my old home. Ma stands at the sink. Amy or Hannah clear the table. I blink, shake my head.

Dawson touches my shoulder, breaking up a hundred memories of a common sight. My heart thuds. My stomach knots. My throat closes up, and my damn mouth won't work right. I look at him and manage a small shake of the head.

He squeezes my shoulder, nods. "Whenever you're ready, son."

"Thanks," I whisper. "Um...thanks for dinner. See you later." I slip away before emotion makes a fool of me.

I step out onto the sidewalk and stroll the short distance to my place. It ain't really my home, just a spot to lay my head. Home's the garage, the house next to it, and the people in it.

My mind goes back to calling my folks and telling them I'm okay, that they don't need to worry. Alone with my thoughts, I sort them out and chase away the damn feelings. At least try to. A coupla weeks ain't enough time to fix a broken family. I gotta fix myself first and foremost. Still, grown man that I am, I can't help but miss Ma every time I take a bite of something Mrs. Dawson makes. I think of Pa every moment I'm with Dawson and almost feel guilty for thinking of Dawson as a sort of father.

But the Dawsons haven't judged me since I entered their lives. As much as I know it kills my family 'cause of what I've done, every tear Ma cried, every frown on Pa's face, every word from Hannah, and every look from Erik tell me they're...what? I dare not name it.

My head aches by the time I unlock the old door to my place. It creaks on rusty hinges as I bang it shut behind me.

"Damn, man, you tryin' to wake up the dead?"

"Sorry, pal," I say as Hank steps into the tiny front room. It's got a sofa, a lamp, and not much else.

He waves me off. "Aw, it's nothin.' Just teasin' ya. I need to get goin' soon."

"How d'you manage to get any sleep around here during the day? It's loud as hell."

"You'd know what hell sounds like?"

"Actually, if you mean hell like prison, then it's more silent than anything. Quiet enough to drive a man crazy."

"That explains a lot." Hank smirks at me.

"Shut it, pal." I punch him lightly in the arm, glad for the distraction.

"Not that it's my business, seein' as I haven't known ya long, but what landed a guy like you in the slammer?"

"Drinkin', back when it was illegal, and then bein' stupid enough to drive on top of it."

"Damn, old boy. Tough luck."

"Yeah, it was pretty stupid." That doesn't begin to describe my biggest blunder.

"Spent a bit of time in my own jail with an old ball 'n chain, if ya catch my drift." Hank winks.

"You were married?"

"Yep, dumbest thing I've ever done. She sucked me dry, that dame."

"What the hell happened?"

"Thought I was really somethin' back in high school, datin' one of those rich girls. 'Course, she didn't go to the public school. Some private, fancy-pants place for her."

"How'd you meet?"

"Neighborhoods are crazy. You can turn a corner, and the world goes from broke-down to rich-city. I was the paper delivery boy. Her house was one of 'em in those rich neighborhoods. Saw her on the porch one summer day and couldn't keep my peepers off her. Soon, couldn't keep my hands off her."

"She sounds kinda like a girl I once knew, though she wasn't rich."

"Girls are trouble, I tell ya. Anyway, don't know what she was expectin' when she right up and married a guy like me who don't have a dollar in the bank. Every penny earned went to her. Wanted to keep her happy, I did. That somehow lasted three years. We lost what little we had. She ran back to Daddy, and here I am, tryin' to pick up the pieces."

"You're still married?"

"Yeah, but hopefully not much longer. What 'bout you, old boy? You mentioned a girl."

"Yeah, she was..." I search for the right words to describe Kat, and in thinking of her, all I see are those damn green eyes on a dead face. "She wasn't who I thought, either."

"Girls never are."

"Well, maybe we just haven't met the right ones."

Hank chuckles. "Don't tell me—you've got your eyes on the mechanic's gal."

"Maybe."

"Not maybe. I know that look. I'd say I'd talk to ya over a drink 'bout it, but I really need to get to work, and you, well, I don't reckon you wanna–"

"That's the thing, Hank. I always wanna drink, but I can't. I'll, uh, let you go."

Hank waves and is out the door. I flop onto the sofa and lean my head on the cushion, staring at the ceiling. Why does a simple talk with my roommate have to open up old wounds? I try think about Kathy, that maybe I'm ready to move on with my life and try my hand again at love, but who am I kidding? Only myself.

CHAPTER 20

For the next several weeks, I steer clear of Kathy. We only see each other in passing and at meals. She won't meet my eyes most of the time. At first, her pretty face lit up whenever she saw me, but as time passed that light died. I wanted to kick myself for how I was treating her, but what did she expect from me? We had one good conversation, but I'm damaged goods.

I'm glad for the cooler weather. Working in that boiling garage in the summer was starting to get to me. I sweated through my clothes within the first fifteen minutes some mornings. Besides the chillier temps, I'm learning lots from Dawson. Cars and I are becoming pals. Dawson's given me free reign to pick any jalopy from the rust pile out back and work on it in my spare time. I don't know enough to fully fix the Caddy there that's only a year older than the one my parents had, but at least the exhaust's repaired!

I'm beginning to feel like my life's on the right track. Maybe, one day, I'll take the next step. Despite my talk with Hank and a deep-seated fear about my ability to be a husband and a dad, I do wanna get married and have a family. I love kids. Every time I see Dawson and his wife together, I want what they have, what my parents have. I don't understand that kind of dedication to another person, but I want to. I wanna be the old man who has someone to go home to when he's done at the end of a hard day's work. When done living, to know life had a purpose.

It's some crazy, deep ache I can't name or talk about.

The first round of holidays starts. Thanksgiving was always a smaller deal than Christmas growing up. Ma'd cook all day, even spend the day before preparing stuff. All us kids had jobs to do–things that started months ago with the canning of apples and cherries and the fattening of a turkey bought in June. I was always sickly fascinated as a kid watching Pa cut the turkey's head off, but I never had the guts to try it. The Dawsons don't have room for animals. After a trip to the Central Market to get most of the fixings, Mrs. Dawson and Kathy, plus her two sisters, set to work in the kitchen.

I have no business in the kitchen, so I hang out in the living room with Dawson and his two sons by marriage. Two kids run around, a boy and a girl, one belonging to each of Kathy's sisters. I half-listen to Dawson and the two younger guys, Dale and Walt, but my eyes and ears are on the kids. I smile, thinking of Erik and me as the troublemakers we were, wreaking havoc on the floorboards of our house and Ma yelling at us to "stop pounding around like a herd of elephants."

Dawson pulls me into the conversation by wrapping an arm around my shoulders and remarking to the others, "Ya met Harry Rechthart here when ya firs' came in. Lemme tell ya that he's becomin' a fine auto mechanic. Maybe I'll have someone ta pass the shop off to after I'm gone, eh? Since neither one o' you boys want it..."

Dale and Walt shift uncomfortably.

I half-smile. "I ain't that good, sir, but thanks." I look at the others to gauge their reaction. Dale's a stick-thin guy with wire-rimmed glasses and not a hair outta place. Walt's rounder and shorter, like his wife, and has a friendly enough face, but he's no talker.

"Nonsense," Dawson goes on. "He might not be teachin' at some high-end college like you, Dale, and he might not be deliverin' goods like you, Walt, but he's a hard worker, this one."

"You're a delivery guy?" I ask Walt, who nods. "My pa was—well, is still, I suppose—a delivery guy. Worked in the business some myself before—"

"Before?" Dale asks.

"Afore he came ta work for me, o' course," Dawson cuts in.

I flash him a grateful smile.

Mrs. Dawson pokes her head outta the kitchen and announces dinner. I can see the relief on the other guys' faces as we all pile into the dining room and take seats. Dawson carves the bird right at the table. Juices drop off the meat and onto the platter. My stomach rumbles. Next to me, Kathy giggles. I glance at her and can't help but smile.

Mashed potatoes, sweet potatoes, stuffing, gravy, and cranberries cover the table. I'm sure this family's been saving up all year for this meal, 'cause it ain't every day folks eat like this.

Dawson finishes carving the turkey and takes his seat.

"Everything looks delicious," says Liza, the oldest daughter.

"And smells delicious," adds Dee, the next daughter, whose thicker waist tells a thing or two.

My eyes are on Kathy as she nods, but it's Mrs. Dawson who speaks. "Why, thank you. It's nothing." She blushes prettily like her daughter.

"Let's say grace 'n dig in, eh?" Dawson says.

After a quick prayer together, I silently thank God for this family and wonder if my own family's gathered 'round a table.

With a coupla kids there, the chaos around the table's a further reminder of my home growing up—a comfort and a curse. Pushing down thoughts of my family, I focus on the moment and join in the fray. I ain't shy about digging in, and talk goes natural around the table with the big group.

"Where's the wine?" asks Dale after some time. "Liza, dear, didn't we bring a bottle to share?"

Wine? My ears perk up at hearing the word. I can almost taste the smooth, dry texture on my tongue.

"Yes, I did," Liza says, a crease forming between her eyebrows. "Mom, where's it at? Did you leave it in the kitchen?"

"It was Kathy's job to make sure the drinks were served," cuts in Dee, shooting her younger sister a glare.

Kathy opens her mouth to talk, but Dawson speaks first. "We ain't havin' none o' that stuff here. We went years wit'out. We can again."

I glance at Dawson with eyes like saucers. His voice is uncharacteristically firm. It's okay, I wanna say. Go ahead and open the bottle. What's one glass?

Just as soon as the thought enters my mind, I wish I could slap myself. One glass? Yeah, right...

"But why?" asks Dale. "I, for one, enjoy a nice glass of pinot noir with a meal."

My anger at myself turns to Dale when he speaks. I wanna kick this hoity-toity clown between the legs. Who talks like this? It's clear that Liza married up. I've got the impression that all Dawson's girls tried to better themselves. I stop my thoughts. "I don't drink, but you guys can if ya want."

Dawson looks at me, his eyebrows raised. I'd say they'd disappear into his hairline if he had more hair up there, poor fella. "Thanks, Dale, but we're gonna stick to what I say 'round here. My house, my rules, 'n all."

The rest of the meal passes without any problems. I learn that Dale teaches math at Case, right here in Cleveland. Head of the department, even. I have about as much in common with him as a cat does with a mouse. I kinda like Walt. If the guy said more than two words at a time, I'd talk to him more about his business. Maybe he knows Pa.

Finally, we finish. Dawson wipes his mouth with a napkin, leans back in his chair, and gives a happy sigh. The buttons are about to burst off his shirt. "Fine meal, Betty."

Mrs. Dawson smiles and raises her eyebrows. "Glad to see you enjoyed it, Ernie. Best lay off for the rest of the day."

"But there's still dessert, darlin'."

"You can't possibly still be hungry."

"There's always room for your cookin'."

She shakes her head as she removes her husband's empty plate and goes into the kitchen. Liza and Dee chuckle with their kids.

"You really put the food away, Grandpa," the girl remarks.

Dale looks disgusted, and Walt has a strange look of appreciation on his face.

Kathy and I exchange an amused glance. "You know, Dawson, your wife has a point," I say lightly. "Looks like you might need some new clothes soon."

Dawson chuckles. "Business's goin' good. Life's good. We had ta cut back like many for years. Now that things're fine 'n dandy, why not enjoy it?"

"Fair point." And it ain't like Dawson's not a generous man.

Dawson shifts in the chair, and it protests under his weight. "'O course, ya may have a point, son. No sense in wastin' good clothes 'cause o' my waist."

We all burst out laughing, even Dale. Mrs. Dawson returns with pumpkin, apple, and cherry pies and serves them up. I try a piece of each and am full beyond measure afterward. I can't imagine what Dawson must feel like, 'cause he doesn't lay off on the desserts.

After the plates are cleared and the leftovers put away, I steal away from the crowd and step outside for some fresh air. A moment later, the front door opens. Kathy joins me.

"That was quite the dinner," I say, looking at the stars. Afraid to look at her.

She sighs, a sound that could mean a hundred different things. My gaze is pulled away from my familiar comfort of star-gazing. Her eyes don't quite meet mine as she says, "I'm sorry if I sound a bit forward in saying so, but I was wondering if I'd done something to upset you. Until today, you'd been acting so strange around me."

"Sorry. I, uh–" I scratch the back of my neck. It's unseasonably mild out. I wish there was a coupla chairs on a porch, but all we've got is a front stoop. "D'you wanna sit?"

Kathy shrugs and joins me on the step.

"Look, Kathy, how do I say this? I like you, a lot, actually. I'm just... I ain't the kinda guy you should get involved with."

"Why? Because of the drinking?"

"What your dad did today was just another example of why he's a great man. Your family's great. You're great." I pause. "How much has your dad told you about why I was servin' time?"

"He said you'd been driving drunk and had an accident."

"Yeah, that's true, but there's more."

Kathy's eyes shine in the moonlight as a gentle breeze plays with her hair. I'm tempted to tuck a lock of it behind her ear, but I keep my hand at my side. My fingers grip the edge of the top step for something to do. I wanna be anywhere but here right now...yet the only place I wanna be is right here with this gal.

"Well? Are you gonna tell me?"

I sigh. "I had a drinkin' problem for years, but my family was none the wiser. Started when I was in high school with the guys I played basketball with. We'd pass around the bottle after every game in the school lot. I've got a sister, Hannah. She's one of those girls who's always been a goody two-shoes, but the older we got, the closer we got. We started double-datin' a brother and sister a while back and goin' to these crazy, wild parties in Millionaires Row."

Kathy smiles. "Millionaires Row? Wow, I've always wondered what it'd be like to live there. Driving down Euclid Avenue with my folks when I was a girl, I imagined I was a princess who lived in one of those palaces. Here, we always struggled...until now. Anyway, I'm sorry. Here I am going on about stuff when it's your story I wanna hear."

"You sure? 'Cause it don't end pretty."

Kathy takes my clammy hand in hers. Her eyes soften. "Yes."

I squirm. "Well, okay. The girl's name was Kat. We dated for months. I thought we were havin' the time of our lives, you know? My sister and Kat's brother got engaged at one point, and it seemed like Kat and me were next. Why not? I loved her...at least I thought I did."

"I'm sorry. I'm guessing she didn't return the feelings?"

I laugh bitterly. "Not at all. Fool that I was, I popped the question. You know, the big one. She laughed, then got mad. How'd I deal with it? I drank myself stupid. Even dumber, Kat demanded I drive her home that night. I shoulda never gotten behind that wheel..." My words stop up in my throat. I choke back a sob. I force myself to breathe. "I haven't talked about this in years."

"I'm sorry, Harry. So, you had an accident and...things ended badly between the two of you?"

"Why are you bein' so nice? You've no idea how bad things went. See, Kathy, how else do I say this? That accident killed her. Is that what you wanna hear?" Anger grips me, and I pull my hand from hers and stand, ready to hightail it outta there.

Kathy grabs my hand and stands. She takes my other hand, forcing me to stand face-to-face with her. I'm paralyzed as our eyes lock.

She leans in and kisses me full on the lips—hesitant at first, like she's testing the waters to make sure there's no shark about to attack. Then she's more insistent, and I carefully respond with a kiss back. When we break away, we're breathless.

She lets go of my hands, opens the front door, enters, and closes it. I stare at the peeling paint on the old door, wondering what the hell just happened.

CHAPTER 21

"That's right, bud. Then she kissed me, and I was standin' there like an idiot," I tell Hank for the second time. I guess he didn't believe me the first time.

We're sitting in our living room, if you can call it that, on the morning after Thanksgiving. Dawson gave me the day off, and Hank doesn't have to go into work until this evening.

"Damn, old boy. So, what're ya gonna do?" Hank runs a hand through his already messy dark hair and sighs into his cup of coffee.

"Dunno." I pull a pack of cigarettes outta my pocket and offer him one. We light up and stare at the smoke, like it holds the answers.

"Girls, women, whatever ya wanna call 'em," says Hank, "a guy can't make heads or tails of 'em."

I chuckle and take a long drag on my cigarette. "She didn't complain about my breath stinkin' from smokin'."

Hank joins me in laughing. "That's somethin'."

"'Course her dad smokes, too, so I guess she's used to it."

"So, what are ya gonna do, Harry?"

"You already asked me that."

"Yeah, and ya didn't give me no straight answer."

"Well, I see Kathy every day. It's not like I can avoid her."

"D'you wanna?"

"Well, no." I grin. "Sounds stupid, but I'm afraid to be with her and want nothin' more than to be with her."

"Ya sound like a lovestruck fool." Hank puts out his smoke and looks at me over the rim of his cup as he drinks.

"Wouldn't be the first time. Damn, why do I hafta feel this way? I used to be the guy who could—bing—turn on the charm like that and woo any girl when I was high-flyin' on the basketball team." I finish off the cigarette and the last of my cold coffee.

"You've gone rusty, Harry. Too much time in prison 'round too many guys. Now, if ya swung for the other team..."

"Don't even say it." I laugh. "No, pal, I'm addicted to girls. Thing was..." I sigh. "Thing was, I was addicted to a girl and to booze. They both nearly damn ruined me."

"Tough luck. Sorry. I dunno if I'm the best guy to be talkin' to 'bout this sorta stuff, seein' as I got my own problems with women."

"Thanks for listenin' all the same. I'd best head down to Dawson's and see if he wants some help."

"Ya said he gave you the day off."

"Yeah, he did, but..." I stand and shrug, my mind going to Kathy.

Hank chucks a pillow at me. "Get goin'. I know what–or who's–on your mind."

I laugh as I block the pillow and toss it back toward him. I'm out the door. The wind that blows off Lake Erie cuts me straight through, the blast to my face almost burning. Today's back to bone-chilling temperatures. I pull the collar of my coat up higher as I walk to Dawson's. Stupid of me not to wear a hat or gloves, but I don't even own any.

The streets are mostly empty. I turn a corner, protected some from the wind by the ancient brick buildings on either side of the street. Smoke rises from the stacks in the distance. A factory whistle shrieks over the calls of the dockworkers unloading another shipment along the Cuyahoga River. Some sorry soul steps outta a bar, swaggering, gripping the wall for support. I step around him, try not to stare, thinking that could've been me.

When I arrive at the garage, Dawson pokes his head out from under the hood of a car he's been working on all week.

"Damn idiot shouldn't be drivin' a car," he mutters as he wipes his hands on his overalls.

"What's got you in a mood?" I ask, half-grinning.

Dawson shakes his head. "Morrison told me 'twas jus' 'a little rattle' in the engine. Whole damn engine's shot. Been fixin' and replacin' parts left, right, 'n center, son."

"D'you want some help?"

Dawson makes to pull a pack of cigarettes outta his shirt pocket, but I'm quicker as I offer him up one and light it for him. After a long drag, he sighs. "Thanks, Harry."

"That's the first time you called me Harry."

Dawson smiles, his frustration gone. "Maybe 'cause yeh've become like a son ta me."

"You've got two sons, well, by marriage." There's a strange warmth in my chest.

"What're ya doin' here, then? It's your day off."

"Just stoppin' by. Figured you'd like the help. Looks like you need it." I laugh.

"Ah, fine, then." Dawson puts out the smoke and goes back to the car. "Com'ere 'n I'll show ya what I've been workin' on."

I follow Dawson to the car and stare at the engine.

"See, damn thing won't engage proper when the car's movin'. Pressure plate's broke. Flywheel can't do its job o' pushin' on it." He continues to explain how everything's connected. This is a part of the engine I ain't familiar with, so I try to pay attention.

"Damn, so many parts. What else was broke?"

Dawson snorts. "Ya don't really wanna know, son. Now, if you're serious 'bout workin' on your day off–"

"I am. And you don't hafta pay me."

Dawson turns his head and smirks. "Free labor, eh? Might be so inclined ta take ya up on that more offen."

I chuckle. "Hey, don't get any ideas, old man."

"Who ya callin' old?" He laughs. "All righ', let's get started, eh?"

"That's the idea." I grin, and we spend the next hour elbow-deep in car parts and grease.

By the end of it, Dawson wipes his brow and shakes his head. "Should do it. Think that's enough for today, son."

"How'd you get into the car business, anyway?" I ask.

Dawson drops onto an old sofa he keeps out in the garage. It's the rattiest thing I've ever laid eyes on furniture-wise. I wouldn't be surprised if there were rats living in it.

"My own pop was in the business. Taught me ev'rything he knew."

"Is he still alive?"

Dawson shakes his head. "No, poor man right up 'n died of a heart attack. Most unexpected thing."

"Sorry."

"What 'bout your pop? All's I know is he's a deliv'ry guy and that you was trainin' under him."

"Yeah, that's right. He broke his leg a while back, while I was in jail. Guess he hasn't been the same since. My folks visited me in the slammer a few times. I never told you, huh?"

"Nope."

"I kept lotsa stuff to myself in there. I still ain't...ready." I pull my gaze away from Dawson's open, honest face and stare at a stain on the arm of the sofa.

"Ah, that 'splains lots... Why you're still here instead o' wit' 'em."

His words go right to my gut–a punch and a hug at the same time. I whisk my eyes back to Dawson. "You never asked questions. You didn't, you know, make me feel like...like..."

"Like you was worth less than others?"

"Yeah." I stare at the dirt floor, sigh and look up at this man who I've got nothing short of praise for. "Why'd you do it, pick me, I mean?"

"Ya really wanna know?"

"I wouldn't ask if I didn't."

Dawson's eyes shine strangely as he looks at me. It's like every joke and smile I've shown to the world have been stripped away, exposing me for what I really am. "Ya remind me o' myself, son, when I was your age. So fulla life, not a care in the world...so ya want others ta believe. Lies. All lies. Am I right?"

"Yeah, too right."

"Spent too many years goofin' off, not takin' my mom and pop serious. Then Pop had a scare–his firs' heart attack. Whole fam'ly was scared. Woke me up, and I got myself righ' with my pop and wit' the Good Lord. Met dear Betty soon after, and she got me on the straight 'n narrow even more. Life was good. Liza was born, firs' grandkid in the fam'ly for my folks. I knew my trade. All was goin' accordin' ta plan. Then...then he died, my pop."

"Wow, I don't know what to say. I guess we hate to let our dads down, not to mention the rest of the family. I've got a brother–older–who always seemed like my folks' favorite when we were growin' up. Always said I wasn't jealous, but I guess, lookin' back, maybe I was. His were some big shoes to fill, in more ways than one." I smile sadly, then laugh softly. "Erik has abnormally large feet."

Dawson bursts out laughing. "Older brothers're like that. Have one o' those, but if ya wanna hear another sad story..."

"You don't have to... I mean, if it's too much..."

"Yeah, maybe you're right. 'Sides, I've got my wife 'n three lovely daughters. 'N you, Harry."

"What about Dale and Walt?"

"Dale's got his head up his ass, if ya know what I mean, 'n Walt, he's a nice enough guy, but the man's gotta grow a backbone. Always hoped my daughters'd marry up. Guess that's true in some ways, but not in the ways that matter."

I consider this and nod. "My brother's not a bad guy. Me and him were always real close as little kids, but things changed as we got older. He actually visited me in prison once. He seemed... I dunno. He didn't have that stick up his ass I thought he did for so long. I guess he finally grew up."

"Like ya did."

"Me?" I laugh and shake my head. "I dunno if I'll ever be grown up, whatever that really means."

"I think you're more grown up than ya think. Yeh've been through hell 'n back. Ya survived, 'n you're here, workin' and makin' an honest livin'."

"Maybe." *But it's only thanks, in big part, to you, Dawson*—the words I can't say.

"Jus' keep at it. One day at a time, son. That's what the Good Lord gives us, one day at a time. 'Times I think that's all we can handle."

"One day at a time. Yeah, that's pretty much how I got through jail."

"Ya best try 'n forget 'bout those days. What's past's past."

"Easier said than done." I stand and stretch, growing wary of the conversation.

"Hey, where's the fire?" Dawson stands as well.

"It's nothin'. I just…" My stomach knots thinking of Kathy and our last encounter. I try not to squirm under her father's gaze.

Dawson's face is unreadable. "Thought ya migh' find Kathy, eh?"

I feel the blush on my neck and cheeks, but try to act nonchalant. "If she's around."

"'Bout time ya worked up the nerve." The corners of his mouth turn up.

"What? You mean, you—?"

"Off wit' ya, then." Dawson chuckles.

Relief washes over me like a warm shower as I wash my hands at the utility sink. I push my sleeves up past my elbows and scrub with the rough worker's soap. Satisfied, I dry my hands, but the black never completely fades. My nails are coated with a layer of grime that I've come to accept these past few months.

"See ya, Dawson." I wave and saunter off toward the house.

That man knows me too well. As for Kathy, I need to get my head on straight and figure out what I'm doing with her. Am I even ready to give it another try with a girl?

And there she is, sitting by the front window, reading. I stand by the front door, locked in a moment of indecision. Just as I'm about to turn away, she looks up. Our eyes connect. She smiles.

I smile back. There ain't no turning back now.

The front door clicks open, and Kathy stands there as the sunlight hits her just right. "Well, are you gonna just stand there, or are you gonna come in?" she asks.

"Actually, I was just thinkin' of standing here."

Kathy raises an eyebrow. "Really? Well, I'll just close the door, then." She makes to do just that, but I slide my hand into the opening to stop her. "Changed your mind?"

"Maybe."

"Hmmm. You know, you don't have to knock. How many times have you just come in?"

"Um, that's not really… I mean, what was that all about yesterday?"

"What was what all about?"

We're dancing in circles here. She's playing the game, and so am I. "Ah, you ain't gettin' off that easy, doll."

"Doll? So, what are you saying, Harry?"

I enter and say, "Can we maybe sit down?"

Kathy gestures toward a pair of chairs.

"Okay, no more games. I changed my mind," I say.

"What?"

"Look, I was afraid, okay?" I keep my voice low as I continue. "I like you a lot, and I'd like to think we're friends and all."

Kathy's face falls. "Oh. Friends, right. That's...that's great."

"Oh, damn, I messed that up, didn't I? Look, what I mean to say is that I hope we're more than just friends."

It's like the sunshine's come out after a week of rain when she beams. "I was hoping the same."

"I just hope you know who you're getting involved with."

"Why is that even on the table? I kissed you first, remember?" She bats her eyes.

"Oh, I remember." I smile and laugh a bit. "Kinda hard to forget."

"So, why the hesitation? I get the impression that you're holding back." Her pout eases into a half-smile.

"Is that why you made the first move?"

"Someone had to do something." The other side of her mouth hitches up.

"I hafta admit—it did take me by surprise. You seemed so shy when we first met."

"I'm not usually so bold."

"Truth is, I used to be a lot more sure of myself around the ladies. Maybe a bit too sure of myself, if you know what I mean. After everything that I've been through, I guess I've changed. I just want you to be sure that you really wanna be with a guy like me."

Kathy's eyebrows draw down as she frowns. "Stop it, Harry. What does it take to convince you that I want to be with you? Aren't you even willing to give us a chance?"

I sigh. "Kathy, you've no idea what I want more than anything...to give us a chance. So, yeah, I just gotta have a little faith, right?"

"And stop being so afraid."

"Okay, you got me there, but this is the last time I'm gonna admit I'm afraid. If you really want me, I'm yours."

"Then shut up and kiss me this time."

I don't need to be told twice as Kathy pulls me by my collar to her and our lips meet. A light turns on, scaring away the darkness.

CHAPTER 22

The day after Kathy and I share our second kiss, I walk into the garage as if I'm floating. Dawson's back is to me, his head buried under the hood of his next repair.

"Morrison come pick up his piece of junk?" I ask, sidling up next to Dawson.

Dawson straightens up and laughs. "Firs' thing this mornin'. Told him ta take better care o' it, that I didn't wanna see him back here anytime soon." He scrutinizes me, pursing his lips. "Somethin's' diff'rent 'bout ya, son."

I grin like a fool, sure I'm blushing. "I guess so."

"Hmm. Y'know, funny thing, that. Somethin' was diff'rent 'bout Kathy this mornin', too... The way she was dancin' 'round the kitchen as she made eggs 'n poured coffee." He pulls out a pack of cigarettes and offers me one.

I take it with calm and collected grace. "Thanks."

We both light up.

Dawson gestures toward the sofa. "Care ta take a load off?"

"I haven't even begun workin', Dawson."

He blows out a long plume of smoke, then looks at me. I'm reminded of the way Ma'd gaze at me over her reading glasses when I was in trouble. "Maybe not workin' on cars, nope, but workin' your charms somewhere...on someone." He drops the cigarette, puts it out with his boot. "Am I right?"

I choke as I take a puff on my cigarette, then cough. My eyes water as I try to regain my composure. "Okay, guilty as charged, sir." I toss my cigarette down and smile. "I was gonna say somethin' today about that, I swear."

A slow smile spreads across Dawson's face. He laughs, slapping me on the back. "Jus' wanted to see ya squirm a bit. But best ya treat my girl like she deserves bein' treated. Ain't every day a man gives his okay for another man ta take his little girl away."

I swallow, the spit scraping my dry throat, reminded of Pa when Amy brought Jack around for the first time. "I swear to do right by your daughter, sir." I know I messed up before with a girl, but this time I mean to make everything right. The words stop up in my throat. Gazing at Dawson, I ask, "Do I have your blessing to see your daughter?"

"Ya do, son. That ya do. Jus' remember what I said 'n hold true ta what ya said 'bout doin' right. I like ya lots, Harry. I don't wanna hafta change my tune."

"You won't. I promise."

Dawson stands, brushing the grime on his overalls. "Betty's gonna hate me for wipin' my hands on my clothes again." He chuckles. "Now, what say you n' me get ta work on this Buick Eight?"

"Damn, that's a nice car." I whistle and run my hand along the smooth side. "Surprised someone with a ride like that'd bring it here. I mean, not that there's anything wrong with here, but you know, rich folks and all..." Realizing I'm babbling, I shut up. My head still spins from my conversation with Dawson.

"Word gets 'round. Even rich folk like ta save a buck these days. Blow their cash on a fancy car 'n then somethin' happens... They ain't got the dough ta take it somewhere nice. Don't bother me a lick. Now, I'm givin' this baby over ta you, Harry. It's the exhaust needs fixin'."

"Righto, Dawson. Hey, uh, why don't you go relax? I got this one."

He chuckles. "Good idea. Was thinkin' of takin' the family to the park. Nice, sunny day 'n all. Ain't gonna be many days like this soon. You wanna join us later?"

"I'll catch up with you at dinner. Go have fun."

Dawson nods and leaves the garage. After he's gone, I realize this is the first time he's given me the place to myself.

* * *

December begins with a snowstorm. Business is bad for a whole week. The advantage to this? I spend more time with Kathy. In the small house, there's not much room for privacy. Dawson and his wife are never more than a room away. The four of us play cards or listen to the evening radio programs. Mrs. Dawson never complains about jazz like Ma did, although Dawson usually nods off within ten minutes of the radio going on. Mrs. Dawson sits with a book in one of the armchairs near the window while her husband snores away in the other. Most evenings, Kathy and I sit on the couch, although sometimes we remain in the kitchen long after dinner, talking over coffee and one cigarette after another for me.

The second week of December, the weather breaks. Dawson and I work all day in the cold, my fingers numb by the time dinner comes. After another busy day, Kathy's parents rest in their usual spots in the living room while Kathy and I sit at the kitchen table. The crackle of the fire and Dawson's snores are the only sounds.

"Has your dad always slept like he could sleep through a war?" I ask.

Kathy giggles. "Yeah, it's pretty bad sometimes. I don't know how Mom sleeps in the same room as him. I don't suppose you snore?"

I shrug. "I wouldn't know. My brother and me shared a room growing up. He never said anything. Why? You afraid I'd keep you up?" Realizing what I've said, I blush.

"That would assume sleeping in the same bed as me." Kathy half-smiles and wrinkles her nose at me.

"Well, maybe...one day? I mean, if we ever, you know, married." My blush deepens, as I know I'm getting ahead of myself.

"Are you asking?"

"Just...dreaming. A guy can dream, can't he?"

"Nothing wrong with dreams." Kathy takes my hand across the table. "Dreams are what keep us going through the hard times...and hope."

"I like the sound of that. I think so, too." I stare into her eyes, imagining her beautiful soul. "Your eyes are the same color as mine." If we ever had kids together, they'd be sure to have blue eyes.

"You have nice eyes, Harry. And a nice smile."

"A crooked smile, more like. My brother, Erik, was graced with the good looks in my family." I laugh.

"Hmm, well, I don't know what your brother looks like, but I don't mind looking at you."

"I'd rather look at you if it's all the same." I grin.

Kathy blushes, giggles, and looks at our entwined hands on the table. "So, what are your dreams, Harry?"

I blink at the checkered tablecloth, the pattern making me dizzy. "I'm still tryin' to figure that out. Compared to where I was a year ago, even six months ago, this is Heaven. What's any guy want but to work hard, do right, maybe marry and have a family? Know he's lived a good life at the end of it all. Stuff like your parents have."

"Thirty years they've been married. I can't even imagine what that must be like, to be totally devoted to someone for that long." Kathy shifts in her chair, facing me more directly. "You know, there were times when things were tough for my family, for my parents. When Dad went to jail, I thought that was the end of us. Mom was so angry, Harry. So furious. She'd cry in her room for hours at the time, ashamed. I thought they'd divorce when Dad got out of jail. I thought we'd lose our home and have to live with one of my sisters. I would've hated that. Mom and I worked where we could, mending clothes, doing odd jobs, but work was hard to come by. No one wants to hire two poor women without men at their sides."

"That's awful. God, I'm sorry, Kathy. The world's a horrible place. What I can't understand is why a smart, kind, pretty girl like you ain't already taken."

"Dad didn't tell you?" she asks in a small voice.

"Tell me what?" Something drops inside me.

Her eyes don't meet mine. "I guess he wouldn't say anything about something like that. He's been very protective of me since... I mean, I'm twenty-four and still living at home. Most women are out by then."

I move my chair closer to hers, place a hand on her cheek, willing her to look at me. "Kathy, what happened?"

She blinks, and the tears spill down her cheeks. "You know this isn't a nice neighborhood. People still talk about it sometimes. I'm amazed it still doesn't stain my family's reputation. My dad's business nearly shut down because of me."

"What? What are you talkin' about?" My heart hammers in my chest.

"I was...I was eighteen, just out of high school. I graduated the top of my class, even though I was classless to some of the richer kids in the school. One of them...a boy named... It doesn't matter what his name was. I'd rather not say it."

I ball my free hand into a fist. "What did the asshole do to you, Kathy?"

She recoils some at my strong words, gasps.

"I'm sorry." I wonder if I sound like this unnamed piece of crap in my anger.

She shakes her head. "It's okay. Well, he said he wanted to take me out on a date, to celebrate graduation. Said he was happy for me, that he always liked me. I knew he hadn't asked my dad's permission, so I lied to my folks, said I was going to be with some friends that night. He picked me up around the corner. I got into his car, thinking we'd go to a restaurant or a park. He kept driving and driving. We left the city limits. I started to grow concerned as it got dark and only farms surrounded us. He pulled off the road, saying the property belonged to his family. The only thing I saw was an old barn. I was stupid, Harry. I shouldn't have stepped out of that car. But I did, and he took me to that barn...and...and..." Kathy's tears overcome her.

From the other room, the radio goes off. Dawson stops snoring. Footsteps follow and Kathy's parents enter the kitchen.

"What's going on in here?" asks Mrs. Dawson. "Kathy, why are you crying? I thought I heard..."

Dawson frowns at me.

Before he can speak, Kathy holds up her hand. "Harry didn't do anything wrong. I was just telling him about..."

Mrs. Dawson falls into the chair next to her daughter and wraps her in her arms. My hands flop uselessly to my sides. Dawson sits, a quiet presence of reassurance.

I pull my gaze away from mother and daughter and stare at him. "I had no idea, Dawson. I'm so sorry."

He sniffs, his eyes vacant and glassy. "So, she told ya."

I nod. "She didn't have to say everything, but I got it. She told me enough."

"See why she's extra special, don'cha?" He grimaces, that pained look only a parent can have when they see their kid hurting.

I nod. "She's the most beautiful woman I've ever known, inside and out."

"'N you're the firs' man who came 'long who I trust, Harry. Jus' figured it weren't my place to tell ya 'bout what happened to my little girl."

Something sparks alive inside me, a fierce protectiveness of Kathy. I have questions, but they can wait for another time.

Kathy sits up, her mom easing back into her chair. "You don't think I'm ruined?" she asks me.

"Are you kidding?" With her parents as our witnesses, I continue, "Hell no! Did you hear what I told your dad just now? That you're the most beautiful woman I've ever known?"

Her tears begin anew. This time, she seeks comfort in my arms. I hold her.

Dawson and his wife exchange a look of understanding and stand.

"Think Harry's got this covered," Dawson says to his wife, wrapping an arm around her. He places a hand on my shoulder as he walks past, then leads Mrs. Dawson to the stairs.

Once Kathy and I are alone, I let her cry into my shirt for as long as she needs. When her shoulders stop shaking, she draws back and stares at the wet spot on my shirt.

"You're gonna need a new shirt, Harry. I've ruined it."

"I don't care a whit about my shirt, Kath. Besides, I think it's time I headed home and let you get some sleep. You must be worn out from all this."

She nods. "I don't know how to thank you."

"You owe me nothing." I kiss the places on her cheeks where the tears fell. "You are quickly becoming everything to me. Maybe it's too soon to say it. I know it's been a couple of weeks that we've been together, but I can't help how I feel. Is it too soon to feel so...so in love?"

Kathy begins to cry again. "Y-you l-love me?"

"I do." I pull her to me. I stroke her hair, tangling my fingers in the curls. I kiss the top of her head like I've just found a sacred treasure.

Only the light over the kitchen table is on. The house is silent and dark, yet in this small, simple kitchen, I am more alive than I've been in years. Kathy's arms are wrapped around my body as she rests her face on my chest. I don't move. My hands stop playing with her hair. Her breathing evens out. Her arms go slack.

I realize she's sleeping. I smile and stare at the single bulb above the table. The cobwebs around it don't hide its light. It shines on every crack and stain on the ceiling, every imperfection made somehow brighter because of its presence.

I give Kathy a little squeeze.

"I have my light," I whisper and let her sleep.

CHAPTER 23

The night I held Kathy in my arms and let her sleep, her head resting against my hammering heart, remains with me every day. Just when I thought I loved her with all that I am, I find more reasons to love her—the way her eyes sparkle when we say hi, her laughter like bells, her thoughtfulness to leave me an extra cup of coffee, her hand finding mine under the table.

At meals, I often catch Mrs. Dawson glancing in our direction, a gleam in her eyes, a slight smile on her lips. She doesn't mention that night that changed everything, but when she lays a hand on my shoulder as she sets a plate in front of me, warmth floods me. It's Ma's touch. She becomes Betty to me.

Most of the time, Dawson and I are elbow-deep in grease as we fix car after car. Like Betty, he doesn't bring up the night his daughter told me her secret. He remains the picture of patience as he teaches me the way around an engine. Sometimes, he steps aside and lets me work out the problem with the car. In my frustration, I glance at him, the question on the tip of my tongue to ask for help.

His grin just widens. "Yeh've got this one, Harry. I trust ya." He winks.

A similar scenario has played out three times in the past couple of weeks. I trust ya. Trust.

As for Kathy, we continue to spend our evenings at the kitchen table long after dinner. A month could be a year for how well we've come to know each other. She is my everything. When I spoke those words, I was never more sure of anything.

Never more sure of anything. I step into the garage five days before Christmas, my hand in my pocket. My fingers slide over the ring hidden by a bit of fabric. Memories flash—a similar ring in my pocket, her rejection, a ring tossed into a bush. I shake my head. No, it ain't like that this time, not at all.

Dawson looks up from the car he's working on. "Somethin' the matter, son?"

I shrug. "Nothin', not really. Just somethin' I wanted to ask you."

"Look like yeh've got ants in your pants." His eyebrows raise. "Smoke?"

I wave him off. "Nah. Actually, Dawson, you got a minute?"

"Suppose so." He grabs an already filthy rag, wipes his hands on it. "What's up?"

My eyes are on everything except him. "You know I love your daughter, sir."

Dawson chuckles. "As sure as the sky's blue." He glances out the grimy window at the overcast sky. "Well, most days." He winks.

I smile, at least I hope it looks like a smile. My feet seem determined to do a jig, maybe all the way home. I swallow and grip the ring, remove it from my pocket before I can change my mind. I hold it up for Dawson to see. "I wanna ask her to marry me, and I, well, if I had your blessing, it'd mean the world to me."

His eyes go large, his face unreadable for a moment. Just when I think I've made a mistake, he booms, "Well, ain't it 'bout time!"

I laugh, disbelief and nerves flowing outta me. "You had a hunch, did you?"

Dawson slaps me on the back and chuckles, a deep rumble starting in his belly and moving up to his mouth. "A hunch, son? More like gettin' right run over by a tractor 'n the plow. Was wonderin' when you'd ask...'n if ya had the nerve ta ask me first."

"Of course, I'd ask you, Dawson. You were...waiting for me to ask?"

"Sneaky suspicion ever since...y'know." He half-smiles.

"Well, just to be clear, I may love your daughter, but I know she's yours first."

Dawson's eyes gleam strangely as he smiles. "She's yours now, Harry. Best ya take good care o' her."

"I mean to do just that, sir."

"I know ya will."

* * *

The Dawson family steps outta church after Midnight Mass. Snow falls lightly as Kathy takes my gloved hand in hers and gives it a squeeze. She swings our arms slowly as we fall in behind the others and looks up at the sky.

"It's Christmas Day, Harry."

A couple of flakes dust the hair around her face and her nose. I'm tempted to kiss them away. God, she looks gorgeous.

"Yep. Merry Christmas."

Kathy giggles. "Merry Christmas. What did your family do tonight, do you think?"

I frown. "They would've gone to church hours ago and are probably all asleep by now. My youngest sister, Irma, is too old to believe in Santa. So...no more tales of ol' Saint Nick."

"That's kinda sad. Do your parents have grandchildren?"

"Yeah, my oldest sister, Amy, she's got two girls. Last I knew, they were the only grandkids."

"Do you ever think about having kids, I mean, one day?"

I search Kathy's face and smile. "Sure, one day, but gotta be married first."

"Yeah, there's that."

"About that..." I fiddle with the ring in my coat pocket, grasp it, release it back into the depths. I hesitate in my walking.

"Something the matter?"

"What?" I pick up my pace and try to act nonchalant. "Oh, nothin'. Just...thinking."

"Penny for your thoughts?"

"My thoughts ain't even worth that much," I joke, but my stomach knots. I wish I hadn't had that extra slice of pie after dinner. *If only you knew my thoughts, Kathy...*

"Hmm..." She shrugs, and then her sisters are upon her, yakking about plans for the morning.

I chuckle. "I'll let you girls catch up." It's as good an excuse as any to try to come up with my own plan of when to propose.

"Best we all hurry on home 'n get in bed," Dawson says to the group. "Santa won't come till you're asleep." He winks at his grandkids.

"You should spend the night with us, dear," Betty says to me, interrupting my thoughts. "Seems silly for you to go home, only to return a few hours later."

"You want me to...really?"

"Of course. I thought Kathy told you about being over early for breakfast and gifts. You don't wanna miss our spread."

"No, ya don't," Dawson agrees.

Dale rolls his eyes at his father-in-law as he stands right behind him. Walt nods with a smile.

"You can sleep with Dale and Walt," Betty explains. "The girls all share a room."

I frown. Part of me wants to protest, as Dale and Walt look about as happy as I feel about sharing a room. "If you're sure..."

"It's no problem," Kathy says for me. That seems to satisfy her mom, who takes her husband's arm. Once the others fall in line, Kathy leans into me and whispers, "I know it's an odd arrangement, but it's like that every Christmas. The kids sleep on cots in the same room as me and my sisters, and the husbands share the other room. We don't have much space to fit everyone, but I want you there, Harry...unless you mean to see your own family."

I take Kathy's hand in earnest and shake my head. "No, my family...not yet. Maybe next year. Besides, your family's mine...I mean, just as good as." *Or will be soon enough.*

"You must miss them, though." Her words are so soft, they barely carry over the light breeze.

I nod, blinking away a sting behind my eyes. My hand grips the ring. "No sense in thinkin' about the past, doll. I've got my eyes set on the future."

We arrive at the house. After Dawson opens the front door, the grandkids rush in, followed by the rest of the crowd. Kathy and I enter last. While her sisters yell in the background at their kids and the rest of the family carries on the general commotion, we stand in the living room. I take her hands in mine, a moment of peace while the ring rests in my pocket as a steady reminder.

"Goodnight, Kath." I close my eyes and find her lips.

"Goodnight, Harry."

We part, but I imagine saying goodnight to her as my wife for many years to come.

* * *

I wake to the smell of bacon, sausage, and coffee. As I sit up in bed, I realize I'm the last one up. No surprise there, since Dale and Walt's snores kept me up late into the night. As much as I try to flatten my hair, it ain't happening. I try to smooth out the wrinkles in my rumpled clothes and double check that the ring is still in my pocket. Relief rushes over me when my fingers find it, but my stomach just as soon churns. I blame it on hunger.

When I join the others in the dining room, the noise level rivals my own family's. The kids are busy running around the tree, arguing over who got the bigger present. Kathy's eyes meet mine across the room, and she's at my side in a moment.

"You want one of those?" she teases, as she nods toward her niece and nephew.

I swallow the lump in my throat and laugh. "You shoulda seen my brother, sisters, and me on Christmas morning."

"Oh, I bet my sisters and I could've put up a good match."

Betty sets the last of the plates on the table and calls us to breakfast. Sausages, bacon, black and white puddings, toast, eggs, tomatoes, baked beans, and fried potatoes in what looks like a creamy sauce fill the table.

"This is a traditional Irish breakfast," Kathy explains to me as we pull up chairs. "Mom makes it for special occasions."

"My mother used to make it quite often when I was a wee lass," Betty says. "Back in the old country, we worked hard for hours on the farm. It was fit to eat a big breakfast then."

"Looks delicious," I remark, my stomach rumbling.

Betty waves me off. "Will you be taking tea or coffee?"

"Coffee is fine, but get the others first."

"I'll take tea, Mom," Liza says, and Kathy and Dee echo.

Betty pours tea for the rest of the family, coffee for me, and milk for the kids.

The stench from the cup at Kathy's setting meets my nose. "What's that stuff? Smells like it'd put hair on your chest."

"As much as that migh' be amusin'," Dawson says, "let's say our prayer, eh?"

I'm silenced, along with the rest of the raucous table. Dawson bows his balding head and says, "Lord, we thank Ya for fam'ly 'n food 'n the blessed day o' Your son's birth. We ask Ya ta bless each ona us. Amen."

We all echo, "Amen," and pass the food.

After our plates are filled, I ask Kathy, "So, what kinda tea is that?"

"You aren't put off easy." She smirks.

"Nope. I come from a family of coffee drinkers. My folks'd tell you tea's too English."

"It's a strong breakfast tea called Lyons. You want to try it?"

"Sorry to say, Kath, but it smells like somethin' I should be cleanin' the floor with."

Kathy giggles. "Don't let Mom hear you say that."

"Say what?" asks Betty.

"Oh, nothing," Kathy says, but her mom doesn't seem convinced.

The rest of the meal goes well. I'm shocked to see there's hardly a crumb left afterward as we all help clean off the table. When the hubbub dies down, Betty shoos us into the living room, where the kids, Jeffrey and Ellis, open presents. Dawson sits in one of the armchairs, looking every bit the king of the house as he watches his grandkids and then his kids unwrap gifts. I kinda feel bad for not getting anyone anything, but Kathy's ring set me back. Any extra money I had since working for Dawson went toward it. My hand keeps going to the ring during all this. I catch Kathy's eye beside me from time to time. She grins, laughs at her niece and nephew's theatrics, and takes my hand.

"Something the matter, Harry?" she whispers in my ear.

Her breath tickles, sending a shiver down my spine. I chuckle. "Nothin' at all. Just enjoying the day is all." *Nothing could ever be perfect enough for you. How do I do this?*

"Your hand's all sweaty."

"It's kinda stuffy in here. I mean...all these people. You, um, care to step outside for a minute? I could use a smoke." *And the perfect opportunity to get you alone.* I shift my weight, trying to find a comfortable position seated on the hard floor.

She laughs. "What's the rush? Besides, there's something I wanna give Mom and Dad." She stands and joins her sisters.

I try to focus on the scene unfolding in front of me. The ring is like a heavy rock in my pocket now.

The sisters hand Dawson and Betty a large, flat present.

"Ya didn't hafta get us anythin'," Dawson says gruffly.

"You know we couldn't let you host year after year without a little something in return," Dee says.

"Besides, it's not like it cost us a fortune," Liza cuts in. Kathy elbows her in the ribs. Affronted, Liza glares at her youngest sister and mouths, "What?"

I smile a bit as Kathy jerks her head in her parents' direction. Her oldest sister is quiet now as she watches her mom undo the wrapping. She adds the paper to the neat pile next to the tree.

Ellis holds a baby doll and Jeffrey a toy plane. Even the kids are stilled in their playing. Once Betty sees what the gift is, she smiles and gasps, "Oh, it's beautiful!"

Dawson grins and pulls his wife to him, kissing her on the lips, not caring a whit that we're all watching. The grandkids giggle. After the kiss ends, Dawson turns the gift around for all to see. It's a family photo.

"We'll hang it over the mantel," Betty says. "Why, it's just right. We haven't had a family picture in...in..."

"Too long," Dawson says. He nods at me and stares a moment too long.

I smile tightly and give a slight nod.

"What's that about?" Kathy asks by my side. "And don't say it's nothing."

Grateful for the commotion around us, I try to come up with a lousy excuse, but Betty saves me by handing me a small package.

"What's this? You didn't...you didn't have to..."

I can't seem to finish my thoughts. It's like the warm feeling inside me has formed a ball and gotten stuck in my throat. Why're the lights on the tree blurring? Why's my head spinning? Why can't I stop for just a sec to screw my head on straight and talk? Surrounded by this family, it's like they're all hugging me at once, and I can't even begin to understand or describe it.

"Nonsense," is all Betty says. "Open it, Harry."

I swallow slowly and nod. Once I remove the paper, I open the box and find a watch inside.

"So yeh'll always be on time ta work," Dawson says.

"But, sir–" I notice that this ain't just any watch. It's old.

"We'll talk 'bout it later, eh?" Dawson gives me a knowing look, and I don't argue. I can feel Dale and Walt's eyes on me. I know what this is, what it means.

"Thank you," I manage to croak.

Kathy stares in awe at my gift. "Dad gave you his watch," she whispers, then looks at me, the question in her eyes.

"I'm just as surprised as you," I say.

Betty shoots up from her seat. "Well, a merry Christmas! I do hope everyone got what they wanted. Now, chop, chop! Harry may have a new watch to keep him on schedule, but we've all got a job to do to keep things rolling along. Let's get this room back in order—except for the wee ones, of course. Girls, we'll need to begin preparing dinner. It won't make itself—"

As the Queen of the Family gives the orders, everyone knows who's really in charge around here. Dawson and I stand at the same time.

"She gets like this ev'ry Christmas. Told her many a time ta relax, but does she listen? Nope."

I chuckle. "Are you having more people over later?"

"Nope, jus' us. Betty's the perfect hostess. Ev'rythin's gotta be jus' right, if ya know what I mean."

"Yeah, I get it. My ma's the same way." My face falls, imagining my family gathered around our—I mean, their—dining room table.

"Ya sure ya don' wanna call your folks?"

"Nah. Look, let's just get on with things. About the watch—"

"Later, son. Ya gotta pop the question first. 'N for the record, Betty knows. Told her las' night."

I nod, my insides both overflowing and empty. Too many emotions. I shake my head and focus on helping the guys clean up the living room. After a few minutes, Dawson tells us to take a break, so we sit and take out the smokes. A little way into the talk, Dale gets up and returns with a bottle of booze.

"Anyone care for a bit of brandy?" he asks, ready to open the bottle.

"Sounds great," Walt says with a lopsided smile. "I'm always up for a bit o' the good stuff."

Dawson looks at me. "Boys, maybe it'd be best if—"

"You know, maybe one drink...a little sip to, uh, take the edge off," I say before I know what's come outta my mouth.

"Son, ya sure?" Dawson asks in a low voice.

"I don't understand," says Dale. "Is there a problem?"

"Nope, no problem," I say, casting a sidelong glance at Dawson.

His frown deepens.

My stomach clenches, as if Dawson is squeezing it with his bare hands. I swallow. "Um, you know, on second thought...you boys go right on ahead. I'm gonna sit this one out."

"You sure?" Dale asks.

"I don't need to drink to have a good time." I know too much about drinking, old boy. I could write books about my messed-up experiences, but I doubt they'd be bestsellers.

"Huh." Dale shrugs. "It's no skin off my back, Harry. You just look like the type of guy who—"

"Who what?" My hackles rise.

"Um, nothing." Dale bites his lip and turns toward Walt, pouring him a bit of brandy.

Dawson gives me a knowing look and leans in. "Ya sure you're okay?"

"Okay ain't the first word that comes to mind, but I'll survive."

"Best be proposin' wit' a clear head." Dawson raises his eyebrows.

"Yeah, still tryin' to figure out the right moment. Any advice?"

He places a hand on my shoulder. "Yeh'll know when."

It's not long before dinner's served. Glee and anxiety mix inside as I sit next to Kathy and hardly touch my food. The rest of the day passes with watching the youngsters play, telling jokes, playing games, and talking about past Christmases.

As the night winds down, Kathy and I find ourselves seated at the kitchen table. The rest of the family has gone upstairs. She shakes her head, giggling. "Wow, I thought Liza would never stop going on about what a great kisser Dale is."

My laughter stops up in my throat. Under the table, my hand fidgets with the ring in my pocket. The other taps on the table. "Dale didn't seem to mind. Must've been all the booze he had over the hours."

Kathy laughs. "Must have been because, well, otherwise…"

"Otherwise he's about as loose as a rigid board?" I can't help but smile, her laughter putting me at ease.

"Exactly. Still, I think you're a better kisser." Kathy smiles slightly, the tease in her eyes.

"Oh, that so? Have you been kissin' Dale to know the difference?" My fingers stop drumming on the wooden surface. The ring molds into my palm, my fingers caressing it.

"No thanks!" Kathy takes my free hand. The smile disappears as she furrows her brow. "But something's been off about you all day, Harry. I know I keep asking, but are you okay?"

A nervous chuckle escapes. "Okay, here goes nothin'. Well, not nothin'…seein' as this is the furthest thing from that."

"What are you going on about?" The crease between her eyes deepens. "You haven't been drinking, have you?"

"Funny you should say that, but no. I feel drunk, though. I mean, drunk in love with you." I remove the ring from my pocket, hold it to her finger as I take her hand in both of mine. "Kathy, what I'm tryin' to say and failin' something miserable at is…I love you like…like… Hell, I don't even know. I'm crazy in love with you, like a man who thirsts for water after he's had only booze. He wants—no, needs—what's good for him, what keeps him goin', what gives him life. Kath, that's you. I ain't fancy, good-lookin', rich, or even that smart, but if I've done one thing right in my life, it's been fallin' in love with you. So, what I'm really tryin' to say here is this: Will you marry me, Kathy Dawson?"

Tears spring into her eyes and roll down her cheeks as the biggest smile I've seen on her beautiful face makes it even more perfect. Her hand trembles in mine. She wraps her hands in mine, the ring crushed between the jumble. "God...yes, Harry. Yes."

I slide the ring onto her finger. She crashes into me, and I wrap her in my arms. We kiss under that single light bulb in that tiny kitchen, that place where history changed us, changes us. When we break apart, her tears continue to fall.

"You're sure, I mean, you know about me..." Her voice is a frightened child's.

"As you know about me," I say, my eyes blurring. The sting of tears wins. "I'd have you if I had to go through Hell and back...and maybe I already have." I pause. "Step outside for a moment with me. I wanna show you somethin'."

We stand, hand-in-hand, and go out the back door.

I gaze at the night sky. "Good, it's clear." I meet her eyes. "I used to spend lots of nights lookin' at the stars when I was younger."

"They're beautiful." She seems to search me. "Like you."

I chuckle. "Don't know about that last part, but yeah, true for those stars. I didn't see them for years. I've been a free man for a while now, and every time I look at the stars, it's like seeing them for the first time." I turn my eyes back to Kathy. "Maybe it's 'cause I'm looking at you now."

Those hopes and dreams that dangle in the night sky come down to Earth as Kathy smiles through tears of pain and happiness at me. My finger slides over the ring on her finger–a promise, our future.

CHAPTER 24

I spend another night at the Dawson house. The next day, our engagement becomes the talk around the breakfast table. Kathy shows off her ring to her family. Her sisters gush over it, and the three squeal and make plans for a wedding we don't even have a date for yet. Dale and Walt are less enthusiastic, but Walt shakes my hand with a genuine smile. Betty hugs each of us while Dawson sits at his spot at the table, his quiet approval evident as he watches the others talk. Before the rest of the family leaves that morning, Dale stiffly extends his hand. Then they are gone. Back to normalcy.

Dawson and I are now in the garage, trying not to freeze. I'm about to get started on an exhaust job when he stops me.

"So ya fin'lly popped the question." He gives me a pat on the back, smiling.

I grin. "Yep. I got the nerve to do it before Christmas Day was over, if only an hour or so before midnight."

"Knew ya had it in ya. Ain't no easy thing for a lotta guys. Remember the day I asked Betty. Was a wreck."

"How'd you do it?"

"Thought I'd take her for a walk on the 9th Street pier...nice summer day 'n all. Black clouds seemed ta roll in off the lake outta nowhere. We was nowhere near shelter. Started pourin' buckets. Soaked us through 'n through." He chuckles, shaking his head. "Thought she was 'bout to up 'n murder me, I did. Her hair was a mess, ruined. Her dress stickin' ta her skin. When we fin'lly found a dry spot, I asked her. She looked at me like I was crazy, then smiled, said, 'I knew you were up to somethin'.' 'Course she said yes."

I laugh. "I'm glad I didn't ask Kathy in a storm. No, it seemed right to ask her here, at home. This place, what it means..." Emotion chokes me, stopping the words in my throat.

He gives an understanding smile. "I got ya. Now, somethin' else I wanted ta talk to you 'bout."

"Okay." I offer him a smoke, but he waves me off.

"Nah, too early. Wanted ta talk to you 'bout the watch." He looks me up and down.

"I ain't wearin' it right now if that's what you're lookin' for. Um, sorry. Didn't wanna ruin a nice watch while elbow-deep in oil and gears."

Dawson chuckles. "'Course not. Ya wonderin' why I gave it to ya 'stead o' Dale or Walt?"

"Well, yeah. I mean, ain't it tradition to pass on somethin' like that to the oldest son, if not son, then son-in-law?"

"Yep, 'tis, but ya know how I feel 'bout those two, 'specially Dale."

"Right, well... Still, I don't know if I can really take your watch, Dawson. That's quite a thing to give up."

"I ain't givin' up nothin'. It's my choice ta pass it on to ya. How many times I gotta tell ya 'fore yeh'll get it in your thick head what ya mean ta me?"

I chuckle. "Okay, okay, I ain't gonna argue, but I'm grateful. You know that. I feel like a broken record tellin' you all the time. I don't know what else to say."

"Ya don' need ta say anythin'. Some things go withou' sayin'."

Dawson's eyes glisten strangely, like he's looking right through me. I can't help but be reminded of the gleam in Pa's eyes.

We spend the rest of the day fixing cars, lost in oil and gears and in all sorts of conversation. Betty serves leftovers for dinner. The evening's quiet with the rest of the family gone. Kathy and I sit in the chairs near the front window after her parents go to bed.

"We should call the church soon and set an official date," she says. The low lamp light reflects in her eyes while she stares at her ring, keeps turning her hand this way and that. "I still can't believe we're engaged, Harry." Her eyes meet mine as she smiles.

"Yeah, it's pretty... I dunno how to even describe it. As for a date, yeah, that sounds good." My insides warm.

She studies me a bit too long.

"What's on your mind?" I ask.

"It's just... Harry, you've hardly talked about your family in the past several months. Don't you think they'd want to be at our wedding?"

I shake my head. "Can I be straight with you?"

"Of course."

"I don't want a big wedding, but if you do, okay."

"I want whatever you do. My parents need to be there—"

"Sure. I ain't arguin' that. I suppose I'll ask Hank to be my best man, even though I've only known him a short while. I'd ask my brother, I guess, if I was gonna contact my family."

"You must've been close, your brother and you."

"We were a long time ago, but things've changed."

"You're sure you don't want your family to be there?"

"I'm sure. You can have your family there and anyone else you want. I don't need anyone there but you." I lean in and kiss this amazing woman and can't believe she wants to settle down with a bugger like me.

After the kiss ends, Kathy giggles. "Well, when you put it like that, maybe we should just elope."

"Mmm, don't tempt me."

"Silly man." Kathy stands. "I guess on that note, I should head upstairs before my parents begin wondering what we're up to."

I stand and wiggle my eyebrows. "Again, don't tempt me."

Kathy kisses me once more and whispers in my ear, her breath tickling my lobe. "I don't mind tempting you. This is just a sample of what you're in for in a few months." She runs her lips along my ear, my jawline, and back to my mouth.

My knees are weak, and I'm heady with pleasure when she breaks away. "Tease," I murmur with a smile. "This is a side of you I know nothing about, but I like it."

"We'll have the rest of our lives to get to know each other. I'm looking forward to the surprises you have for me, too."

She saunters away, and I see myself out. The moment the cold blasts me in the face, my thoughts of what I wanna do with Kathy once married blow away. The snow's picked up. Even though it's a short walk home, I'm chilled to the core by the time I enter the blessed warmth of my little shack.

As I catch my breath, I find Hank sitting there. He looks up from his book and smirks, lazily tapping his cigarette into an ashtray. He raises an eyebrow and offers me a smoke. "If you don't look like a fella who's slain, I dunno what does."

I drop onto the sofa next to him and take the cigarette, lighting up. After a few drags, I say, "I'm gettin' married, old boy. You wanna be my best man?"

* * *

1935 starts with snow and more snow. The snow ain't the only problem.

"But I wanted a spring wedding." Kathy's face drops that dismal January evening.

We're seated around the kitchen table after dinner with her parents.

"I'm sorry, dear, but that's just not possible," Betty says.

"But a year! Six months, at least..." Kathy looks for all the world like she's gonna cry. "I can't wait that long, Mom."

"Those are the rules of the Catholic Church, Kathy. I didn't create them, but there you are. They're in place to make sure couples don't rush into marriage. Father Davis will want to meet with you and Harry several times between now and the wedding. And there's the matter of Harry converting."

I don't care about having to convert if it means marrying my girl. Hell, I'd walk down the aisle naked if that was her custom. All she has to do is ask.

Kathy looks at Dawson. "Dad?"

Dawson holds up his hands and shrugs. "Don' look at me, darlin'. I had ta follow the same rules when I married your mother."

Kathy sighs and snaps her gaze to me. "Harry and I can't wait that long, can we?"

The pleading in her eyes stings me. "Well, I...I told Kathy she could have whatever sort of wedding she wanted, but if–" I turn my gaze to Dawson and Betty.

"No buts," Kathy cuts in. "We just won't get married Catholic."

Betty gasps. "Now, let's not be hasty, dear–"

"Come on, Mom. What's it matter? A wedding is just the start of a marriage."

"What's it *matter*?" Betty's cheeks flush as she stands. "It matters because it's tradition, young lady. It matters because it's your heritage and what your sisters did and I did and my mother before me. The groom is to marry according to the bride's custom. Any marriage outside of the Catholic Church isn't recognized as a true marriage."

"Now, Betty, darlin'," Dawson says, "maybe it'd be best if–"

"If what, Ernie? We just let them go down to the city courthouse and sign some papers?"

"I ain't sayin' that."

"With all due respect, Betty," I say, "my folks weren't married in the Catholic Church, and they've been faithful to each other for thirty-five years."

"Well, that's all fine for your family, Harry, but where I come from, things aren't done that way." Betty walks outta the kitchen.

"Dad?" Kathy asks in a brittle voice.

Dawson sighs and runs a hand through what remains of his salt-and-pepper hair. He rubs his face with a handkerchief, blowing his red nose. "Damn cold." He meets our eyes across the table. "Give her a day, Kathy. Ya know your mom can be righ' stubborn. Best go check on her." He stands and leaves.

"This isn't how I wanted it to go, Harry. It's our wedding, our marriage. Who cares about some stupid rules?"

"Hey, it'll be okay. I'm all for breaking a few nonsense rules, but I don't wanna put a barrier between you and your folks, either. I know what that's like."

"Dad doesn't really care one way or the other. It's all Mom."

"I've never seen her like this."

Kathy laughs humorlessly. "Oh, trust me. Mom can really bring out the claws when she wants. Dad's always been an old softie."

"I can imagine. Dawson doesn't strike me as the type who'd harm a fly."

That gets a laugh outta Kathy.

"Listen, whatever happens, we'll be fine. Okay?"

"Okay."

But her glassy eyes and frown tell a different story.

* * *

The next three days, Betty and Kathy don't say a word to each other. I can't imagine what living under the same roof must be like right now, but going inside during meals is enough time to wanna look the other way.

Out in the garage, Dawson keeps shaking his head, muttering, "Women."

"How d'you survive in that, what's going on in there?" I finally ask.

"Put it outta my mind, son. Jus' turn off the switch. Betty tells me I don' listen ta her half the time anyway."

"Sounds familiar. Ma gets on Pa about that, too. Well, she did. Guess she still does."

Dawson laughs. "See what yeh've got ta look forward to? Kathy ain't so nitpicky, but any o' my daughters can be spitfires, like their mom."

"How d'you stay married for thirty years? What's your secret?"

"Take a break. Migh' as well freeze ta death sittin' on the couch 'stead a standin' over a broke car."

I follow Dawson to the beat-up sofa and plop down.

He offers me a smoke, and we light up. "Ain't got no mysterious secret. Ya gotta learn to stay in love."

"Okay," I draw out and chuckle. "How do I do that? Fallin' in love's the easy part."

"I'd drink ta that if ya weren't, ya know… Anyway, I think yeh'll find havin' kids puts a big strain on your marriage. Gets the wife all tired-like and in a mood all the time. Understandin' as the husband tries ta be, she don't wanna hear it most o' the time. Other things pop up—extended fam'ly interferin', givin' their own two cents and whatnot. Tough economic times… Ya know how that went over for me, son. Betty stuck by my side, but 'twas my lowest moment, that. Think a lesser woman would've up 'n divorced me."

"You were just tryin' to provide for your family."

Dawson blows out a long stream a smoke and sighs. "Yeah, but don't excuse what I done. Been tryin' ta make up for it ever since."

"Does Betty, uh, say anything about your prison time? Ever remind you?"

"Nah, she ain't one ta rub it in. 'Times, I think, in those sweet eyes o' hers, there's a sorta sadness there. But the way she cares for us all, the cookin', all the times she held our girls... Harry, she's the glue holdin' us t'gether."

"I get that. I think Ma was the same way. 'Course, I didn't appreciate it growin' up, not really. Pa worked all day, so he wasn't around us kids all the time like Ma."

"Same thing here. Even though the shop's righ' behind the house, I'd be out here workin' from dawn 'til dusk most days. 'Times, I'd jus' be steppin' through the door, and Betty'd hand off ona the girls ta me. She'd be tryin' ta get dinner on the table, and someone'd be screamin' or whatnot. But then they grow up...so fast. Betty 'n I took our vows serious-like. When times got tough, we'd hafta remind each other o' that... o' what we fell in love wit' ta begin wit'. It ain't jus' a pretty face or a girl who can cook for an army... It's holdin' fast to a promise ya made."

I put out my cigarette. "Thanks, Dawson. I'll try to remember that. I love Kathy, and I wanna be the sorta husband she deserves."

We stand. Dawson claps me on the shoulder. "Ya will be, son. Ya already are. Now, let's get back ta work, eh? This clunker ain't gonna fix itself."

* * *

We close up shop for the day hours later.

"Ya sure ya wanna stay out here freezin' when there's a hot meal waitin' inside? Mad or not, Betty's cookin' don' suffer 'cause o' her mood."

I shake my head. "Nah, Dawson, you go on ahead. I'm good here for a while. Besides, it's been weeks since I had a chance to work on that Caddy out back."

"Ya still hopin' ta get her up 'n runnin' for your folks one day?"

"Yeah, that's the plan." I shrug.

"Well, all righ'. Don't stay out too late. Wind's bitin'."

"Go on, Dawson. I know you're probably starvin'."

Dawson rubs his belly and laughs as he leaves. "Ya know me too well."

I smile at the back of him as he disappears into the dark. Damn jalopy of a Caddy won't start to move it, so I go outside to freeze my ass off for a few minutes, anything to avoid being in the same room as Betty and Kathy. As I set to work on the car out back, that sun's setting. The back light on the garage doesn't help much, so I don't have long. Still, the cold inside's worse than outside right now.

I tinker here and there, taking apart and tightening parts. My mind's not on repairing anything but the broken relationship between a mother and her daughter. Maybe Dawson's waved a magic wand, and when I go in, all will be hunky-dory.

After a few more minutes, it's too dark to see, so I close the hood and head toward the house. I stop just outside the back door and listen. It's silent.

I debate on going home and scrounging up something that ain't moldy from our tiny fridge, but Dawson and Kathy are probably expecting me. I turn the knob.

Three faces look up. Dawson smiles and waves me over, his mouth full. Kathy's smile doesn't reach her eyes. Betty grimaces and stares back down at her soup.

I wash up and slide in next to Kathy. "Sorry I'm late. I told your dad to tell you not to wait up."

"It's okay," she says. "And we didn't wait." She giggles.

"There's still plenty, dear." Betty stands, picks up my bowl, and begins ladling her potato soup into it.

"I can do that. Don't worry about it."

"Nonsense, Harry. You and Ernie have worked hard all day. One day, Kathy will take care of you, but for now, let me do it."

I glance at Kathy and raise my eyebrows. "Does this mean–?"

Kathy nods, but doesn't speak.

Betty finishes her task and drops back into her seat. She doesn't touch her spoon or make any movement to pick up her tea cup.

"Oh, pride be damned!" Dawson exclaims. His spoon clatters on the floor as he tosses his arms up.

The rest of us must look like raccoons as we stare at him, startled.

"W-what?" I ask.

"Betty, jus' up 'n tell the young man."

"Yeah, Mom, tell Harry."

Betty sighs, her face pinched. She rubs at her forehead like she's got a headache. "Okay, fine. After– after some deliberation, I've decided it's up to you and Kathy what you want to do with getting married."

"Could you sound any less happy, Mom?" Kathy asks sarcastically.

"This wasn't an easy decision to make, Kathy," Betty says through clenched teeth. "Don't push me."

"Oh, enough's enough," Dawson growls, his usually kind face twisted like it hurts to speak. "Harry, Kathy, ya have our blessin'. Betty, darlin', we've been over this."

"Fine, Ernie. But that doesn't mean I have to be happy about it."

"Mom, it'd mean the world to me if you could just be happy for us," Kathy says in a small voice.

I take her hand beneath the table. "I think what Kathy's tryin' to say, Betty, is that we want you to see our marriage as true and meaningful as any, Catholic or not. I don't wanna get between a girl and her folks, but you all've been like a family to me. I hate seein' you not getting along. I've broken my own family enough. I hate that. Families shouldn't...shouldn't fight. You're too good of people to let this ruin your love." I stop, shocked at what I've just spewed. "Sorry, it ain't really my place to say somethin', but there you have it. I'm shutting up now."

Kathy and Betty have tears in their eyes.

Dawson, while stunned, smiles at me. "Harry, ain't never heard truer words." His eyes shift to his wife and daughter. "Betty, Kathy, please..."

Betty pulls a handkerchief outta her apron and wipes at her eyes, then blows her nose. "I'm sorry. So sorry for– for putting you through this. Let's put this behind us. Nothing would make me happier than to see you two married."

Kathy stands, walks to her mom, and hugs her. "Oh, Mom, thank you. Thank you so much."

Dawson and I exchange proud smiles as we watch the women we love make up. When the hug ends and the tears are done, Dawson says, "Well, now that that's outta the way, what's for dessert?"

Betty shakes her head. "Men. One-track mind. Kathy, you're sure you want to marry? He'll eat you out of house and home." We all laugh.

CHAPTER 25

A pril arrives, but winter hasn't released its hold yet. I wonder if our wedding will mean Kathy walking through a foot of snow. All her visions of a spring wedding seem on the fritz on April Fool's, even though we've still got four weeks until the big day.

"I do hope the daffodils are in bloom by then," says Kathy that evening over a cup of after-dinner tea, or coffee in my case. "They're usually so beautiful just in time for Easter if it's late like it is this year."

"Don't worry. Easter's a week before our wedding. It won't snow when it's almost May." I stir my coffee as we sit at the table long after everything's cleaned up.

It's hard to believe that it's been three months since Betty and Kathy saw eye-to-eye about our wedding while around this same table. We decided to marry in a Methodist church, since that's my background. Betty slowly warmed to the idea. When she met the pastor, she said he would do just fine. Funny enough, Pastor Willis was somewhat reluctant to move so fast, but we agreed to meet with him every week before our wedding. For us being strangers with the pastor before those meetings, Kathy and I quickly grew to like him, and all seemed to be moving forward just dandy since.

I tuck away my thoughts on the matter. And there's no sense worrying about a bit of snow when we didn't know if we'd even have a spring wedding a little while ago. I puff on a cigarette, leaning back in the chair. In the other room, the drone of the radio entertains Dawson and Betty.

Kathy doesn't seem convinced. "I remember it snowed once in May when I was a kid."

"Really? I don't think it's ever snowed past my birthday on the 10th." Another birthday means another year since I killed Kat, but I push those thoughts away as well. Too much on your mind, Harry, old boy. To Kathy, I hope I'm the picture of calm and collected. Poor girl's got enough on her mind without me adding to it.

"Well, I'm going to pray for a beautiful day. My sisters both had lovely days when they got married in the spring."

I stop stirring my coffee and meet Kathy's eyes. "You do realize we'll still be married at the end of the day, even if there's a tornado?"

"Don't jinx us, Harry!" Kathy laughs as she smacks my arm.

"Ow, you pack quite the punch, darlin'."

"It wasn't a punch, just a little hit."

"Mmm-hmm. Anyway, stop worryin' about it, Kath. I still can't believe you wanna marry me. What'll Hank do? He'll need to find a new roommate."

Kathy shakes her head and giggles. "He'll live." She makes a face. "Ugh, do you have to smoke inside, Harry?"

I frown as I put out the cigarette in the ashtray. "Sorry, I'll try to blow it the other way. Never seemed to bother you before. Besides, your dad smokes."

"I know. It's just that... It's a bad habit."

"Kathy..." I can't help but feel my hackles rise a bit.

"Sorry, I think it smells awful."

"I can keep it outside if you like or not do it around you. Sorry...it calms me. It's not like it's gonna kill me or anythin'."

"Hmm, well, do you ever think of quitting?"

I sit up in my chair. "Why? Is that really a problem?"

"We're going to be married now. Maybe it's time, you know, you stopped smoking."

"What's smoking gotta do with gettin' married? My breath stink?"

Kathy purses her lips. "Well, it doesn't smell like roses. Your clothes, your hair, everything... I'll be washing your stuff soon."

"Is this really about my smoking?"

"Okay, no. I just...I'm thrilled we're getting married, really I am. But I'm also nervous. What if I'm an awful wife?"

"Look, if the smoking's that bad, I can quit. But you're already everything amazing. You shouldn't worry so much."

"Well, okay. Let's just focus on our big day, huh? I'm pretty sure everything's in place."

"You've got your dress, I take it?"

"Of course, but you're not seeing it until I walk down that aisle. It's bad luck for the groom to see his bride in her dress beforehand."

"You don't really believe that, do you?"

Kathy laughs. "Come on, let's go see what my parents are listening to."

We leave our cold, empty cups behind and join the warmth of the living room. As I sit next to Kathy on the couch and hold her hand, I watch Dawson and Betty as they sit next to the radio. Dawson's large hand massages Betty's shoulder as she leans into him. They probably don't realize they've got an audience. I hope that's Kathy and me in twenty or thirty years.

* * *

Kathy's got nothing to worry about when our wedding day comes, every bit full of flowers and sun as she wanted. Hank and I drive in his jalopy to the church.

Hank looks me up and down as we step outta the car in the church lot. "Well, ya clean up somethin' nice, Harry, but ya look like ya just swallowed a lemon."

"It's nothin'...well, it's somethin', but nothin' I can do anything about now. Too late to tell my folks I'm gettin' hitched today." My hand brushes over Dawson's watch on my wrist.

"There's a phone in the church. Ya could call 'em."

"Nah. Let's get inside."

We wait in one room while somewhere else in the church Kathy gets ready with her mom and sisters, at least that's what I'm told. When the organ starts playing before the ceremony, Hank and I enter and take our spots. The bride's side isn't very full, maybe twenty or so people. A few of the folks shoot looks in my direction, probably wondering who this guy is Kathy's marrying, why she ain't in a Catholic church, and why the groom doesn't have anyone here for him.

"Well, damn, look at her," Hank whispers in my ear as the music changes.

I swallow hard and smile. I'd tell him it's probably not a good idea to swear in church, but my mind focuses on the vision of beauty coming toward me. I don't know the first thing about fashion, but she looks like an angel in her dress. Her face draws my attention more than anything, her radiant smile and shining blue eyes. The veil frames her face and covers the back of her loose hair. Dawson looks every bit the proud father as he walks his youngest down the aisle. When the pair reaches the front, the music stops, and the ceremony starts. I don't really listen to what the pastor says. Dawson steps away early on, leaving only Kathy and me. The rest of the people in that church don't exist. We say our vows, make a promise with rings, and share a kiss.

Then it's over, just like that. She's Mrs. Harry Rechthart. Well, she's actually Mrs. Harold Rechthart, but I'll be damned if anyone ever calls me by my awful full name. Outside, applause greets us. The bells chime. We kiss again and get into the back of her parents' car to go home.

Dawson drops in behind the wheel and chuckles. "Well, it's done! Congrat'lations, ya two!"

Betty sits much more delicately in the passenger seat a moment later.

"Thanks, Dad." Kathy beams, gazing from her dad to me.

"Ya sure ya wanna live at the house, son?" Dawson asks. "Ya migh' be able ta afford somethin' ta get ya started soon."

I try not to blush. "Soon enough, Dawson. I really appreciate you taking me in like a lost puppy."

"Already done that months ago." Dawson laughs.

The truth of his words hits me, even though it's nothing that should come as a surprise. Still, a man's got his pride, and now that I'm married, the need to support my wife is real. Maybe that's why I feel like Dawson's words are like bricks falling from the sky, aimed right at my head.

Dawson glances at me in the rearview mirror. "Ah, relax, son. This's a happy day. Plenty o' time for worryin' later."

He's right. Kathy takes my hand and squeezes it. We can do this married thing 'cause we're gonna do it together.

Back at the house, Betty outdoes herself with the dinner. It's just the immediate family.

"You didn't have to do all this, Mom," Kathy says as we tuck in for the meal. She's changed outta her wedding dress and into a pretty pink everyday number that makes her cheeks look even brighter.

Betty waves her daughter off, like preparing a ham and all the sides is small potatoes. "We wanted to, dear, for both you and Harry. Besides, the shop's been doing well enough for a while now. We can afford a nice meal now and then."

Dawson takes up his usual spot at the head of the table. I sit at the other end, the esteemed second man of the house. "That's righ'. It's in no small part ta you, Harry, that we can do this."

"Well, I try, Dawson. Still, my mechanical skills have a long way to go. Mr. Watson seemed none too happy last week when he had to bring his car back 'cause of my mistake."

He laughs. "Been tellin' Watson ta get a newer car for ages. Not your fault or mine if he don' listen ta reason."

"But it was an exhaust repair, and you've handed those pretty much over to me."

"Are we here ta talk 'bout exhaust repairs or celebrate your weddin', son?"

I chuckle. "Okay, fair point." I look at Kathy, who smiles at me and shakes her head in amusement. "Glad you can put up with this banter," I say to her, my stomach fluttering.

Kathy's smile widens more as she reaches for my hand. "Harry, if I didn't love you, I wouldn't put up with it."

That gets a chuckle from everyone at the table, even Dale.

"Let's get this dinner started then, shall we?" asks Betty. "If we sit here talking much longer, it'll go cold, even on a warm day like this."

That said, we stop wasting time and dig in. In place of wine is grape juice. I am half-tempted to ask Dawson to break out some wine. It's Kathy's and my wedding day, after all. One glance at Kathy, however, and I change my mind. I want a clear head to remember every moment of today. I see the way Dale and Walt frown into their cups. Let them. I smile at Kathy, then at Betty and Dawson, as I eat. Really, they're the only ones whose opinion matters.

After dinner, we don't have a wedding cake but rather strawberry pies Kathy's sisters made from canned berries from their gardens. We sit in the back yard, the garage half-hidden by a large oak. Between cups of coffee and cigarettes, the talk flows like some sorta river that's been going forever. The air cools as the dark falls. We watch the kids run through the grass.

"Just think," I whisper to Kathy, "that'll be our kids one day."

Kathy can't stop smiling. "I hope so."

"It will be. It doesn't hafta be long."

"Hmm, I'm not sure this is a conversation we should be having near my family." She giggles.

"Something funny over there?" asks Liza loudly.

"Nothing at all," Kathy shoots back, and we share a laugh.

I imagine Liza and Dee exchanging an eye roll, but in the dark, I can't tell.

"So, did your wedding day go like you wanted?" I ask my lovely wife. The smoke trails lazily in front of me as I exhale away from her face.

"Every bit. I can't believe how nice the evening is."

"See? And you were worried about snow."

Kathy laughs. "Well, can you blame me? Maybe you can teach me not to worry so much."

"I'll do my best. And while we're at it, maybe you can teach me how to be a good husband...'cause, Kath, I'm gonna try my best, and I hope that's good enough."

Kathy kisses me. "You're more than good enough, Harry."

* * *

Late that night, we share the double bed in what was once Kathy's room. Her sisters and their families went home an hour ago. Dawson and Betty followed them shortly by going to bed. She lies on her side, her head propped up by her arm. I take in every inch of her, imagining sharing ourselves for the first time. I am on the verge, about to jump off a cliff into the sweet abandon that is Kathy.

"Can you believe it? We're married." Her eyes dance in the low light from the bedside lamp.

I lean in and kiss her. "I'm the luckiest guy alive."

The smile falters on her lips. Her eyes go glassy. A tear slips past, trailing down her left cheek.

"What's wrong, doll?" I cup that cheek and kiss her again.

"I-I never thought this day would come."

"What? Why not?" My heart hammers, afraid she's having doubts.

A tiny, nervous laugh escapes. "Not because of you. You misunderstand. I mean, I didn't think I'd ever get married, period. I couldn't imagine anyone wanting me." Her gaze shifts to the mattress.

I wipe another tear away with my thumb, kiss the spot where it fled from her eye. "You remember what I said all those months ago? That you're the most beautiful person I know?"

She lifts her gaze and tries to smile. "Yeah."

"I meant that, Kath. Every word. I ain't romantic. I mess up a lot. But you're the one thing I know I got right. You deserve to be treated like a queen. To never hurt again."

"I don't deserve you, Harry."

"Hush, now. None of that." I pull her to me.

Our kisses deepen. Her hands caress the length of my exposed back. Our breathing heavy, we pull apart, resting our foreheads on each other's.

"We don't hafta do anything you ain't ready for," I whisper.

"No, Harry. I...I'm ready." Her smile seems uncertain.

"You sure?" I run my hand through her curls.

"It's you. It's time we made our own memories."

I kiss her again, then ease her down onto the mattress, with the deliberate care of handling something sacred. I close my eyes and let my heart and body show her my love.

CHAPTER 26

July 1938

"D'you hafta go, Daddy?"

My daughter tugs on my pants. I look down at two large eyes staring up at me, begging me not to go. I pick Gloria up and toss her in the air. She giggles as I play our favorite game again and again, until I kiss her belly and then her nose. I hug her and set her down on the floor. "Hey, pumpkin. Daddy's gotta work, remember?"

"But Mommy's no fun 'more, not wiff him." Gloria pouts, arms crossed over her chest.

I almost laugh. Getting down on one knee, I place my hands on her shoulders. They seem like giant's hands, holding this fragile, tiny person. "What's wrong with Mommy? She loves you, too. You're the big sister. Show Mommy what a big girl you are and help her out, eh?"

Gloria budges a bit. "Well, okay...but I don't hafta like it...or him."

"He's got a name. Little Lucas is only a month old."

"All he does is poop, pee, 'n sleep...'n cry."

"You couldn't do much when you were that little." I stand. "Now, run along. Papa won't be none too happy to be kept waitin'."

Gloria darts up the stairs. I watch her go, unable to believe I've got a wife and kids. Still living with the Dawsons is somewhat embarrassing for a guy like me, what with wanting to make ends meet and all, but one step at a time. Kathy asks me from time to time if I'm gonna tell my folks I'm married, that they've got grandkids. My answer's always the same: Not yet. I ain't ready.

As I step outside, I wonder when and if I'll ever be ready. It's been four years since I got outta the slammer. The sounds of the city are well underway, despite the early hour. The sun pokes over the skyline. It's gonna be another hot day. I shake my head, trying to imagine what my family's up to at this very moment. Are Ma and Pa getting on okay? Is Pa still working? Are Erik and Lily still living in Columbus? Did they start a family? How old are Amy's kids? God, I can't even remember... Irma's a young woman. And Hannah... Did she marry?

So many unanswered questions. My family's become a memory, a group of people who're strangers and yet not. I blink away the wetness in my eyes and blame the humidity.

Readying myself for another day of sweltering in the stuffy garage, I walk the short distance to the old building. I step inside. "Ready to sweat, old boy? And I do mean old, Dawson. You're pushin' sixty!" I laugh at my bad joke as I eye up the inside of the garage. The car we've been working on fills most of the space, but where the hell's Dawson? I step around the side of the car and ask, "Dawson, you here?" My foot brushes against something on the floor. I look down, meaning to kick a spare part outta the way.

"Oh, my God!" I fall to my knees. They smart from crashing into the cement floor. My hands fumble as I grab at Dawson and check for a heartbeat. He's still warm, but there's nothing there. Just dead silence.

"N-no... Dawson, wake up, damn you! You hear me? You can't do this..." Death lies on the ground right in front of me, and it's claimed one of the good ones. My eyes sting. As much as I wanna sit there and sob, I can't. I stand. Betty, Kathy...the rest of the family...

I walk back to the house in a daze. This can't be real, can't be happening. Maybe if I turn around and go back, I'll find Dawson standing there with that crazy grin on his face, asking me if I'm ready to start working on cars for another day, 'cause that's the way it's been, the way it's always been.

I open the back door. Betty's back is to me as I enter the kitchen. Each step smacking the floorboards is like a bell tolling doom.

She startles, turns. "Oh, Harry. Is something wrong?" She frowns.

"Um, Betty, I gotta tell you something..."

"What is it? Dear, you look like death washed over."

"Dawson, he's–" Why can't I say it? My throat closes up. I shake my head, trying to push the damning emotion away. But my eyes are traitors as the tears leak out. "He's... Betty, he's gone."

"What?" Her voice is brittle, like the smallest puff of wind will knock her over. She clutches at the back of one of the chairs for something to hold her up.

I go to her, steady her with my arms. "Betty, I'm... I just walked in...and– and there he was..."

"What do you mean he's gone?"

"He's dead, Betty. I found him on– on the floor."

She goes white. She leans on me as we go out the back door. We make the short trek to the garage. Betty doesn't say a word. The humming of the city around us is the only noise. Once we enter the garage, she spots Dawson's foot hanging out behind the car. Her cries are muted at first, but with every step, they increase in volume and intensity, until she kneels next to the man she's loved for thirty-some years. She cradles his head on her lap, bent over him as she mourns. I step away, feeling like an intruder.

As if it ain't bad enough that I gotta be the messenger once, I go back to the house to deliver the news to Kathy. My heart thumps in my head. I can't believe it. Gone. He's really gone, and without him, what's that mean? He made this home what it is. Without Dawson, now what? I continue on as if walking through a haze, a hellish dream.

I'm thinking too much, like always, as I take the steps two at a time. I knock on the door to our bedroom.

Kathy calls out, "Yes, what is it?"

I open the door. Kathy is feeding our son. They look so peaceful, the opposite of the chaos in my head. She glances up and seems surprised to find me standing there. "Harry? I thought you'd be Mom." Her gaze goes to the open window, which faces the back yard. "I thought I heard someone cry out a little while ago." She looks at me, the question in her eyes.

I step into the room and sit on the end of the bed. "Where's Gloria?"

"She went to her room to play with her dolls."

Lucas is asleep in Kathy's arms.

"Will he be okay for a few minutes if you put him in the cradle?" Every forced-calm word comes undone the more I speak.

Kathy looks down at our son and smiles. "Of course. I was just finishing up." She stands and walks the short distance to the cradle, placing Lucas in it like he's the most precious thing in the world. And he is, besides Gloria. She straightens and comes to my side as I stand. "Now, what's this all about?" She furrows her brow as she buttons her blouse. We creep outta the room.

"Just come with me." I keep my gaze ahead, afraid that one look at Kathy and I'll crumble. I reach for her hand with my shaky one.

When we arrive at the base of the stairs, Kathy stops me with a hand to the shoulder. I turn toward her. My eyes shift from the floor to her face and to the floor again.

"Harry, you didn't answer my question."

When I open my mouth, all my words dry up. "Kathy, I–"

"Good God alive, you look like someone's just died."

I feel the crease between my eyebrows deepen as my forehead draws in scrrow, that sadness running down the rest of my face as tears. I shake my head and squeeze her hand. "Kathy, Dawson...he-he's dead."

She doesn't move. "N-no." Then she runs outta the house.

I follow at a slower pace, having no desire to return so quickly to the spot of this tragedy. Once I step outside, Gloria runs out the back door, oblivious to what's happening a few feet away. She comes to me, tossing her little arms around my legs.

"Oh, Daddy! I heared ya come inside. Can ya play? Pease, pease, pease!"

I'm torn between staying with my daughter and finding my wife. When Kathy's sobs mix with her mom's and escape from the garage, I pick up my little girl and hold her close. "Let's go inside for a bit, eh?"

"Don'tcha gotta work, Daddy?" She looks back at the garage, frowning. 'Hey, why ya cryin'?"

"Daddy's just tired. And it's too hot to work today, pumpkin. Let's go in and check on your brother. What d'you say?"

As I enter the house, I cast a mournful gaze toward the garage. As much as it pains me to leave Betty and Kathy to pick up the pieces for now, I can't let Gloria see her darling papa lying on some dirty, unfeeling floor like a piece of garbage.

Dawson, old man, words can't say what the hell I'm feeling right now, but I'm gonna miss you something awful. That don't begin to cut it.

* * *

Several hours later, after Dawson's been taken away, the family sits around the living room. Dawson's chair by the window is empty. Even the kids are quiet. Kathy's sisters and their families joined us mid-afternoon. Betty and her girls pushed themselves through the motions of making dinner, and we ate what little we could. Every bite was like eating sand.

The orange glow of the sunlight comes in through the picture window. The air's stagnant and hot.

Finally, Betty speaks. "So many memories in this place. It's like the ghosts of the past are haunting me as I sit here and remember."

"Like what, Mom?" asks Liza softly.

"Oh, where to start? That year your father insisted on picking out the largest Christmas tree on the lot. We could barely get the thing through the front door!"

"And then when we did, it was too tall." Dee laughs quietly, blinking a bit too quickly for it to be the light bothering her eyes.

"You wouldn't let me cut it any shorter," Liza says to Dee, and the two sisters continue to laugh.

"But Dad always had his heart in the right place," Kathy says.

I take her hand and give her a nod that only she can see.

"Aye, that he did, bless him," Betty murmurs, removing her glasses to wipe at her eyes with a handkerchief.

"Remember the popcorn garland we'd spend hours making as kids?" Dee asks.

"Yeah, whatever happened to that? We need to start that tradition up again," Liza puts in.

The kids seem to perk up a bit when talk of Christmas comes, even though that's months away.

"We'd eat the popcorn after Christmas. It was so stale." Kathy smiles wistfully.

"My family did the same thing," I say before I realize what I've said.

If ever there was a time to pick up the phone and call my family, it's now. But even as the realization that Ma and Pa might be dead, too, grips me and tears my heart further, I stay rooted to my spot on the floor.

The sisters stop laughing. Silence takes hold.

Then Betty speaks: "It's not been a day since he left us, and I already miss his laughter. Besides his time in jail, bless him, we spent not a day apart all these years."

"He could make anyone smile," Dale admits, and I'm shocked to hear such words of kindness from him.

Walt nods. "He was always better than my own pop."

Kathy looks at me, maybe willing me to speak up about fathers and such, but I can't say it. I can't say that I loved Dawson more than my own pa. Neither can I say the other way's true. I love them both, and I mean that in the present tense. Yeah, 'cause Dawson ain't gone forever.

"I think he'd want us to remember him with smiles instead of tears," I say, "hard as that is."

If I drank, I'd lift a glass in Dawson's honor. As the thought enters my mind, I glance out the window into the street beyond. A small store on the corner sells beer and wine. I can almost see myself walking there, the pull for one measly drink growing.

I shake my head. Kathy side-looks at me, frowns.

"It's nothin.' Just...y'know...today and all."

She gives me a watery smile and squeezes my hand. "We'll get through this...together."

I nod. If only I believed that.

CHAPTER 27

The next few days blur one into the other. Well-meaning family and friends are in and out of the Dawson household with food, hugs, and condolences. I mostly keep to the background, watching my kids. These folks don't know me, not really, and part of me wants to tell most of them that they didn't know Dawson like I did. Their kind words seem forced, like they don't know what else to say. How many of them have come outta obligation and nothing else?

But that ain't fair. I'm in a bad place. As time passes and it settles in me that Dawson's really gone, I'm less at peace with it. The funeral's the usual affair, but I find I'd rather be alone to mourn my second dad. Only Kathy and Betty–plus my own kids, though they're too young to understand–are welcome in my circle of bitterness.

Anytime I see Betty or Kathy in tears or sitting silently, I mentally berate myself for feeling like I do. They've got years on me of knowing Dawson. Guilt eats away at me like an infestation, and I'm miserable for the first time since I was in the slammer.

Two weeks or so after Dawson's death, the house is dark and quiet. Everyone's gone to bed but me. I wander out back to the garage. I haven't opened the garage since Dawson's death, and I don't know if I will. I should. The family's counting on me to be the breadwinner now. With a flashlight in hand, I run my fingers over the unused parts sitting on shelves, left to bake in the daytime heat and collect dust.

With a sigh, I turn back for the house. As I'm about to enter, Kathy stands there.

"What were you doing, Harry?"

"Sorry, I...I dunno. Just hangin' out in the garage."

She takes my hand and leads me inside. We sit in the armchairs by the front window. "I'm worried about you."

"Don't be. I'm fine."

"Harry, I don't know how else to say this, but... Well, are you planning on taking on any more customers soon? Mom's getting worried about the bills."

"I've made some deliveries here and there," I offer. "It ain't much, but it's something." It's a measly excuse and nothing more. Over the past couple of years, I've done some deliveries for Walt, putting what Pa taught me into practice. It was meant to supplement our income and nothing more, not be the sole source of money.

"I know, and that's great and all, but it's not enough. Mom's wondering if she ought to do some sewing jobs."

I sigh. "She doesn't need to do that. I'll reopen the garage tomorrow."

"I didn't really come looking for you to talk about the garage. I know you're not fine."

It's too dark to see her face clearly, but I feel her eyes on me. "I shouldn't be doing this... He was your dad, not mine. I'm a lousy husband, Kath. I'm barely working to support you, and your poor mom's letting us live here. If anyone should be upset, it oughta be you and your mom."

Kathy sighs. "I don't think there are rules on how a person's supposed to mourn someone. It's okay, Harry. I just wish you'd have told me sooner. We've always been able to talk."

"You're the best, you know that?" I lean in and kiss her.

"I've been told that." I hear the smile in her voice. "Now, let's go to bed, eh? If you're really gonna reopen the garage in the morning, you'll need your sleep."

I follow Kathy up the stairs to our bedroom. After shrugging outta my clothes and into a T-shirt and a pair of boxers, I slide under the sheet and hold this amazing woman close.

But even with the assurance of my wife, something's still off.

* * *

As promised, I open up Dawson's Garage in the morning. I ain't expecting much business, since it's been closed for so long. I sit and wait, sweating and thinking. In a way, it's like being in jail again.

They say you don't know what you've got till it's gone, and ain't that the sad truth?

Finally, a customer pops in just as I'm about to close early for the day.

"Howdy," says a middle-aged man as he steps into the garage. "Uh, is Dawson around?"

I stand, pushing the chair back on its wheels with my quick motion. "No. Haven't you heard?" My words are short, impatient.

"Heard what?"

"Dawson died a coupla weeks ago."

"Oh, well…" The man shifts from one foot to the other. "I was hopin' he could take a look at my car."

"What's wrong with it?"

"Well, that's why I've brought it here. Keeps stalling every time I'm driving."

"Probably something wrong with your carburetor."

"Okay, then are you the man I need to see to take care of that?"

"That'd be me, Harry Rechthart. Dawson, he taught me himself." Speaking of Dawson to a stranger's hard enough, but I keep my voice controlled. All this man wants is for his car to be fixed. That's all he ever came here for. That's all Dawson ever was to him: a repairman. Yep, that's Dawson in a nutshell. Taught me a lot and not just about cars. Fixed me. Now I'm broken again, and where are you to fix me when I need you, old man?

"Um, excuse me, Mr., uh, Rechthart?" The man's voice interrupts my thoughts.

"What?"

"So, are you gonna take a look at my car?"

"Yeah, sure. Sorry. What's your name, sir?"

"I'm Henry Gregory. Been bringing my car to Dawson for years to be serviced. I don't remember seeing you. You new?"

As we walk outside to Mr. Gregory's car, I reply, "Been here about four years, give or take."

"It's been that long since I stopped by? Well, damn. I heard about Dawson's time in, uh, prison. Always surprised me to hear he'd ever swindle anyone."

My gaze drops to the ground. "Yeah…not one of his finer moments, but we all screw up sometimes, right?"

"True enough, young man, true enough." We stop by the car, a decade-old Model T, those dime-a-dozen cars. Mr. Gregory shifts again, his hands buried in his pants pockets.

I toe at the gravel with my worn shoe as the silence draws out. As if I need to kick myself into gear, I snap outta my daze and go to the car, opening the hood.

Mr. Gregory comes to my side and starts rattling on again. "If I'd have known Dawson's time was short, I'd have stopped by more often, you know, just to say howdy and how-do-you-do. He was a good man. All the more reason I couldn't believe he was in jail."

"It's the carburetor, all right. I can get her fixed and back to you tomorrow if that works." I stare at the engine as I speak.

"Tomorrow? Wow, that'd be great." Mr. Gregory's voice lightens.

I tear myself away from the car and slam the hood shut. "It's not like I've got a lotta business, sir." I manage a half-smile, but my heart's not in it. In what feels like another life, that Harry'd make some stupid remark about booming business and pass it off as a joke. That guy feels dead right now.

"Right, well...I'll be off, then. Thanks, Mr. Rechthart."

I watch Mr. Gregory leave, unconcerned if he's got a ride home, is taking a bus, or is walking. After a few unsuccessful attempts to start the car up, I manage and pull it into the garage. Once there, I flop back into the chair and glare at the car like it's the reason for my ire.

I spend the next couple of hours tearing down the engine, not thinking that I'm doing more harm than good. Some people beat a pillow when they're angry. I guess I rip apart cars. Although I've removed the bad carburetor, I'm of no mind to put a new one in today. Instead, tired of sweating and brooding, I close the garage up and flip the sign to closed, an hour before Dawson's usual closing time. I'm too worked up to go inside, so I decide on a walk. Maybe it'll do me some good.

I take off, not telling anyone. Just a little walk and I'll be back in time for dinner...

The dockworkers are finishing up for the day. The streets grow quieter as the evening settles over the city. Soon enough, a different type of folk will roam these parts of town. Sometimes I wonder if Kathy and I oughta move into a nicer neighborhood, invite her mom to come with us, but there's no way Betty'd leave that house. I don't think Kathy would either, so I don't bring it up.

I turn a couple of corners, tipping my cap at a few people I've seen around. I keep walking. As much as I try to focus on the sky or the people or the buildings–anything other than the fact that Dawson's dead–I can't. By the time my feet ache, it's nearly dark. I realize I must've been walking for three or more hours. I stop and find I'm standing right in front of a bar. A few guys are on their way in, probably looking to escape their families after their work for the day's done. I walk inside and take a seat at the bar.

The bartender wipes down a cloudy glass as he looks up at me. "What'll you have, then?"

"Just a beer."

"Sure thing, young man."

What the hell am I doing? Kathy's probably worried sick. But then, something inside me ain't ready to return home.

A minute later, the bartender sets a mug down in front of me. The amber-colored liquid looks like gold. As I lift it to my lips, it tastes like Heaven. In between sips, I light up a cigarette and take several drags. Before long, my sips become swigs, and the mug's empty. It's like a switch is flipped on now that I had a drink. When the bartender asks if I want another, it's an easy yes.

The more I get into the second mug, the less I think. And that's a good thing. I'm tired of thinking, thinking, and overthinking. Damn mind won't give me a moment's peace.

I'm well into my third mug now, and my tongue's loose. I smile easy at the guy sitting a few seats down from me. "Y'know, spent too mucha my life mis'rable. When I was in prison, talk 'bout torture. They keep you silent, see. Drive a guy slowly crazy 'cause he can't talk."

The man snorts and looks into his mug. The guy serving the booze don't seem to mind giving us poor suckers what we want, and before long, a fella who looks like he could be good ol' Dawson's brother walks in and buys us all a shot of whiskey.

"To our misery!" he shouts, and we echo and drink it down. It burns, but it's a fire that cleanses away all that rot of being down and out.

The bar fills as the night drags on. I'm lost as to how many drinks I've had. All's I know is, damn, I feel like a king! I feel free for the first time in years.

These guys are my pals. We swap stories of past loves and drinking to the memory of vixens who broke our hearts and trampled on them.

"Her name's Kat. Meow! She's somethin' special, I thought, yeah, but then, well...she laughed...laughed! Wanted t'marry her, I did, and she laughed!" I laugh, and there's chuckles all around. But as I laugh, it turns sour. Like everything, nothing good lasts.

"Boys, it's closing time," the bartender announces. "Everybody out."

We moan about our sorry states, but slowly the crowd breaks up. I step outside, swaggering with every step, holding onto the wall. Once on the sidewalk, those guys who were my buddies for a few hours no longer care a damn about me as they saunter away. I lean against the brick wall, overcome with dizziness. I puke on the cement and then slide down the wall, almost sitting in my vomit. The smell's downright awful, so I puke more. I force myself away from the stench just enough to breathe, but I ain't moving. The world spins, the buildings like monsters closing in on me in the dark. My head's killing me, so I close my eyes. Then the tears come.

"Oh, Kat...Kat...Kath...Kathy..."

Then blackness.

* * *

"Ow."

I open my eyes to darkness. I rest against something hard and unyielding. I reach behind my head to touch a wall. Coarse brick.

What the hell?

My eyes adjust for a few moments until I can make out the forms of buildings against the night sky. There's no moon out tonight, and there are few street lights.

What am I doing outside?

I try to stand and have to use the wall for support as a dizzy spell overtakes me. I touch the back of my head where it's sore from using a brick wall as a pillow.

Then I remember. It's a haze, but a simple turn to the right gives me the proof I need. The entrance to the bar's right there, the bar where I drank like the damned fool I am. I slide back down the wall and bury my head in my hands, my knees drawn up like I'm a little kid who's lost and scared. I stay like this for a while, afraid if I stand again, I'll puke. Afraid that standing will mean walking home and facing Kathy.

"What've I done?" I moan, rubbing at the sides of my head.

My hair tangles in my fingers, and I realize my cap's gone. Probably lost it in the bar.

I force myself to stand, steadying every step with the help of the wall. Slowly, I make my way back home, which is hard enough in the dark, let alone while hungover. When I arrive, it's like I'm standing on death's doorstep and God Himself's judging me.

I swallow. My throat's parched, so the saliva scrapes its way down to my empty stomach.

"Be a man, damn you, Harry." I turn the knob and the door opens, but not without a creak.

Before I can close it, Kathy's upon me. "Oh, good Lord above!" she breathes, clutching at me and pulling me to her.

I put my arms around her and bury my face in her neck, sobbing into her hair.

"Harry, what happened? When we didn't see you in the garage, we grew worried, and–" She stops and takes a step back. No longer safe in her arms, I stand there, exposed. "You've been drinking."

"Kathy, I'm...I'm sorry."

"Come up to the bedroom, Harry." It's a command, not a request. Kathy's normally quiet, kind voice holds steel in it. "But first, a shower, I think."

I sigh and follow her up the stairs. After a quick shower, I enter the bedroom.

She's sitting on the bed with her arms crossed over her chest. "So, what happened?"

"Can we maybe turn off the light? It's killing my eyes." I try to right myself by wiping at my face.

Kathy flicks off the overhead, leaving a much dimmer bedside lamp on.

"Thanks." I sit on the edge of the bed. "It's obvious what I've done."

"But why?" Her tone speaks of angry desperation.

I stare at my hands. "I don't know."

"What's that supposed to mean?"

"I don't know. I–"

"How could you? What were you thinking?"

"I– I don't know."

Kathy groans and balls her hands into fists, clenching and unclenching her teeth. "Tell me. And don't you dare say you don't know."

"I just thought I'd take a walk to clear my head. This guy came into the garage right as I was thinking of closin' up for the day, and he had no idea that Dawson was dead. No idea, Kath! He started talking about him and then left, and I was in that damn garage all day, sweatin' and thinkin' about your dad. So, yeah, I just wanted to go for a walk, okay? A stupid walk, and I kept walking and walking, not realizing how late it was getting. Before I knew what I was doing, I stepped into a bar. Just one drink, I told myself. I'd take the edge off and be done with it, but one drink turned into two and then three...and, well, you can fill in the blanks."

"Oh, Harry..." Kathy drops onto the bed beside me and hugs me.

I return the hug, and we sit like that for a while, holding each other in silence.

"I never thought I'd give in like that again...not to that level." I pull away enough to look her in the face. "I mean, sure, I've had moments where I thought about it, about having one drink. But it's been years since I actually touched the stuff."

"I don't think you've dealt with your grief."

I shake my head. "I've got no right to feel like this. He was your–"

"Yes, we've been through this. He was my dad, but I'd be blind, deaf, and a downright idiot to not know he was as good as a father to you. My dad was just that kind of person. He'd walk into a room and make everyone smile. You couldn't not love him." She wipes at her eye and smiles slightly. "I've had plenty of moments where I've cried, but you know what keeps me going?"

"What's that?"

"Remembering him as he was, that he wouldn't want to see us sad all the time. Mom pulls herself up by her bootstraps every morning. She told me that when she first wakes up, she sometimes forgets he's gone. That's when she allows herself to cry. Five minutes, she tells herself. Five minutes and then it's done. We've got lives to live. Don't throw yours away."

"Yeah, I've done plenty of throwing mine away already." I take a deep breath and let it out. "This is hard to admit, but I guess it never really left me–the urge for a drink, the reckless behavior... I'm a father now. I'm supposed to be a man, and I'm no different than I was ten years ago."

"That's not true."

"How do you know? You didn't know what I was like back then, Kath–the sorts of things I did, the people I was around."

Kathy cups my cheek. "I know what you were like then because I know the type of person you are now. You're still you, struggles and all. You think I don't have a few of my own setbacks?" She drops her hand.

I laugh weakly. "You're perfect."

Kathy purses her lips.

"What?"

"You, no one else, made me believe I could be loved, truly loved. I felt used, disgusting, for years. Then I met you. I never thought I would have kids of my own or a husband to love them and me like you do. Yet here we are."

"I'm sorry, Kath."

"And I question myself a hundred times a day if I'm doing right by our kids. I'm always asking Mom for advice, for help. I feel inadequate to do the job correctly. My mom seems like a saint compared to me."

I chuckle weakly. "You sound like my sister, Hannah."

"Hannah sounds like someone special."

I sigh and glance toward the window at the dark beyond it. "Yeah, she was...still is, I'm sure. She sold herself short for years, comparing herself to our older sister."

"That sounds familiar. You've said you always felt inadequate around your brother. What's his name again?"

"Erik. Yeah, I did. Funny thing is, Erik and me were the best of friends when we were just kids, but remember me telling you that Hannah and I got close as we got older?"

Kathy nods.

"Well, she was there most of the time when I was going to a different bootlegging party every weekend or so. She saw how I was when I drank. She tried to tell me to stop, but did I listen? Nope. You know how that ended."

"I do, but that doesn't change how I feel about you. You think I'd stop loving you, ever?"

"'Course not. But the urge to drink's always with me. It's like...like it's waitin' right around the corner, and all I've gotta do is turn that corner, and bam, I'll run right into it with open arms."

"How about this? When you feel like you need to drink, come to me first. We'll talk, no matter what time of day it is. Can you do that?"

"Yeah, I can. At least I hope so."

Feeling done in, I flop back into the pillows, their comfort never more welcome. Sure beats a brick wall behind the head. Kathy puts out the light and lies next to me. We kiss, and she's asleep before I am. I thank God for this amazing woman once again, but the longer I lie there, the more restless I am. I leave the bedroom to use the bathroom and go to the kitchen for a glass of water. As I lean against the sink with a splitting headache, I wonder if I can keep my promise, and also, how the hell am I gonna open the garage in a few hours?

CHAPTER 28

Mr. Gregory is none too happy when he shows up the day after dropping off his car, only to find I haven't touched it beyond removing the old carburetor.

"You mean to tell me I wasted my time coming down here today?" A vein on his forehead twitches.

"Sorry, sir. Uh, somethin' came up, but if you give me another day, I'll have her right as rain for you. Promise."

"Hmph." He crosses his burly arms over his chest. "Well, you'd better, that's all I can say. I never would've gotten such awful service when Dawson was in charge around here, son."

Son. The way he says that, the way he throws Dawson's name into the mix sets me on edge. It was like he's only here to mock me. "I'm sorry. I'll knock half the price off. It won't happen again."

"Best not." He makes to walk for the exit, then stops. "You oughta change the name of this place, 'cause it sure ain't Dawson's Garage anymore." With those words, he leaves.

His words slap me in the face. The sting remains, goes deeper than his accusation. Heat boils inside me, but I force it to do something usual as I bury myself in the car and get the thing fixed.

* * *

The next day, there's still next to no business. One guy stops by in the morning, and when he finds out Dawson is gone, he turns without so much as a "sorry to hear that" and leaves. I light up cigarette after cigarette, trying to calm my nerves. I want to hit someone. Instead, I kick at old car parts out in the junk lot behind the garage. I glare at the mostly fixed Caddy I worked on for years. I walk and walk some more, making sure to close up whenever I leave. Maybe a customer or two came by while I was out, but I don't care. I stop at the corner shop, pick up some bottles of beer, and hide them in the garage. In between smoke breaks–breaks from trying to think, I guess–I sneak the beer in.

By the afternoon, Mr. Gregory returns to pick up his beauty.

"I trust you've finished up?" he asks.

"Yeah, she should be as good as new." I sit behind the wheel and start the car up. I tell him what he owes me, and after he pays, Mr. Gregory slips into his car and seems pleased.

He doesn't give me any thanks, but I'm glad to see the back of him. Since it's nearly closing time, I tidy up the garage and wonder about the future. Part of it seems cruel to keep the name as Dawson's Garage. Still, the better part of me makes a silent promise that I'll keep it. It was and always will be Dawson's Garage, as long as I don't mess that up.

I frown at the two beers that are left, ask myself what I'm doing. If I had half a mind, I'd chuck them, but as I close the door, I keep them hidden behind car parts.

I continue in this way for days, days that turn into weeks, into months. I've always got just enough alcohol to keep me calm. Business at the garage steadily picks up as fall starts, but several customers return, unhappy because I've messed something up. Kathy thinks my mistakes are due to my grief. I let her believe that.

In the early mornings and often in the evenings, I make deliveries. I'm glad for the extra cash, as the garage ain't raking in the funds it used to. No one seems to notice that I'm drinking, and I'd like to keep it that way. To keep the smell of beer off my breath, I smoke after finishing a beer and chew on gum. Kathy's almost always busy with the kids or helping her mother in the house, so she hardly ever comes out to the garage. Dawson always said it was too dirty a place for women, and I guess he was right.

I've just finished fixing another car and sent another customer out the door. I step outside for some fresh air and a smoke, surprised at the bite in the wind. Gazing at the sky, I see that clouds are rolling in. I take one last drag on the cigarette and put it out under my boot. As I'm about to turn back to the garage, the rain starts. I take this as a sign to close up shop for the day.

While I close the garage doors, a car barrels toward me. I jump outta the way. The car stops just short of hitting the building. A man gets out and slams the door, and he runs through the downpour into the garage. I stand there, too stunned to speak.

"That rain's really coming down, isn't it?" the man asks, not looking at me.

"Uh, right. Is there something I can help you with, sir?"

The man's outta breath as he removes a handkerchief from his pocket to wipe at his forehead. He's probably in his fifties, grey peppering his otherwise brown hair.

Something about him seems familiar. He's too busy fretting about his person to meet my eye as he says, "Car keeps overheating. I had to get it somewhere quick, so I stopped at a gas station down the road. They told me about this place. Are you Mr. Dawson?"

As he asks the same question I've now heard several times over, he looks at me, then gasps. "You." All worry about his car leaves his voice. Only accusation remains.

Oh, shit. "Hi, Mr. Jones." Of all the stupid things I could say.

"What the hell are you doing here? Why aren't you rotting in jail where you belong?"

I take a step back. "I served my time, sir. You knew what the sentence was." I try to keep my voice even. Maybe he'll just leave and be done with it.

Mr. Jones glares, but stands his ground. "Three years? That's hardly long enough, don't you think? Is that all my daughter's life was worth? Three stinking years?" The anger gives way to brokenness.

I could let his words fuel a fire of hurt that I've kept burning inside for years, but that ain't fair. "You don't have to stay here, sir."

Mr. Jones sends another glare my way. "Car's not gonna start for at least another hour. I don't fancy getting soaked while trying to find a bus in this neighborhood as it gets dark."

"I can drive you."

He snorts. "Yeah, sure, and let you kill me like you killed her?"

"Maybe I deserve that. You have every right to hate me, but don't you think I hate myself more? There's not a day that goes by where I don't think of what I did. I'm offering to help you, for whatever it's worth because..." My voice softens and shakes. "Because, damn it all, the man who this garage's named after helped me when I was down and out. He taught me a thing or two about trying to do the same for others."

Mr. Jones stares, her mouth hanging open.

I reach for a beer bottle and hold it up. "Guilty as charged, Mr. Jones. You got me right. I'm just some drunk who screws up again and again, so maybe you'd be smart not to take my help after all."

I toss the beer bottle aside, listening to it shatter. I grab another off the shelf and let it drop. More glass breaks. "There, gone. You happy? This boozer has nothin' to drink, so am I safe?" I laugh humorlessly at my lie, feeling the damning stare of numerous hidden bottles on the shelves.

Mr. Jones backs away from me, hands held out as he shakes his head. "You're crazy. Rain or no rain, I'm getting the hell out of here. I'll worry about my car another time."

I continue to laugh as he runs into the rain and out of sight. I stop laughing and walk to his car, setting my hand on the hood. It's hot as hell. A door slamming breaks my concentration, and I look up to find Kathy walking toward me with an umbrella.

"What are you doing standing outside in this rain?" Before I can answer, she grabs my clammy hand and pulls me under the umbrella. We return to the house.

Once inside, I take off my soaked shoes. "But I didn't close up the garage."

"It can wait until this rain lets up some. You'll catch your death in those wet clothes. Go change."

"Yes, Mother." I smirk, trying to downplay the recent events in my mind.

A few minutes later, I return with dry clothes. "Where are the kids?"

"Both napping, would you believe? And Mom is, too. She seems to tire easily these days."

"Good for her taking a nap. I guess that leaves you with the job of making dinner?"

"Yes. I was just putting some chicken in the oven when I looked outside and saw you. Whose car is that? I saw a man run off shortly before coming out." Kathy pulls some potatoes out of a sack and washes them.

I sigh, dropping into one of the kitchen chairs. "That was...someone I wish I'd never see again. I have no idea what to do with his car. He said something about dealing with it later. Either way, it's gonna have to be moved before anyone else can pull into the garage."

"So, who was he?" Kathy stops washing the potatoes and sets them aside, turning to face me.

"He was...Kat Jones's dad."

"The girl you, um..."

"Yeah, her. I'm sure you can fill in the blanks when he realized who was running the garage."

"Ugh, that's awful, Harry. I'm so sorry. Are you going to fix his car?"

"Should I?"

"I don't know... Maybe it'd give him a little satisfaction."

"Fixing his car ain't gonna bring his daughter back."

"No, but maybe he can let go of some of his anger toward you. Look, I'm not saying you owe him anything. I know what happened was as terrible for you as him–"

"You don't know anything about it." I stand, knocking the chair over.

"Harry..." Her face crumbles. Lucas starts to cry upstairs.

I can't even look at her as I turn and run back into the freezing rain. I go to the garage and find an old pair of boots. Idiot that I am didn't even have anything on my feet when I made the smart decision to dart outta the house. The boots aren't gonna be much help because the soles are coming apart, but it's better than nothing. My coat's upstairs with the rest of my dirty, wet clothes, lying in a heap on the bathroom floor. Already chilled to the bone, I consider going back to the house.

I frown at Dawson's greasy coat hung over an old tire, but I pull it on. It's too big and smells of motor oil, but again, better than nothing. Is this what I've sunk to, taking what's better than nothing? Maybe nothing would be a blessing right now. To feel nothing. To think nothing. Just plain nothing.

With the hood pulled up, I slam the garage doors shut and walk away from everyone who matters to me...well, everyone but my family that I haven't had the courage to talk to in years. One thing I didn't forget was to move my wallet from my old pants to my new ones. How convenient. I head to the bar I visited several weeks ago.

The same guy works behind the counter. As I step in, recognition lights his face. "Ah, you're back."

I smirk. "Yeah, maybe too long since I paid the bottom of the beer mug a visit, eh?" I sit. "I'm thinkin' something stronger than beer today, though, old chap."

"Name's George, sir. What name d'you go by?"

He must be making talk with me 'cause other than the fella in the corner who looks passed out, I'm the only guy here. "Harry's fine. I ain't formal or anythin'."

George pours a shot of whiskey and sets it in front of me. He chuckles. "This place's the furthest thing from formal, young man. You look down and out. This one's on the house."

I pick up the shot glass and toast to him, smiling. "Much appreciated, Georgie, pal."

The burn of the whiskey on the way down warms me. "Thanks. D'you think you can serve up another, this time on my tab?"

"Sure, Harry. That's what fellas like you come here for, right? Lay all your sorrows out on the bar for us to see. I'm sure some other guy'll be joining you before long. The day shift's about to let out." While George takes the shot glass and refills it, he continues, "You wouldn't believe the stories I hear."

He sets the shot in front of me. I take it, throwing my head back and then clunking the glass down on the counter. Running a hand through my messy hair, I say, "I bet. Sure they don't hold a candle to mine." I laugh.

"That's why you're laughing, right? Laugh enough and it doesn't hurt quite so much."

"Yeah, somethin' like that. Life's a joke, though, eh? If you can't laugh at how screwed up your life is, you cry about it. No man wants to cry like some baby, so laughter it is. I'll have another."

George's smile doesn't reach his eyes. "Easy on the drinks, son. This is the last shot, and then it's only beer, got it?"

"Right." I frown. "Keepin' an eye on me like some daddy figure?"

"Something like that." He returns in short order with another shot, then leans on the counter with his elbows. "Y'know, I get why you boys do it—the drinking, I mean. I'm happy to help you take the edge off, but most of these fellas who come in here are years ahead of you in their misery. They might as well dig their graves and be done with it, but not you. No, there's something different about you. I've seen enough long faces over the years to know. You can't be a day over thirty."

I knock the shot back. "Twenty-eight, act'lly, but who's countin'?" As the booze starts to go to my head, I wonder if I look older than I am. I shrug.

"Point is, son, you've got years ahead of you. Don't mess up your life."

I chuckle. "Bit late for that, don't you think? I messed up years ago when I killed a girl in a car crash. And yep, before you ask, I was drinkin.'"

George's face slackens. "That's a serious thing. It's no wonder—"

"Yeah, it's no wonder I just left my wife and kids to come here."

"Maybe you should go back to them. You aren't intending on leaving them for good, are you?"

His words pierce my heart like a knife. I open my mouth, but no words come. I sigh, blaming the booze for not doing its damn job as tears leak out.

George sets a clean rag in front of me. "I'm thinkin' you need this more than another drink, son."

"Stop callin' me that." I pick up the rag and wipe my humiliation away. I toss the rag back on the counter. "There, I hardly used it. Bet you can still put it to good use cleanin' those dirty mugs of yours."

George smiles sadly. "Mugs are easy to wipe clean compared to a guy's life. So, did you wanna talk about it?"

"About what? My jail time for what I did, or the lousy husband and dad I am?"

"Seein' as the past's the past, why don't you focus on what the problem is right now, eh?"

"The problem is, Georgie, that the one man I looked up to for years up and died on me. Surely you knew him—Dawson, Ernie Dawson."

"Owner of Dawson's Garage? Yeah, nicest fella. I was sorry to hear it. So, you knew him well, then."

"That's puttin' it mildly. He's my father-in-law...was. I'm supposed to be runnin' his garage now and supportin' my family, and instead I'm here."

"Well, here's a bright idea. Why don't you let me pay your tab, and then you pick up your sorry ass and go home?"

"You throwin' me out?" I almost stand to leave, but dizziness overtakes me.

"It's your choice, but if I were you, I'd get the hell outta here. I get plenty of business without a young man like you ruining his life more because I'm helping him."

"Hmm." I stare at George as he turns his back to me and wipes around the sink. Then a couple of guys wobble in, probably already liquored up, and take seats at the bar. George's attention goes to them. I stare at the wood grains on the old countertop, try to imagine how many guys have drunk here over the years, what their stories might be, and how they ended up. Most are probably buried six feet under by now.

One life. That's all I've got, and what am I doing with it? It's easy to say what I should be doing. It's another thing to do it. I push the empty shot glass away and stand, pushing past the dizzy spell. George turns as I make to walk out.

I catch his eye and say, "Hey, thanks...just, you know, thanks."

George smiles slightly and nods.

When I step outside, the rain's stopped. Crazy thing is that there ain't a cloud in the sky now. I take a deep breath of fresh air and steel myself. I take the first step...then another...turn the corner...and walk right into another bar.

CHAPTER 29

The bartender at the second place becomes my new best friend. He doesn't ask questions, won't meet my eyes as he gets me one drink after another. Beer has lost its effectiveness, so it's straight-up shots that warm me as I sit in that dingy, musty bar. The smell reminds me of my prison cell. The bar is quiet, though. No screaming like in jail at times. These sorry fellas are likely wailing on the inside if they're anything like me.

When the bar closes, three other guys and I wobble out onto the streets. The darkness is thick. I wander without purpose or thought, as if walking through a haze. I float like in a dream, my mind blissfully empty. A lazy smile covers my slack face.

After some time, I turn onto my street, these buildings as familiar as the back of my hand after all these years. My head begins to pound. I wince. "Damn."

I stop, resting my hand on the wall of a brick dwelling to steady myself. This is the moment where I question why the hell I drank, where every pathetic boozer asks himself why he did it, knowing he'd feel like shit when the short-lived euphoria ends.

Kat laughs at me, then snarls her rejection. I toss the ring in the bushes.

A humorless laugh escapes my dry lips. I push off the wall and haul myself the rest of the way home. When I reach the front of the house, I pause, stare at the dark windows. Kathy must be in bed. I continue on to the garage, flick on the light. It buzzes, going in and out, the bulb either loose or about to die.

The inside of the garage spins. Car parts lining the shelves seem to fall off. I stumble toward the shelf with the exhaust pipes. Dawson's voice haunts, explaining how the exhaust system works...my first lesson. I shake my head, push the pipes aside, grab a bottle of whiskey.

"Hello, old buddy," I murmur. I drop onto the tattered sofa and bring the bottle to my lips.

A LAUGHING MATTER OF PAIN

The smooth, strong liquid burns at first, then warms. When my head stops hurting and the pleasant dizziness returns, I stop, gaze at the bottle. An inch remains. What the hell? Why not just finish it off? The perfect way to end this night. It goes down easy. The bottle clatters to the floor, but doesn't shatter.

A light goes on upstairs in the back of the house. I grin. "Kath's up."

I stagger outta the garage, across the yard, and enter through the back door. Light shines down the stairs. With my arms out, I steady myself through the kitchen and into the living room, gripping the rail as I take the steps. Standing at the top is Kathy. She frowns as she reaches for me, takes my hands.

"Harry, where have you been? I saw the light on in the garage." The concern on her face disappears as she sniffs. "You reek of alcohol." She releases my hands roughly.

"Aw, don't be like that, doll." I chuckle. "Was just havin' a bitta fun is all. Miss me?" I lean in to kiss her, but she steps away.

"Come into the bedroom, Harry, and lie down. We'll talk about this in the morning." She makes to head for the room, but I grab her arm, pull her toward me.

I wrap her in my arms and kiss her. "C'mon, Kath. Let's go to the bedroom, yeah, but I can thinka better things to do there than sleep."

Kathy tries to shove me off.

I chuckle. "Like it rough, eh? I can give it." I lead her to the bedroom.

"Harry, let go. You're hurting me."

My hand holds her wrist. "I ain't hurtin' you. Just want you to come with me. Give your hubby a little love, eh? Missed you, too." I yank her down onto the bed and fall next to her, laughing. Pinning her under me, I lean into her and start kissing, moving down her neck. I fumble with the buttons on her nightgown, ripping them right off. My hands trail to her chest. "God, you're beautiful, Kath."

"Harry, s-stop." Tears stream down her cheeks. Her voice wavers.

"C'mon, doll. I ain't gonna hurt you. Just need some good ol' lovin' is all." I undo my belt, unzip my fly, grind into her. "Undies needa come off, Kath."

She bites on her bottom lip so hard, it bleeds. She clenches her teeth, the scream hardly concealed. "Harry, please..." She pounds my chest with her fists, tries to push me off.

It's like someone hits me in the head with a boulder. I blink, stupefied. Her face is flushed, tears covering her cheeks, losing themselves in her hair as she lies on the mattress. She sobs, her eyes screwed shut as she continues to hit my chest. I recoil, leave the bed completely, and bang into the wall. I slide to the floor, drawing my legs up to my chest as my own tears start.

For a long time, neither of us says a word. The happy haze of the booze wears off into a pounding headache and nausea. When I can't hold it in any longer, I run to the bathroom and puke.

It's a wonder the kids or Betty haven't woken up through all this. A small mercy.

I return to the bedroom. Kathy is curled on her side. Her sobs have stopped. Glassy eyes meet mine. She flinches as if struck.

I sink onto the edge of the bed, resting my elbows on my thighs. I bury my face in my hands and sigh, run my hands through my hair and over my bristly cheeks. "God, Kath, I-I'm so sorry."

"I don't care."

I reach for her.

She shudders and pulls away. "Don't touch me."

"I said I was sorry. It won't happen again, ever. I swear it."

Kathy sits, glares as she holds the top of her nightgown shut. "And I said I don't care. I think it would be best if you slept on the couch."

I stand and nod. "I get it. I'll, um…" I walk toward the door, rest my hand on the frame for support. The room tilts. "Kathy, you know I love you." The sting in my eyes releases in fresh tears. "I love you."

"Just go." Her voice is broken. I've broken her.

I nod, but she doesn't see it. She's turned away from me, bent over and rocking herself as the sobs wrack her body. I want to reach out to her, to hold her, to caress her, to hug her, to love her…but the few feet between us might as well be a canyon.

A door opens. Betty stands in her room, staring at me with wide eyes. "What's going on?" The accusation in her voice slugs me in the stomach. Lucas begins crying behind the door to the kids' room. Betty frowns and goes to her grandkids' room, shutting the door.

Just as I start to shake my head, my stomach tightens. I return to the bathroom and throw up again, then I haul my sorry ass downstairs and lie on the couch, staring at the pair of armchairs near the window.

My mind drifts back to better days when Dawson and Betty occupied those chairs, listening to the radio. How many times did Dawson fall asleep, his snores enough to wake the whole house?

Then there were times when Kathy and I sat in those chairs, talking late into the night as the fire burned low. Stolen kisses and silly remarks and stupid jokes passed between us. Those days were golden, numbered…now as dead as Dawson and the cold fireplace.

My gaze falls on the family picture above the mantel. We never got a new picture taken, but below it rest pictures of the grandkids and Dawson's daughters with their husbands, including me. Even me.

My head throbs against the pillow, so I sit up, rub my face. "What've I gone and done, Dawson? You'd be so disappointed in me. After everything you did, I…" But I can't finish that thought.

A dizzy spell overtakes me, and I lie back down. Close my eyes. Betty and Kathy's low voices carry down the stairs. Lucas has stopped crying. Tears leak out from my eyes. I can't keep the emotion in. Somehow, the house goes silent and sleep wins.

* * *

"I guess that's a day wasted. No money coming in today."

I wake to Betty's angry voice. Sitting up, I blink, gazing around at my surroundings. My back is sore, and my head feels like someone hit it with a hammer. It takes a moment to realize why I'm in the living room. Flashes of last night come: one bar, then another, an empty bottle in the garage, me pushing Kathy down on the bed, her cries and tears, her mom's frown.

From the kitchen, Kathy replies, "I don't know what to do, Mom." She sounds like she's been crying.

"Whatcha talkin' about, Mommy?" Gloria asks.

"Don't you worry about it, baby," Kathy says. "Just eat your breakfast, okay?"

"Well, something needs to be done," Betty says. "Things can't go on like this."

I stand and amble into the kitchen, sure I look a fright. The women gasp upon my arrival. Betty turns away, clanking dishes in the soapy water in the sink. Kathy holds Lucas to her breast as she sits at the table, her gaze on our son. Only Gloria smiles.

"Daddy!"

It's enough to undo me.

"G'morning, sweetheart." I drag my feet over the wooden floor to my daughter and plant a kiss on the top of her head.

"There's coffee if you want it," Betty says without looking at me. "Oatmeal on the stove."

I nod, muttering my thanks. Silence hangs thick in the room as I grab a cup of coffee and fill a bowl with oatmeal. When I sit and pull the chair to the table, it squeaks over the floor, compounding my headache. I spoon oatmeal into my mouth, make the motions of chewing and swallowing, but it's like eating sand. After a few bites, I sigh and push the bowl away. I down the coffee, stand, and take the dishes to the sink.

"Just put them there," Betty says, nodding toward the counter next to the sink. She continues to focus on the dirty water.

"Thanks for breakfast. I'll, um...just gonna take a quick shower and then I'll get the garage open."

"You're sure that's a good idea?" Kathy asks.

Her words pierce me. I stop in my tracks as I'm about to exit the kitchen. "What d'you mean?"

"Mom, can you take the kids outside for a little while?"

Betty sighs, wipes her hands on her apron, and turns toward her daughter. "If that's what you think is best." She glares at me, then smiles at Gloria as she takes Lucas from Kathy. She coos at him, then takes Gloria's hand. They pull on coats and leave through the back door.

"Kathy, I'm sorry." I take a step toward her. "Please–"

"Are you sure you're sober enough to fix cars? How do I know you won't go down to the corner store and restock your secret stash?" She crosses her arms over her chest. Her blouse is buttoned back up after nursing Lucas, like a shield against me.

I sigh and take a seat. "Can we talk about this?"

"You've been lying to me for how long, Harry? After last night, seeing the light on in the garage, I went out there this morning and found several bottles, including an empty whiskey one. And it doesn't take much imagination to figure out you were at the bars last night. You got home after three in the morning! And Dad's business has been suffering for months now. That's why you were making so many mistakes. So many unsatisfied customers. It wasn't because Dad wasn't around to watch you anymore or because you were grieving. It's because of the drinking."

"Kath, if you'd just let me explain–"

"I think your actions have done plenty of explaining. What if Gloria had walked in on us, had seen her father drunk? Is that the type of dad you wanna be, the kind of husband? Mom says I should kick you out, if we didn't depend on your income. You don't wanna know the names she had for you. As for Dad, what do you think he'd say if he were alive? He'd be thoroughly disappointed in you. He gave you a chance. He treated you like family. And this is how you repay him, by drinking...and– and nearly ra–?"

"Now, wait right there!" I stand, the chair clattering to the floor. "I didn't do that! I may be a drunk, but what kinda monster d'you think I am?"

"But you almost did, Harry, and that was enough." Her voice wobbles.

"I didn't mean to hurt you. I was drunk. I wasn't thinking right." The words fall from my lips like the pathetic pleas they are. Betty's glare comes back. "Does your mother know what I almost...almost did?"

"What's it matter? For your information, no, I didn't tell her that. Knowing you were drinking was enough for her. I'm sure if I enlightened her, she'd want you out for good, and we'd suffer trying to survive...probably move in with Liza or Dee. The garage will close, my dad's work and legacy dead with him."

"Kath, we can work through this. Please."

"You hurt me long before last night. You weren't thinking for months before you lost control completely." Tears stream down her cheeks. How I long to kiss them away, but every tear damns me, drowns me, stabs me.

I take a step toward her, reach for her. "But, Kathy...I–I love you."

"Maybe love isn't enough."

A LAUGHING MATTER OF PAIN

My breath hitches in my throat. I try to swallow the lump, but it grows. If a man's heart could stop beating from words that speak the death of love, I would be a dead man. "W-what're you sayin'?"

"I don't know." She withdraws from me, burying her face in her hands.

Beyond the window, Gloria's happy shrieks come, a slam against me for every mistake I've made, of the good life I had and threw away.

"Give me ten minutes. I'll pack my bag, and if I'm lucky, Hank will take me back in. If not, I'll find some other place. I'll keep the garage goin', but won't step into your house." Your house. Not our house.

"I didn't say you had to go."

"You didn't have to." I leave the kitchen and go upstairs to collect the scraps of my life, to pack them away.

* * *

When I return downstairs, Kathy is nowhere to be seen. I go to the back door and look out the window. Dawson's '25 Ajax is gone. The yard is empty.

Before I know what I'm doing, I approach the phone like it's about to disappear if I don't reach it fast enough. My hand hovers over the phone like it's a bomb about to go off. I grasp it and dial.

Two rings and a man's voice answers. "Hello?"

I breathe into the receiver once, twice, three times.

"Hello? Is someone there?"

Four breaths, five. Six.

"I can hear you. Who is this?"

Just as I start to say, "Pa," he hangs up.

I sigh into the dead receiver and put it back.

I don't have the resolve to make the call a second time. I grab my bag and exit through the back door. Stepping into the overgrown grass, I gaze at the garage. Mr. Jones's '24 Chevy sits right in front of it. Part of me can't believe it was just yesterday when he pulled into the driveway.

It would be so easy to walk away from all this...yet so hard. I could pretend the past four years never happened and live on the streets. I certainly can't return to my own family.

But as I stare at the garage, Dawson seems to stand just beyond the threshold. He grins at me like it's the first time on that sunny day all those years ago when he saw me, a man just outta prison. His blackened face couldn't hide his wide smile and kind eyes–eyes that watched me for hours, days, as he trained me how to fix a car. Eyes that never judged me. Eyes that saw something worth fixing in me.

"I owe it to you, Dawson, to keep goin'. Most especially now." I take one step and another to the garage and set my bag on the couch. Glaring at Mr. Jones's car, I say, "Okay, you piece of trash, you're gonna start. I'm gonna fix you."

I struggle for fifteen minutes to start the Chevy. I pull the car into the garage, then slam the door and return to the sofa to smoke. My hands shake as I go through half a pack, imagining Mr. Jones returning to get his car and shoot accusations at me...or much worse, for Kathy and Betty to return and kill me with the truth of what I am.

By mid-afternoon, the car is fixed. I toss a wrench aside and drop onto the sofa. Betty and Kathy haven't returned, nor have any customers come to the shop. The spot where Dawson always sat is forever indented. I pat the cushion. "Miss you, Dawson." I light up again and close my eyes, letting the smoke do its work as it goes in and out. Dawson sits next to me, telling me how his older brother screwed up big time by letting his drinking win.

"Poor guy didn't have no chance, Harry. Never even tried ta figh' it."

"I'm sorry. That must've been tough."

"Yep, 'specially since I was the man 'o the house, next in line 'n all." Dawson shakes his head, his blue eyes glistening in the cool morning air. "Which's why, son, ya need ta keep that promise to yourself. Ain't nothin' good ever come from drinkin' too much. 'Course, ya don' need me ta tell ya that."

"Yeah, I know that too well. I owe—"

He waves me off. "Nah, was jus' doin' my little part. 'Twas you who took the chance ta be a better man. Ya make me proud."

That conversation was six months ago. I open my eyes to emptiness, the physical kind echoing what's inside. My vision blurs as I stare beyond the garage into the sunlight.

A man calls out, "Hey, you in there, you son-of-a-?"

I stand and shout, "Don't dishonor my ma's good name, Mr. Jones." I step up to him and continue, "Say whatever the hell you want about me, but don't go bringin' others into your hate."

Mr. Jones snaps his mouth shut as his eyes shift from me to his car. "You fixed it?"

"Yeah, I fixed it." I kick at some dirt on the floor. "Now you can get the hell outta here and drive it off my property." My property...is it?

"But– you fixed it?" Shocked, Mr. Jones drops into the driver's seat and starts up his beauty. The engine sounds smooth and new. He turns it off. "Why?"

"'Cause that's what I do, Mr. Jones. I'm a repairman."

Mr. Jones leaves the safety of his car and stands in front of me. "How much do I owe you?"

How much? How can I put a price on the damage that's been done by me? "Just get it outta here."

"But–"

"You heard me." I cross my arms over my chest and stare him down.

"Well, uh...thanks." Mr. Jones has the gall to look embarrassed as he gets back into his car and backs out of the garage. Once he's on the street, his tires squeal.

I watch him disappear down the street. I'm a repairman. That's what I do. I fix things. That's who I want to be.

"Here's hopin' I can fix my family, Dawson."

CHAPTER 30

I walk between the kitchen and the living room, restless. Every time the rumble of an engine comes down the street, I run to the window in the hope it's Betty, Kathy, and the kids. The hour grows late. My stomach growls. I force down some burnt toast and a few apples, missing the hot meal that always waits for me after a long day's work. Sitting at the kitchen table, I smoke cigarette after cigarette until I run out. The clock ticks overhead, another hour gone.

It's 9:00. Kathy and her mom ain't coming back tonight.

I stare at the phone and the paper with the numbers of family and friends tacked on the wall next to it. They're likely with one of Kathy's sisters. I could call, but the thought of listening to another voice accusing me of what I already know ain't appealing.

I ball my hand into a fist and pound the table. "Damn it." With a groan, I rest my elbows on the tabletop and run my hands through my hair.

Shaking, I stand, grab my coat, and go out the back door. The evening is chilly but not uncomfortably so for October. I walk to Hank's, then remember he ain't there. Still working the night shift.

"Need cigarettes." I check the pockets of my coat and come away empty.

The corner store is closed. I walk, my legs growing unsteady. I pass two more small shops and come away with what I already knew: closed.

A bar's sign flickers a hundred feet away.

"Just gonna grab a pack of smokes," I mutter.

I enter, glad it ain't the same bar where ol' Georgie started judging me last night. The bartender is busy talking to a group of guys. The haze of cigarette smoke is a balm to my nerves. I stop at the vending machine near the door and insert my money. When the pack drops, I smile in relief and turn to leave.

"Hey, pal. Ya jus' steppin' in?"

I turn, expecting the bartender to be gazing at me. Instead, a guy in his sixties stands not ten feet from me. "You," I say. "I've seen you before."

He grins. "Like to hit all the joints up, sonny, but you ain't jus' leavin' now, are ya?"

"Actually, yeah. I think that'd be best."

He laughs, the familiar sound tearing me up. "Aw, c'mon, don't be like that. Whaddaya say? Jus' one drink. On me. I insist."

My mind drifts back to all those months ago when I hit the bar for the first time and this guy bought everyone a round of shots. "I don't know if–"

He wraps an arm around my back and pulls me to an empty spot at the end of the bar. "Yo, Jimmy. I'm buyin' for this young fella. Poor guy looks like he needs some comfortin'."

The bartender half-smiles. "Righto, Rick. See you got another youngun on your sleeve."

Rick laughs, smacks the bar top. "Start off with a beer. See where the night goes."

The bartender clunks two mugs in front of us. I stare at mine, frowning. The deep aroma wafts off the top of the mug, easing my nerves a bit. The amber liquid froths, almost spilling over.

Rick picks up his mug. "Cheers, eh?"

"Right, cheers." I bump my mug to his, but set it back down.

"What's the problem, fella? Say, what's your name? Look familiar..."

"If you're who I think you are, maybe that's 'cause I knew your brother."

Rick's face goes slack. His smile washes away like he's been doused with cold water. "What'd ya say?"

"You heard me right. You didn't even have the balls to come to his funeral. You know he died a few months back, right?" I glare at Dawson's sorry excuse for a brother.

"Yeah, I heard. Was sorry for it, but I know where I ain't welcome, fella. So, that's where I seen ya...working wit' Ernie in that garage of his. Ya got a name, sonny?"

"It's Harry, and I'd like it if you didn't call me sonny."

Rick laughs. "Whatever ya say. Ain't no skin off my back." He chugs down most of his beer, wipes the foam from his lips. The resemblance to Dawson is uncanny: the same blue eyes, the same thinning hair, the same build, only Rick's gut is likely from years of boozing.

I wanna tell him how pathetic he is, but the bigger part of me just feels sorry for the guy. I push the beer away and stand. "I should go."

"What's the hurry? Ya look right down 'n out."

"Not that you'd get it, but your brother was a great man. Losin' him messed me up. And like you, I got a drinkin' problem, but maybe I'm man enough to do somethin' about it."

Rick scowls. "Ya don't know what you're talkin' about. Wanna know the truth of it?"

"What's that?"

"Bein' the oldest son meant all the expectations was on me. My old pop wanted me to follow in his footsteps. Maybe I didn't wanna. Ernie was jus' like my pop in the end. Both of 'em uptight asses. He used to know what a good time was, then he up 'n got a stick up his ass jus' 'cause our pop had a little heart scare."

I sit down, glare at him. "Accordin' to your brother, it was more than just a little scare. He had a heart attack. That's what got Dawson thinkin' he'd best get his life on the right track. And if I heard right, another heart attack took your poor father's life soon after. Same damn thing that killed Dawson." I pick up the beer, take a gulp.

Rick's frown lifts at the corners. "Ah, see? Ya did need to take the edge off. How's that feel goin' down?"

I clunk the mug down. "Did you hear a word I said?"

"Aw, c'mon, fella. Seems you 'n me got more in common than you'd like to think. Can't help our lot in life, can we? Some fellas are born with talent, good looks, money, whatever. Somma us ain't so lucky. Don't we jus' gotta do what we can with what we got?"

"To a point, I suppose, but if your brother taught me one thing, it's that you gotta keep tryin', keep betterin' yourself. And Dawson was more than my boss. He was my father-in-law, more like a dad, actually. I married his youngest daughter, your niece." I drink more beer, this talk of Dawson with the man who could be his twin and yet is so different messing with my head.

Rick chuckles. "And that's why you're hangin' out in a bar?"

When I set the mug down the second time, I push it away. "I think I'm done talkin' with you...and done drinkin'."

"Maybe for tonight." His grin widens.

"Hey, what's your problem, pal?" My fists clench at my sides.

"Ya tell yourself you're done drinkin' every day, right? Ya lie to everyone 'round ya, but most of all, ya lie to yourself. If you're anything like me, sonny, you ain't done, not by a long shot. Might as well be honest with your sorry self."

I laugh humorlessly. "Yeah? That what you've done, be honest with yourself? Look how fine and dandy you've turned out. Thanks, but no thanks. Turnin' into you's the last thing I'd want."

He chuckles again. I wanna hit him. "More lies, sonny."

"Stop callin' me that." I stand. "You'll never be the man Dawson was."

Rick stares at me. The ruckus in the bar fades away as I gaze back at his glassy blue eyes, trying to imagine what they've seen, the pain they've witnessed. For a moment, it's just him and me, two drunks locked in our own little world.

"Tried bein' that kinda man. Didn't work out so good, so why bother?"

His words pelt me as I storm outta the bar. A few guys on the sidewalk send startled glances at me.

"What the hell are you lookin' at?" I yell.

They laugh.

"Lookin' at a horse's ass."

"Seein' a sorry son-of-a-bitch who needs a few!"

I shake my head, walk off. As I take the route back home, my encounter with Rick plays through my head. My rage burns away with every step and turn I make. By the time I reach my street, only pity fills me. Rick spoke of lying to himself. Poor guy knows he ain't happy.

And it scares me how much of myself I see in him.

When I arrive home, the house is dark. No surprise. No way Kathy's gonna return home at midnight.

I enter through the front door and turn on the lamp between the armchairs that flank the front window. I flop into one of the chairs with a sigh. Resting my elbows on my knees, I bury my face in my hands. No tears come. I'm drained. My gaze goes to the family portrait above the mantel.

"It's late." I stare at Dawson's smile as sadness and fondness wash over me. "Goodnight."

I go to my room. The starkness strikes me the moment I step in. My grimy clothes fall to the floor, forgotten. A moment later, I turn off the light and pull the covers over my naked, broken body. I shiver, reaching for Kathy in the emptiness beside me.

Sitting up, I turn on the bedside lamp and open the night table drawer. Dawson's watch looks up at me from the contents. I smile sadly and withdraw the watch, cradling it. I shake my head, the weight of Dawson's gift in my trembling hands. Returning the watch, I close the drawer, turn off the light, and pull the covers over me in the hope of losing myself to sleep.

Hours later, I lie awake, the absence of Kathy hitting me every time I turn to touch her, to whisper to her, to kiss her.

When I do fall asleep, I awake from nightmares that I've killed Kathy, too. Those green eyes turn blue and do more than accuse. They stab through my chest, rip my heart out. They rob me of any chance of making right. Hopelessness the closest thing to death.

CHAPTER 31

The ring of the phone wakes me. I startle at first, then groan as my head spins from lack of sleep. The insistent ring bellows up the stairs, seeming to rattle the whole house as I pull on a robe and make my way outta my room and down the steps. By the time I reach the phone, it stops.

With a sigh, I walk into the kitchen and turn the light on. In the pre-dawn light, the garage barely stands out from the rest of the back yard as I stare out the window. I swallow thick saliva as I grip the edge of the sink.

"This is it, old boy," I tell myself. "Time to prove you've got what it takes."

The void filling the house hits me all over again as I go through the motions of making breakfast. I set the pot of coffee to boil and work on trying to fry a couple of eggs without burning them. The dependency on Ma, Betty, and Kathy all these years for something as simple as a meal eats away at me. Eating, yet another thing I took for granted. Didn't know the value of it until it was ripped from me. Or more like, I threw it away. Like so much.

While I wait on breakfast, my gaze drifts to the phone. Was it Kathy or Betty calling? Surely no one else would've called this early. I go to the phone, pick it up, start to dial Dee's number. Of the sisters, Kathy seems to get along better with Dee. The smell of burning eggs strikes my nose. I curse and replace the phone, darting to the stove to save my pathetic breakfast.

A little while later, the food sits in me, doing only a half-decent job of easing my nerves. I wash the dishes and clean up the rest of the mess I've made. By the time I'm done, the sun is up. And my head hurts.

After a quick shower and pulling on some clothes, I return downstairs. I can't keep my eyes off the phone, as if willing it to ring.

I put on my coat and go to the garage to open up for the day. I take the remaining bottles of booze and dump them out in the junkyard behind the garage, then toss them in the trash.

When I return to the garage, the disorganization of all the car parts lining the shelves seems to yell at me to fix it. I begin to work, waiting for someone to arrive with a damaged car.

When the morning passes without a single customer, I begin to wonder if word's gotten around that I'm a drunk. Business has already suffered since Dawson's death. Kathy's words come back.

"That's why you were making so many mistakes. So many unsatisfied customers. It wasn't because Dad wasn't around to watch you anymore or because you were grieving. It's because of the drinking."

Yet the drinking and the absence of Dawson go hand-in-hand. I light a cigarette and stare at the overcast sky. All morning, I've wondered if the phone is ringing in the house, yet every time I ran into the empty place like I needed to save someone from a fire, silence greeted me.

I toss the cigarette to the ground and stomp it out, then close the garage for lunch. I pass the house and go to my old dwelling place. After several knocks on the door, a drowsy Hank answers.

"Harry, what the hell ya tryin' to do? Can't a guy get his beauty sleep?"

"Hey, you got a minute or ten?"

He steps aside and gestures for me to enter. I sit on our old, holey sofa.

He joins me. "What's up, pal? You look like you've just come back from the dead."

I laugh. "Don't suppose you got any food?"

Hank beckons me into the tiny kitchen. "Don't know if ya'd call it food exactly, but here's what I've got."

I follow him and join him at the fridge. A plate of leftover meat looks inviting. I pull it out and go to the table.

"Well, since ya woke me up, I might as well join ya. Sure I can rustle up somethin' from here that ain't growin' mold." He laughs.

I nod. "Thanks for the food." I waste not a moment digging in.

"Sure ya don't want me to heat it up?"

"No, I'm good. Starvin', in fact. I think I could eat just about anything right now."

He shrugs as he puts something in a pot and heats it on the stove. He grabs a couple of soda pops outta the fridge and passes one to me. Hank sits. Resting his elbows on the table, he asks, "So, why ain't ya eatin' somethin' nice and warm back home? Are ya in hot water with the missus?"

I swallow, take a swig of pop. The discomfort of the carbonation and the large lump of meat going down take a while to pass. "I, um... You might say that."

He frowns. "In all these years, pal, ya ain't never come runnin' back to this old hole. Must be pretty bad. Don't ya have a business to run?"

"Lunch break." I smile weakly and try to eat, but my appetite dies. I push the plate away and light up.

"What gives? Ya were starvin' a minute ago. C'mon, Harry. We've known each other how long?"

"Sorry, you're right, of course. I'm just... I don't even know where the hell to begin."

"I find that usually the beginning's as good a place as any." He half-smiles, stands, and gets his food, then rejoins me.

"Very funny." I can't help but laugh a bit. "Well, you know my drinking troubles. Truth is, old boy, I've been hittin' the bottle again ever since Dawson died."

"Damn, pal. Wish you'd've told me. I'm guessin' Kathy found out?"

"She knew a while ago. I hit the bars one night, came home hammered. We talked. Thought we had it sorted out. Turns out that was a big lie. Been drinkin' on the job for weeks now, months. Business is sufferin' 'cause of my stupid choices. Found myself back at the bar a coupla nights ago, and...I came home worse than ever. Did something damn near unforgiveable to the woman I love." I hang my head.

Hank stops as he's about to take a spoon of his soup. "What the hell happened?"

I sigh. "I ain't at liberty to spill all the details. It involves some pretty serious shit, stuff that happened to Kathy years before we met. I hurt her. Bad. Now she's taken the kids and her mom and left. Guessing they're stayin' at one of her sisters' places."

"Oh, damn." He doesn't quite meet my eyes.

"Yeah, it's bad. Don't blame you if you wanna toss me out on my ass, comin' here beggin' for scraps like a bum. Maybe that'd be for the best...if I just live on the streets and drink my sorry self to an early grave."

Hank's spoon clatters to the table. "What the hell're ya talkin' about, fella? D'ya hear yourself? This ain't the Harry I know." He glares at me, challenging me to fight back.

But I don't have that kinda resolve. "I'm tryin', okay? Maybe it ain't good enough. I ran into Dawson's older brother at a bar last night, and nope, I wasn't there to get drunk. Needed cigarettes. I knew his brother was a drunk. Saw firsthand what a mess his life was. Even lied to him that I wasn't gonna be like him."

Hank stands. "Get up."

"What?"

"Ya heard me right. Stand up."

"What? You really kickin' me out?"

"Just listen to me for once, Harry. God, you can be such an idiot sometimes."

I stumble to my feet, thinking he's gonna land a good one on my face. "Wha-?"

Instead, Hank grabs my shoulders, shakes me. "D'ya hear yourself, pal? Wake up and be a goddamn man."

I raise my arms, knocking his grasp away, and step back. "What the hell d'you know about it anyway? You've never had a drinking problem."

"No, but ya think I ain't never seen it firsthand? Hell, plenty of the guys I work with show up to work liquored up...or don't show up at all and go to the bars instead. My own dad was a boozer. Made sure we all knew it, too. Came home late, angry at the world, at his own family, thought everyone and everything were against him. Loved to take off his belt and leave his mark on my brothers and me. Loved to hit my mom if she didn't give him what he wanted. I'm guessin' ya didn't do that kinda shit, am I right? Tell me I'm right, Harry. Ya didn't hit your wife or belt the hell outta your little kids." Hank shakes, his hands fisted at his sides. His voice trembles as much as him. The glassiness in his eyes spills over onto his rough cheeks.

I shake my head. "God...hell no. I'd never... Hank, old pal, I had no idea. You never told me."

"Ain't exactly the kinda stuff a guy wants on the front page of the paper. As for whatever haunts poor Kathy, I think I get the hint. Ya ain't like my dad. Ya gotta go back there and make right, whatever it takes."

I nod. "I'm tryin'. What I said, about livin' on the streets..."

He meets my eyes. "I know. I know ya ain't the type."

"I...I should go. I'm sorry for, you know..." My tongue rests heavy and thick, the words as slurred in my mind as if I've had a few.

Hank waves me off, tries to smile. "Just get goin'. I'll talk to ya later. Don't starve, and for the love of God, fix things with her."

"Thanks for the food. I'll see you later."

I exit in silence and don't look back. Hoping I haven't ruined the rest of my friend's day, I return home and take the time to cook some bacon without burning it. Just as I'm about to sit down for a late lunch, a car pulls into the driveway. My heart skips, but then I realize it ain't Kathy.

I go out the back door and find a man stepping outta a Chevy Confederate.

"Can I help you, sir?"

"Sure hope so." He goes on to explain the problems with his car, finishing with, "Was told this was the place to come. My neighbor brought his car to Dawson for years. Sure am sorry to hear the news about his passing." He removes his hat and places it over his heart.

"That's nice of you to say." I gaze at the hat, at the man's somber face. "I should have it fixed for you tomorrow morning if that's fine. Ain't had much business."

"I see that. Say, what's your name?"

"Right, sorry. Where's my manners? Harry Rechthart at your service, sir. What name might I call you?" I hold out my hand, for once not covered in grime.

He shakes it. "James Franklin. What d'you think it'll cost?"

I tell him the amount.

"That it? I'm robbing you."

"Nah, it's fine. You got a ride?"

He nods. "Gonna catch the streetcar. I'll be back tomorrow." He waves and walks off.

I watch him go, then return to the kitchen and devour my lunch. After a quick cleanup, I stare at the phone, wondering if it rang while I was out. My hand burns to pick it up, yet my mind is at war with my heart. I glance at the broken car in the garage. My feet move to the phone before I know what I'm doing. I dial Dee's number. After several rings, I sigh and hang up, then go outside to fix something I know I can handle.

CHAPTER 32

By the end of the day, Mr. Franklin's car is fixed, but my relationship with my wife sure ain't. I sit at the kitchen table long after dinner for old time's sake. The smell of bacon hangs in the air. The greasy meat sits in my stomach like a rock, but it's the only thing I can cook...sorta. I tried calling Dee's house right before dinner, but no answer again.

Now I stare at the smoke hanging in front of me. My coffee has gone cold, barely touched. Another day gone. Another lonely night ahead. What about tomorrow?

Smashing out my cigarette, I stand and turn out the light. There is little sense in hanging onto old memories when the present hits me like a train speeding down the tracks with every step I take through my sad house.

In the darkened living room, the rolltop desk rests opposite the wall with the sofa. Should I send a letter? Would that be easier than talking? Yet I fear putting a pen to paper and writing out all my mess-ups.

I shake my head in disgust and go upstairs to clean up, wishing a simple shower could wash away the inner grime the way it does the dirt on the outside.

After I'm physically clean, I crawl into bed, my head splitting from going a whole day without a drop of booze...for the first time in months. The headache grew worse as the day dragged along, but I was able to ignore it by working on the car. Without purpose and alone in the night, part of me longs for the bars.

It would be so simple, old boy. Just get dressed and go down the street but a little ways. Ain't no big deal to take the edge off like you've been doing. Hell, it's what you know, how you deal with the shit piles of life.

"Shut up."

I close my eyes, try to imagine I'm a kid again and sharing a bedroom with Erik. Those were simpler times, maybe better times...yet the best of times were the last four years with the Dawsons, until...

My mind drifts to Hannah. She tells me she won't cover for me again. She gazes at me in shame and pity, the concern written in her hazel eyes for my decisions. Her eyes go green. Kat leers at me, laughs.

"Ah, Harry, you're good for a fun time and nothing else! Here, have another!" She pushes a glass of wine into my hand.

I drink, but don't taste the smooth, dry flavor. Instead, the coppery tang of blood covers my tongue.

Kat screams, then stares, glares at me with those accusing eyes as blood trickles down her broken face.

Those green eyes turn vivid blue. They strike me straight through, a knife to the heart. I stagger outta the Caddy's driver seat, stare down at my chest and find a jagged piece of glass from a bottle of booze sticking outta my skin. My breaths come labored and short. My vision goes blurry and black around the edges, until my attention is snapped by a voice.

"Yeh've disappointed me, son. What the hell do ya think you're doin'?"

I gaze up at Dawson. He's a hundred feet away, the judge with a gavel behind the bench. Behind him, the jury box is filled with Pa, Ma, Erik, Hannah, Amy, Irma, Kat, Kathy, Betty, Hank, Gloria, and Lucas. Twelve people meant to condemn me.

"The verdict's in, son," Dawson continues. "Guilty."

Guilty, guilty, guilty, thuds my heart.

I try to pull the glass blade from my chest, but it won't budge.

"Guilty," says Dawson.

"Guilty," echoes the jury.

The blackness closes in as I fall to my knees and scream. My eyes open. The scream continues, then stops as I shut my mouth. But the bellow doesn't stop. It takes me a moment to realize the phone is ringing.

I stumble outta bed, unaware of the time, but knowing it's gotta be the middle of the night. My nightmare hangs with me, tugging me backward with every step.

By some miracle, I don't fall down the stairs. I reach the phone and pick it up.

"H-hello?" It hurts to speak.

Silence, but the hiss of the connection.

"Kathy, that you? P-please, just...say somethin'."

"Harry." She chokes back a sob.

I lean against the wall, slide down to the floor, the phone cradled in my hands, hot on my ear. Tears spring into my eyes. I swallow, but the lump in my throat grows.

"Kath, thank God."

"I'm sorry for calling so late. Dee, Mom, even Walt, they...they don't want me to be in touch with you."

"I'm glad you called. No, more than glad, I'm—"

"Harry, we need to talk. I can't sleep."

"Yeah, we do need to talk." I sigh. "Can't say I've been sleepin' well." My nightmare flashes through my head.

"How...how are you?"

My heart melts as more tears form. "I should be askin' you that. God, Kath, I'm so sorry. I know I messed up big time. Hurting you and the family's the last thing I wanna do."

"I've had some time to think. I believe you, but what happened, it's still a big deal, Harry. You're not drinking, are you? You don't sound like you've been. Leaving you by yourself like this wasn't my idea. I tried to tell Mom this wasn't the answer, but she wouldn't hear it. She wasted no time in filling Dee and Walt in."

My insides turn to ice. "Who else knows?"

"No one. And I'd like to keep it that way. But getting back to my question. Have you been drinking since I left?"

"I'd be a liar if I said it hasn't crossed my mind. I always want a drink, Kathy. That's what it's like being a...drunk. I took two gulps of beer the other night, and that's it, I swear. I dumped out everything in the garage and got rid of the bottles."

"But what's stopping you from going and getting more? How do I know you won't just go back to the same behavior, hit the bars up again? How can I trust you?"

I hear the tears in her voice. They stab me like the broken booze bottle in my dream.

"What's stoppin' me, Kath...is you. Is Gloria and Lucas. And Betty. And Dawson. And everyone else who's given a damn about me all these years. Kath, I– I love you. I need you in my life, 'cause I can't do this without you. I don't wanna go another day without you and the kids here."

Her sobs intensify.

A muffled voice comes from the background.

"I have to go."

"Kathy, wait–"

The line goes dead.

"Damn it." I stare at the phone as if that will reconnect me to Kathy.

With a long sigh, I hang up. My gaze goes to the stairs, to the darkness. I don't think I could fall back asleep if I tried, and the thought of having more nightmares is all the more reason to stay awake. Instead, I go into the kitchen and flip on the light. The clock tells me it's 4:07. Realizing I left my dirty plates in the sink from the night before, I turn on the water and wash them. I spend the next hour wiping down every surface in the kitchen, trying to remove the grease spots around the stove from my attempts at cooking. Betty and Kathy always kept the house in order. Keeping it clean seems the least I can do.

My stomach grumbles shortly after 5:00, so I fry up more bacon and try my hand at eggs again. My second attempt goes better, so breakfast isn't horrible. I clean up the dishes again, wondering how women can do this after every meal. The work seems tedious. I laugh at the ridiculousness of my thoughts.

Maybe because it's so common and everyday. Maybe because I took a simple thing like clean dishes for granted.

I shower because I have little else to do but allow my mind to drive me crazy. Then I go out to the garage and continue yesterday's task of organizing and junking parts that are no good. By sunrise, the garage almost resembles the place Dawson kept. I open for the day.

The next three days pass in a similar manner. As if by some luck granted by God, the customers flow in with their car troubles. The work keeps my mind off drinking, off my family, off my problems. I can almost feel Dawson standing next to me during every step as my dirty hands work with the car parts like Hannah's nimble fingers played the piano or I dribbled the basketball. This is good, honest work. This is fixing. This is taking care of my family, at least in the only way I can for the moment.

Yet when the sun sets and the world grows dark, I grow dark with it. My mind goes to my family, all of them, the one I haven't seen in years and the one I haven't seen in days. When no call comes from Kathy, I wonder how long she can go without returning home. How angry can Betty be to keep her daughter from me? Kathy's words come back to me about how mad Betty was at Dawson for his misgivings, how her parents' marriage almost ended. I remember Betty's disapproval at first over our desire to marry outside of the Catholic Church, how she went days without talking to her daughter. But she forgave Dawson. She gave her blessing for our marriage.

As I sit at the kitchen table, cigarette in hand, my mind goes to the night Kathy told me she was raped. The hurt, the protectiveness, the almost betrayal in both of her parents' eyes, if only for a moment, as they entered the kitchen and heard their daughter's cries reverberates through me. I made a promise to them and Kathy that day to love her.

"And what have I done?" I ask the silence.

I put out the cigarette, my mind weary from thinking too much. Thinking will kill me if drinking doesn't. Resting my elbows on the table, I run my hands through my hair and release a heavy sigh. My over-dry eyes grow heavy. As sleep is about to claim another victim, a pound from the front door shakes me awake.

"What the hell?" I stand and gaze into the living room.

The knock comes again.

"Who the hell'd be comin' here this time of night?" I shake my head and walk toward the front of the house, thinking maybe it's Hank.

A LAUGHING MATTER OF PAIN

Maybe I'm crazy to answer, but at this point, I ain't got much to lose. I open the door. A familiar face gazes at me. For a moment, I imagine myself delusional, that Dawson is back from the dead and has returned home.

"What do you want?" I ask. "Did you know I lived here?"

"Hey, pal. Jus' wanted to talk. Ain't no crime in that, right? And yep, seen ya 'round enough to guess. Add that to what ya said 'bout bein' married to my niece...'n, well, I figured it out. " Rick gives me a lopsided smile.

He doesn't reek of booze, but the night's young. I step aside. "Come in...I guess."

He enters and looks around at the living room, his eyes resting on the family portrait for a moment. "Nice place ya have here."

I close the door and cross my arms over my chest. "It's really more your brother's place than mine. I don't feel I have the right to own it."

"Hope I ain't disturbin' nothin'. Saw the light on 'n thought I'd try my luck."

"Well, call it luck if you like, but there's no one else here to disturb."

"Where's the rest of the fam'ly?"

"Not that it's any of your business, but they're stayin' with Betty's middle daughter. Seems my behavior's driven them away. You'd know a thing or two about that." I glare at him.

Rick holds his hands up, shakes his head. "Look, sonny–"

"Told you not to call me that the other night, or were you too drunk to remember?"

"Whoa, okay. Hot-headed young fella, ain't ya?" He chuckles.

"What's your point?"

He sighs, all traces of laughter dead. "Look, wanted to tell ya...I was there."

"Excuse me?"

"At the funeral, ya know, in the background. Didn't step in no church or nothin', but at the graveyard, was hidin' behind an oak that's been there since I was a boy."

"Oh...well..." I trail off.

"Visited that cemetery plenty of times over the years, 'though mostly drunk." His gaze is on the floor. His breaths come with effort, the heaviness of regret pushing in on him from every angle. He looks up at me. "What did Ernie tell ya 'bout me?"

"Not much." I gesture toward the armchairs.

We sit.

"He pretty much said you had a drinking problem and left the family. Dawson picked up the family business because you wouldn't...or couldn't."

"He tell ya I once had a girl?"

"No."

"Yep, pretty thing, too. Sweet as sugar and bright as the sun. We was engaged at one time. Good thing she never up 'n married me. Broke her heart 'cause I wasn't man enough to change." He pauses, maybe considering what to share next. "See, thing is, I seen what Ernie built. Kept away from fam'ly gatherins'. Truth is, sonny, I knew I had no right to be there with those folks. Wasn't 'cause I didn't care...jus' easier to turn to the bottle than to face 'em."

"Why're you tellin' me this?" My stomach drops.

"Think ya know. Call it a moment of clarity, those rare times in between drinks."

"Well...um, thanks." I squirm in the seat, his words too close to my reality. "Do you need anything? Don't have much in the fridge, and I ain't offerin' you a drink."

"You got a smoke?"

I smile. "That I can do, sir." I pull the pack of cigarettes outta my pocket and offer him one.

Rick takes it and lights up. He goes quiet.

"It ain't too late, you know," I say, maybe more to myself than him as I puff on my own cigarette.

"What's that?" He stares at me, startled.

"I mean, you always have a choice, right? To turn your life around? You wanna know how I met your brother?"

"How's that?"

"In prison."

Rick blows out a long stream of smoke. "Well, damn. Ya know, when talk got 'round these parts 'bout Ernie rippin' people off, couldn't quite believe it."

"Doesn't seem like him, does it?"

"Not by a lick. Almost wanted to clap 'cause good ol' Ernie done screwed somethin' up for once."

"My point is, he chose to do right from then on, and what's more, he helped me. And here I am."

"What ya done that landed you in the slammer?"

Kat's eyes flash before me. "Somethin' bad, bad enough I'd rather not talk about it if it's all the same to you. Gettin' back to what I was sayin' earlier, it ain't too late to turn your life around. I messed up big time again a few days ago, but I ain't touched a drop since that beer you got me. Don't intend to, either."

"Well, good for you." Rick's tone drips with resentment.

I sigh and shake my head. "I'm not tryin' to preach or tell you I'm better or somethin' stupid. Not sure what you want me to say."

Rick puts out his smoke in the ashtray, stands, and smiles sadly. "Ain't your fault, sonny." He turns for the door.

I stand, step toward him. "Wait."

He stops and turns, gazes at me with haunted eyes. "Can see why Ernie liked ya so much."

Before I can say a word, he's out the door. I'm left standing there, staring at the closed door, his words cutting straight to the heart. Tears prickle in my eyes. My legs wobble and I sink back into the armchair.

"Damn you."

CHAPTER 33

When Sunday arrives, I wake early again because sleep either won't come or is filled with nightmares. Another night has passed without a call from Kathy. Rick hasn't come knocking at the door late at night or any other time. I have never been more alone, even in jail.

After breakfast, I stare out the window at the garage. Dawson never opened the garage on Sundays, and I followed that routine. My gaze roams to the phone again. I go to it, my hand hovering over it for several seconds.

"Oh, the hell with it. Enough is enough."

I go upstairs and change into my Sunday best, shave, and comb my hair. I take Dawson's watch outta its drawer and slide it on my wrist. I wind the timepiece until it starts ticking. For a while, I sit on the edge of the bed, my eyes on the little clock, watching the second hand make its progression. Minute by minute. Hour by hour. Day by day. My head spins at how much time I've allowed to slip by without wearing this watch, this gift, this reminder of Dawson. Somehow, the excuses of not wanting to ruin it by wearing it in the garage fall flat. A pang goes through me as I recall how I didn't even wear the watch at Dawson's funeral. Maybe it was too painful, the hurt as fresh now as it was three months ago, yet with that watch on my wrist now, its weight is a reminder of a promise I made to Dawson to love his daughter with everything I got.

My gaze travels to my wedding band. The ring hugs my finger as the watch hugs my wrist, yet it's the arms of these people those things symbolize I long to feel around me again. The ring is but another promise, this one made to Kathy, the only woman I could ever love as I have, as imperfect as that love might be.

When my vision begins to blur, I blame it on staring too long. I shake my head and stand.

A few minutes later, I go out and hop on the next bus. My hands lock and unlock during the trip, my palms sweaty. Breakfast sits uneasy in my stomach. I'm sure the growing headache is due more to nerves than the on-and-off throbbing in my head

I've felt since going sober. When the bus reaches the stop I need, I step off into the chilly October morning.

Several well-dressed people pass on the street, likely on their way to church. I pull my coat closer and walk. The wind off the lake bites at my face, seeming to tell me that coming here was a bad idea.

I make a couple of turns until I stop in front of a brick bungalow that's identical to all the others on the street. Dawson's Ajax is in the driveway, along with Walt's truck.

Taking a deep breath, I steel myself and take the short walk to the front porch and knock. Children's laughter and footsteps come from within. I smile, hearing Gloria's little voice mixed with her cousins'. The door opens. Jeffery stands there, his eyes large. Before he can speak, Gloria peeks around him. Her cute face breaks into a huge grin.

"Daddy!"

"Hi, pumpkin." I get down on one knee, reach out for her.

She exits the house and runs into my arms.

"Jeff, how many times have I told you to let a grown-up answer the door?" comes Dee's voice. Kathy's sister stops just beyond the threshold and gasps when her eyes land on me. "What are you doing here?" Dee's younger son, Michael, hangs off his mom's leg.

"Who's there?" comes another voice—Walt. He joins his wife. "Oh, it's you." His kind face contorts into a frown.

I stand, holding Gloria, her little arms around my neck. "I'm sorry for just showing up like this, but I wanted to see my family. Is Kathy here?"

Walt crosses his arms and tries his best to look intimidating. Nearly a head shorter than me, that's hard to do. "What do you want with her?"

The crease between my eyebrows deepens. "She's my wife. I think what I need to tell her is between us."

"She's busy," Dee says. "Maybe you should call next time, instead of coming by uninvited."

Her words strike me like bullets. "C'mon, guys." I set Gloria down, and she joins her cousin. Even little Michael scampers off, apparently bored with the adult conversation. "How long have you known me?" I hold my hands out.

Walt sighs and drops his arms. He steps aside. "Dee, maybe we should—"

"What? Just act like everything's fine? You know how Mom feels."

"How I feel about what?" comes Betty's voice. When she sees me, she scowls. "Harry." She looks drawn, worn down.

"Betty, please, I need to talk to Kathy." I ignore the others and take a step toward the door.

"Kathy's feeding Lucas."

"I can wait."

"I don't know if that's a good idea."

I gaze at Walt and Dee. "This is your house. If you really want me to leave, I will, but I ain't givin' up on trying to talk to my wife. Can you at least tell her I stopped by?"

"Let him in," Walt says.

"What? Are you crazy?" Dee asks.

"Maybe, but let the man have a word, Dee. For God's sakes, he's her husband!"

Floored at the tone this guy who seemed to have no backbone takes with his wife, I want to applaud him. I bite my lip.

"Oh, fine." Dee scoffs and steps aside to let me in. "But I don't have to like it."

I enter, the walls closing in on all sides. Their gazes are hot on my skin. Everyone is dressed nicely.

"We're leaving for church in ten minutes," Betty says, then exits the room.

"Where can I find her?" I say to Walt.

Dee shakes her head and goes the same direction as her mother.

"I'll show you." He walks toward the bedrooms and gestures toward a closed door. "She's in there. I'll leave you alone."

"Hey, uh, thanks." I try to smile.

His smile is pained. "I think I saw your dad the other day. Was droppin' off some boxes at Higbee's. Looked like the guy you told me about. Drove a truck with the name 'Rechthart' on it."

My chest constricts. I nod. "It probably was him. Did he...look good?"

"Seemed to. Anyway, I'll leave you to it." He turns to go, stops and turns back toward me. "It's good to see you, Harry."

I nod dumbly as he leaves. I turn to the door and stare at the white paint. When I rap on the door, the muffled sound of someone shifting comes from inside the room.

"Who is it?" asks Kathy. "Mom, if that's you, I'll be out in a second. I know we're supposed to be going to church, but–"

"Kathy, it's me."

Silence. Then: "Harry?"

More movement, the rustle of clothing. Then footsteps. The handle clicks and the door opens. Kathy stands face-to-face with me, our son in her arms.

My heart melts upon seeing them. I hold my arms out. "May I hold him?"

Her frown lifts the slightest bit at the corners. "Of course." She passes Lucas to me, and I hold my son like he's a newborn again. "He's grown since I've seen him."

She smiles, almost undoing me. "He's eating like he's starving. I'm sure he's going through a growth spurt."

I make silly noises at my son, who coos and laughs at me. I turn my eyes to Kathy. "I've missed you, all of you."

She blinks quickly and nods. "How are things going at the house, the garage?"

"Fine. I'm tryin' to keep the house nice, but probably failing. The garage is going steady."

"That's good."

"And you? The kids?"

"We're managing. I think we're wearing out our welcome, though. To be honest, I don't know how much longer I can stay here."

I pass Lucas back to Kathy. She takes him, and I place a hand on her arm. "Then don't stay here."

She frowns and withdraws like she's been burned.

I pull my hand away and hold both up in front of me. "Kathy, come on now. Talk to me. Stop acting like I'm a stranger." My arms drop to my sides, my shoulders slumped.

She sits on the bed, her gaze out the window. "I don't know where to start."

"Kathy?" comes Betty's voice from the hallway. "We're about ready to leave."

"I'm not going to church."

"Kathy–"

"Just a minute," Kathy says to me as she stands and goes to the door. She steps outta the room.

Betty and Kathy's voices are heated whispers. A minute later, Kathy returns empty-handed.

"Where's Lucas?" I ask.

"Mom's taking him to church. The rest of the family's going to Mass, but I'm staying here."

"You're staying? To talk?" My heart leaps.

"I guess." She sighs, running her hand through her hair. She sits on the bed again. "First things first, have you been drinking at all since I last talked to you?"

"No. Not a sip."

She studies me for a while and nods. "I believe you."

"So, you trust me again?"

"I'm not sure, Harry. I want to believe you won't go back to a bar or stash away bottles again, but..."

I sit on the bed, careful to keep some space between us. "When we married, we made a promise to each other. Your dad told me marriage wasn't easy, but it's based on that promise you make...to love each other through it all."

"I'm not sure if that includes an addiction, Harry."

"What're you sayin'? You wanna divorce?" My mouth hangs open, my brow creased.

"I don't want that, but... Oh, God, this isn't easy, okay?" She sighs. "Every night away from home, from you, tears me apart. I wish none of this had ever happened. You drinking... Dad– Dad dying..." She trails off, her voice lost in tears.

I reach for her without thinking. I hesitate, but before I can second-guess myself, I pull her into my arms. She stiffens, then relaxes as she buries her face in my shirt and cries. She clutches at my clothes with her fingers, her grip unsteady. I'm reminded of that night all those years ago in the kitchen when I declared my love. I long to kiss away her tears, to caress her cheeks, to run my hands through her hair...to cherish her and never let go.

"You really are the most beautiful woman I've ever known."

She sniffs, withdraws enough to look up at me. "That's what you said when–"

I kiss her tears. She lets me. She stays with me.

"Yes, and I still believe that. I'll always believe that. I've done the unforgivable. I've hurt you deeply, and I can never take it back...but God, do I wish I could. Meeting you, loving you...the one thing I got right in my life, Kath. The one thing."

She sobs into my shirt, hiding her face.

My voice breaks as I continue, the tears on the verge of falling. "I wish I could say I'd be a better man, Kath–that I'd be everything you and the kids deserve. God knows I've tried to be that man these past four years. All I can do is try. And I'm tryin' somethin' hard. I don't ever wanna hurt you like that again. I love you with all I've got, but I'm puttin' myself in your hands now. I've got no right to make any demands of you. If you'll have me, I'll give you everything I've got, but if...if you're done with me, I understand." The tears win. My throat closes.

She continues to cry into my shirt, but her arms snake around me, holding tight.

I pull her closer still, until my face is buried in the crook of her neck. "Please...please..." My whispered plea is but a breath into her ear. I have no words. Only tears.

She withdraws, her arms going slack. For a moment, I wonder if she's gonna up and leave. Instead, she takes my face in her hands–her soft, warm hands on my moist cheeks. She gazes into my eyes, that clear blue so unlike the condemning green. "I forgive you, Harry. I love you. I think it's time we came back home."

My voice fails. My eyes can't see right. My mind can't believe what it's hearing. My body doesn't seem capable of moving. I sit there in awe, my mouth open. More tears flow. Then I pull her to me again and kiss the top of her precious head.

Finally, when I can find it in me to speak, I say, "Just when I thought you couldn't get any more beautiful, you prove me wrong."

CHAPTER 34

How do you fix a man? One day at a time. That's what I do, just take it one day at a time. Kathy and the kids returned home with me that Sunday I came to Dee and Walt's place. When we left, Betty and Dee stared us down like we had just committed the worst sort of crime. Kathy's eyes glistened with unshed tears the whole drive home. When I tried to comfort her that night after the kids were in bed, she shook her head, wouldn't talk about it.

I knew her mother and sister had some choice words for her. Even behind closed doors and in hushed voices, it was obvious they didn't approve of Kathy's decision. Betty stayed with Dee for the next several weeks. As for my little family, we carried on. I worked and stayed sober as fall passed into winter.

Maybe it's a battle to not drink, but when I look into my kids' faces and see how they look at me, like they believe for all the world that I'm the best dad in the world, I put down that bottled urge to drink. I can't forget Kathy, either, not for a minute. Now, instead of reaching for a bottle to drown my sorrows, I find my wife.

As another year draws to a close, I sit back and reflect. Christmas has come and gone. The first round of holidays without Dawson wasn't easy, I'm not gonna lie, but we got through them 'cause we were together. Seems even Dale ain't quite the hoity-toity ass I thought when I first met him. He knows not to bring wine into the house, and it seems everyone's fine with that. "For the best," Betty would say, all the while glaring at me. She never did quite forgive me, even after she returned home after Christmas. As for Walt, we've struck up a kinda friendship over the years. He appreciates me taking on extra deliveries when he can't keep up, and after my drinking problem, he turned into an even better friend.

Every time I'm out with Walt's truck, I wonder if I'll bump into Pa. Is he still out there, driving around with a busted-up leg at the age of sixty-five? I never run into him, despite what Walt told me about seeing him a few months back.

The rest of my family's never far from my thoughts. It's now New Year's Eve, and Betty's gone up to bed. She hasn't been the same since Dawson died, somehow less with us and more bitter than anything, even before I broke my bond with her.

Kathy comes down the dark stairs and joins me on the sofa. A fire burns low in the grate. "The kids are in bed...finally."

"Lucas again?"

"Yeah. Those teeth just need to break through, and hopefully he'll be happier again."

I smile. "Must be hard being a baby."

"Must be, so maybe it's a good thing we don't remember." Kathy frowns as her eyes shift from me to the fire.

"What's on your mind?" I ask quietly, putting out my last cigarette for the night. I wrap an arm around her and pull her to me.

"Mom was coughing a lot this evening. It sounded like she had fluid in her chest."

"She should see a doctor."

Kathy nods, her brow creasing. "Harry, what if–?"

"Don't say it, Kath. No one knows what the future holds." I kiss the top of her head as she leans into me.

"True, but..." She shifts, withdrawing from my arms. Her eyes search mine, seem to dance in the low light.

"But?"

"Harry, we've been through so much together."

"I couldn't have done it without you." Without Dawson.

"If there's one thing I've learned from it all, it's that life's too short. Harry, when do you think you'll talk to your family again?"

I sigh. "I've been thinkin' about them for years, but especially since Dawson left us."

"If I get Mom to go to see a doctor, I want you to see your parents."

"Good luck with that." I laugh softly. "Betty's as stubborn as an ox when it comes to doctors...and a lot of other things." My joke dies on my lips as the weight of my words settles in me. "I hope she's okay. I'd hate to think..."

Kathy shakes her head. "I'll get her to a doctor." She pauses, bites her lip. "So, will you call your parents?"

"It's a new year tomorrow, right? Maybe it'll be my resolution instead of tryin' to stop smoking." I grin, hoping to lighten the mood.

"That's not funny, Harry." Her lips quirk.

"Was I tryin' to be funny?"

"You know you were. Now, kiss me, you funny guy."

"But it ain't midnight yet." I smile.

"Shut up." Kathy leans toward me, and my eyes slide shut. I don't need to be told twice.

Seconds after our kiss ends, the little clock on the mantel strikes midnight. We kiss again, and after we break apart, we nestle close, staring in the dim light at the family picture above the clock. Dawson seems to wink at me, but maybe it's just the flicker of the firelight.

* * *

Betty sees a doctor a couple of days later. It turns out she has pneumonia. She spends a week in the hospital and gets out. Relief floods the family.

But then two weeks later, it's back to the hospital. In and out. In and out. It seems like Betty just can't kick this thing.

Kathy keeps hoping that come spring with the warmer weather, her mom'll be okay. But by March, Betty's condition worsens. The hope Kathy and I had for 1939 fades as we watch her mom fade. It seems like Betty's not gonna come home this time, at least not to her earthly home. This time, I'm man enough to be the support Kathy needs instead of falling to pieces. I sit with Kathy at Betty's bedside at the hospital. A kind neighbor who's got young kids has let ours stay the night.

Walt looks pale as he stands behind Dee, who's fallen asleep in one of the chairs in the ward. Dale paces. Liza watches him while she silently cries, the blowing of her nose the only interruption. Kathy's closest to her mom. Betty is sleeping. A curtain's the only thing separating us from a dozen others who are laid up in bed.

"How much longer do you think it'll be?" Kathy whispers. Her eyes search my face in the dim lighting.

"I dunno, Kath." I take her hand.

"You don't know what'll happen," Liza says to her sister. "Maybe she'll be okay."

"Don't give me false hope, Liza," Kathy says.

"I'm not–"

"Maybe we should just shut up and be with Mom, huh?" Dee's eyes open.

"You heard that?" asks Liza.

"Every word. Mom wouldn't want us arguing in her last hours."

Watching Kathy suffer, I feel helpless. The guilt that Betty and I never really reconciled eats away at me.

The sisters go quiet. The hours pass, and some time shortly after midnight, Betty takes her last breath. Kathy sobs into my shirt as I hold her.

"I'm so sorry," I say, whether to Kathy or Betty or both, I'm not sure.

Kathy looks up at my face, her eyes locked on mine. "Call your parents, Harry. See them, before it's too late." Then she buries her face in my shirt again.

I hold her, kiss her head. "I will, Kath. I promise."

In the following days, I don't try to offer up any cheap words of comfort. I'm just there for my wife in the way I wasn't when her dad died. It's sad that it's taken me this long and the loss of my in-laws to make me realize what a fool I've been. I thought I was saving my family from hurt by staying away all these years, but with every tear on Kathy's face, I wonder if all I did was hurt them all the more by not being there.

Even then, it takes me another couple of weeks to get my crazy head on straight. The house is empty without the older generation here. It doesn't feel right that I'm the man of what's supposed to be the Dawson house. Still, after Kathy and the kids are asleep, I sit downstairs in Dawson's tattered armchair and smoke a few cigarettes every night, my mind turning over a hundred different thoughts.

On this night, I pull out a worn, old picture of my family from my wallet. I'd almost forgotten it was there after all this time. I stare at the younger versions of us and shake my head. Ma and Pa are a decade younger. I was just graduating from high school, thinking I had the world all figured out, that I was so smart.

I laugh softly as how wrong I was. What a hollow sound.

"See you soon, Ma, Pa...everyone."

CHAPTER 35

I stand on the familiar slate sidewalk in the dark, staring at a house that fills me with equal parts happiness and sadness. Kathy asked if I wanted her to come with me tonight, but I told her this was something I had to do alone. As if some invisible clock strikes the final hour, I take a deep breath, run my hand over my new beard, and steel myself to face my family.

One foot in front of the other. I stop at the bottom of the driveway and put my foot on the big rock that's always been there. My childhood home and my family could be that immovable rock–constant, forever there. But as I look down at my foot resting on that old rock, it doesn't seem so big anymore. Funny how a few years can change things. Can change a guy.

I clench and unclench my hands at my sides, tell myself this ain't no big deal. Try to convince myself of the lie. But no more lies. No more hiding behind jokes and smiles to disguise the pain. No more hiding behind the booze.
It's time.

I make the short trek up the driveway, Pa's truck the only vehicle parked there. The glare from the front porch light shows it's rusted through in spots. I keep walking, deciding to try the back door.

I come face-to-face with the window on the door. The board Pa put up years ago to cover the window's long gone. I smile slightly at memories of Erik and me breaking that damn glass again and again with stray balls before the board was put up. That was a lifetime ago. Or so it seems.

I knock and wait. When no one answers, I half-wonder if they've gone to bed. Part of me's ready to dart away and pretend I never came, but the larger part beats some sense into yellow-bellied Harry. My stomach flip-flops. My palms sweat as the world seems to spin. It's moments like these when the thought of a stiff drink comes to mind.

I knock louder. Heavy, slow footsteps, like they're dragging. The inside light turns on, and the knob clicks.

I'm bathed in light as the door opens. Then I'm nose-to-nose with Pa. For a split-second, his face screws up in confusion or fear—like he's seeing a ghost. Then he stands straighter, and ten years seem to drop off him as his cane clatters to the floor. The spark reignites inside him as his eyes light up.

"Dear Lord above… Harry!"

Before I know what's happening, two arms pull me inside, but it's not Pa who's hugging me. I hear her sobs into my shoulder and look down at the grey head of Ma, her bun in the same place it always was. I snake my arms around her, and time melts away. How often have I dreamed of this? And yet, I was afraid, so very afraid for so long.

"Harry, oh, Harry." She pulls back enough to look up into my face, placing her hands on each of my cheeks. "You've got a beard."

I can't help but chuckle. "I can shave it off if it bothers you."

Ma shakes her head. "Is it really you?"

"Y-yeah, Ma, it's me." My voice is thick. My tongue feels like it's grown twice its size.

"Oh, my son! My son! You've come back!" Ma's tears continue as she hugs me again.

I pat her on the neck. "It's okay, Ma. Really." As emotional as this is, I can't help but exchange a smile with Pa. Ma hasn't changed a bit.

"Okay, Lucy, let the boy, uh, man, breathe." Pa gently removes my mother from me and leads her to a chair.

Like her, I think my legs are about to give out, so I drop into a chair as well.

Pa leans on the table, his cane forgotten on the floor. He looks me up and down and nods. "Yeah, you've become a man, Harry. Can't call you my boy any longer."

"He'll always be our boy," Ma says quietly.

Just then, a dark-haired young woman enters the kitchen. It takes me a moment to recognize her. "Irma…"

"Harry?" She takes a few more steps into the room, her hand going to her mouth. "Oh, my goodness. Harry!"

"Hi, Irma… Wow, look at you, all grown up."

"You came back."

"Of course I came back." I say it like it should've been obvious, like I'm still talking to my littlest sister and she's only five.

Just as I'm about to stand, Irma sits.

Pa shrugs and pulls up a chair, maybe thinking we're all about to have a long-overdue family meeting.

The back door opens. A young woman with long, dark blond hair enters, her hand clutching a stranger's. The man looks several years older than her with his slicked-back dark hair and round glasses. The woman is beaming. "Ma, Pa, I'm getting mar–" She freezes as she stares at me, her mouth gaping. "Harry?"

My nerves start firing as I sit up straighter and lock gazes with her. I know this face, but she's not the girl I once knew. I run my hands nervously through my freshly cut hair.

"Harry, aren't you going to say anything?" asks Irma.

"Hello, Hannah." I swallow thick saliva down my dry throat.

Hannah's eyes glisten as she continues to look at me. "It's good to see you, Harry. I've missed you." She tries to smile, but her face crumbles as tears spill over.

"Yeah, um...you, too." My voice wobbles, as do my legs under the table. I'm glad to be sitting. I look down at the table as shame washes over me. I search for something to distract me. "I..." My eyes dart around the kitchen. "I've only been here five minutes. I have something to show you all." I take a picture of Kathy, the kids, and me outta my coat pocket and pass it off to Ma with shaky hands. The others move in around her and gaze down at the picture.

Now that they have a clear picture, literally, of my new family, I find some of my resolve. "I've been married for four years now. This is my wife, Kathy, and these are our kids, Gloria and Lucas. I've made a life for myself. I've taken what I learned from Pa's business and put it into practice, and I've also opened my own auto repair shop in the shed behind my house."

It's funny the stuff I leave out: no mention of Dawson or his family, or that the garage is really his, or that my drinking was still a problem, or that the delivery stuff's really just on the side. Maybe I wanna impress Pa, make him think I've followed in his footsteps. Anything to not disappoint these people surrounding me.

"All these years," Hannah says, tears still falling. "You've had a family all these years, and we didn't know."

"You have a beautiful family," Pa says. "We'd love to meet them."

"Gus, we have grandchildren we didn't know about." Ma's voice is choked. "Harry, please, dear, you must bring the rest of your family around."

"It sounds like you've done well for yourself," Pa adds. "I do hope you'll stay around this time."

"I hope so, too," Hannah puts in. "But, Harry, you have a family. Why did you stay away so long? I'm sure I speak for us all here when I say we would've loved to meet your family, to know you were happy. To know something, anything."

"I knew what I was, Hannah," I say, my eyes on my hands in my lap. I sigh, then force myself to stand. "But I wasn't always happy. It wasn't always good times all these years. I...I'll tell you everything one day, but not now. Not now. I-I just can't." I meet her eyes. "I wasn't about to show my sorry face again until I'd proven I was worthwhile."

If they knew the first thing about what I've been through, what I've done in their absence, the lies I've told, the lives I've hurt besides theirs, the number of bottles I've drank... My head spins as I overthink my life yet again. Then Kathy's pretty face flashes through my tired mind, her blue eyes pleading with me to see my family, to forgive as she's forgiven me, to love as she's loved me. "Ya make me proud, son," Dawson says, somewhere deep in my memory.

Irma comes forward. "I believed in you, Harry. Had I been old enough, I would've visited you, but I don't think the rest of the family ever meant to hurt you."

Aw, Irma, kid...I don't blame you. Too bad I don't say it.

Hannah steps closer and places a hand on my upper arm. "You'll always be my brother, Harry. *Always.*"

My body trembles as sweat drips down my brow. I blink too quickly, and the room spins like I've had too much to drink. Any second now, I'm going to dart out that back door and not look back. It's too much. Just too much. I can't...

"Harry, stop," Ma says as she cries. "We never wanted any of this pain. Dear Lord in Heaven, I'm sorry for letting my grief get in the way of my love. Please, forgive us, forgive yourself."

Two sturdy, old arms pull me into a hug. Shocked, I stand stiffly for a few seconds, but then my knees grow weak. I clutch onto Pa like I'm a little kid who's just been found again and sob into his shoulder. A mixture of shame for wishing he was Dawson and for being back home with my own pa surges through me like the booze I've drunk down too many times.

"Harry, I'm so sorry you've been through so much pain," comes Hannah's voice. "But you should know that you were always worthwhile. Don't doubt that for a second."

I pull away from Pa and nod. Hannah's face mirrors my pained smile as Pa sits again.

I look at my sister, really look at her. She's beautiful. Her hazel eyes shine, whether with tears or hope, I ain't sure. Maybe both.

"There's been enough crying here for one night." I reach out to her and take her in my arms. When the hug ends, I glance toward the man Hannah entered with, then back at her. "But you were gonna tell us something big when you walked in tonight, and I'm afraid my showing up here kinda ruined all that." I half-smile. "C'mon, Hannah-panna, spill the beans."

Hannah laughs through her tears. "Oh, Harry, how I've missed your crazy lines." She smiles at her man. "Well, according to Edward, Ma and Pa shouldn't be all that surprised, but I'm getting married!"

Pa stands and pats Ma on the back as she cries happy tears, then walks to Hannah and her man, clapping them each on the shoulder.

"It's about time, eh, Edward?" he says with a wink. "Hannah, if you'd known how long we've been waiting since he first came to us and asked our blessing, you'd understand it's been driving us crazy. Congratulations, you two."

My chest clenches at Pa's words...so like Dawson's when he spoke of me asking for his blessing to marry Kathy.

Ma blows her nose, interrupting my thoughts. "I'm sorry. Excuse an old lady, dear." She looks right at this Edward guy as she speaks, then at Hannah. "Edward had the gall to tell us he was 'just in the neighborhood' when he came by to ask for your hand. We knew what he was about the moment he entered without you around."

Hannah grins. "Yes, he told me the story himself. Silly man."

Irma comes to Pa's side and hugs Hannah and her future brother-in-law. "Wonderful news. I didn't know a thing. This sure was a shock to me, just as Harry's showing up here tonight."

"Well, it seems this night is just fall of surprises," I say. "Congratulations, guys." I hug Hannah and shake Edward's hand.

"Thank you," Edward says, smiling.

"Quite a show we put on for you, Edward," I joke.

"Oh, Harry," Hannah says a grin.

"But hey," I say, "maybe we all needed a good cry before we could move on." I sigh deeply, my eyes on the ceiling, imagining Dawson up there in Heaven with the Good Lord. I can see his approval, and that's all I need. "God knows I've done that many times over these past several years."

"I'm ready to move on if you are," Hannah says.

I nod, half-smiling and turn toward this stranger who's gonna be my brother-in-law. "Welcome to the family, Edward. Are you sure you want to marry into this?"

Edward smiles. "Every bit of it."

I like this guy.

CHAPTER 36

"You didn't have to wait up for me."

The moment I enter, Kathy stands from her spot in the chair by the window, her book falling to the floor. "How did it go? I can't tell from your face."

I sigh in relief as my face melts into a smile. "I did it, Kath. I saw my family." I lead her to the pair of chairs, and we sit. I recount everything that happened in that old kitchen.

"Wow, that must have been quite the reunion. Your sister sounds like she was pretty broken up, although in her shoes, I'd probably feel the same way." She smiles, but her voice carries a serious undertone.

"Gee, thanks." I half-grin. "But I get it. Hannah had every right to be hurt, but we're fine now. Promise. Ma didn't let me leave without inviting us all there for Easter. She's thrilled to have more grandkids. My family can't wait to meet you."

"That's wonderful, Harry." Kathy takes my hands. "Do you wish you'd have gone to them sooner?"

The question hangs unanswered for several seconds. I stare into the darkness, hoping for an easy answer. "Maybe. If nothing else, I think Dawson and Pa would've hit it off something great."

This reply gets a chuckle outta Kathy, but I'm avoiding the real issue. Finally, I say, "I don't know, Kath. There were plenty of times I wished I'd've called. I did, once. Pa hung up 'cause I didn't say anything. Still, I guess my shame was too big to overcome until now."

"So, are you happy, Harry? I mean, really and truly happy?"

"I'm a messy work-in-progress, but compared to five years ago, yeah, I'm happy. I've got you and the kids, my family back, and your family. Can't really beat that."

We stand and kiss.

"That's enough thinking for tonight. Let's go to bed," I say.

As I follow her up the stairs into the dark, I whisper, "I still haven't seen Amy...or Erik."

* * *

Easter arrives. Standing in the yard, Kathy and I eye up the old Caddy I've spent years fixing.

"Well, it's ready. Are you sure you're okay to drive, Kath?"

"I'll be fine, Harry." The teasing tone in her voice draws a smile outta me.

"All right. I just can't wait to see the look on my folks' faces when I drive up in this thing."

"They'll be proud of you, Harry. Not only because you fixed a whole car, but because you fixed your life. I think they already know the second half of that."

"I hope so." I watch Kathy as she goes inside the house to get Gloria and Lucas.

A little while later, Kathy and the kids pile into the Ajax while I take the wheel of the Caddy. I've been behind this wheel before to test it out, but that was just a quick drive around the block. Still, there's a haunting feeling being in a car so much like the one I crashed. I shake my head to clear the memories that've stayed with me too long.

"I can do this," I murmur as I start up the car.

The drive takes all of about fifteen minutes. We park on the street and meet at the end of the driveway.

"It looks just like you described it," Kathy says, gazing up and down tree-lined Madison Avenue.

"Daddy, is Granma gonna do a egg hunt?" asks Gloria as she tugs on my arm.

"I dunno, pumpkin. Let's go inside and find out what she's got planned. One thing I do know is she's gonna be super excited to meet you and Lucas."

We take the short walkway to the front door. Kathy admires the large porch as I knock. Seconds later, Ma opens the door, Pa right behind her. Their faces break into smiles, and the hugs begin.

"Oh, come in, come in!" Ma exclaims. "You must be Kathy. And oh, this darling little girl must be Gloria..." She pats my daughter's head and then takes Lucas from Kathy, kissing him on the cheek. "He looks just like you did as a baby, Harry. What beautiful children. Gus, we have more grandchildren!"

Pa chuckles. "Yes, you said as much when Harry visited the first time, Lucy."

The next few minutes are a whirlwind of taking coats, leading us farther into the house, Kathy dropping off a cake she made, and Ma fussing over us. Irma comes down the stairs and beams, nearly crushing me in her arms.

"Harry! You came back again."

"Hey, kid, I promised I would."

Irma lets go and half-smiles. "I'm not really a kid anymore."

"No, you're right. You went and grew up on me while I was away, but I promise, Irma—no more of that. I ain't leavin' you guys again."

"I'll hold you to that. Come check out what Ma's got prepared for dinner." Irma leads me to the kitchen. I almost don't notice Amy. My older sister hasn't changed a bit. If anything, I hafta do a double-take to make sure it's her and not Hannah.

"Harry," she says, smiling slightly.

Ma and Pa have taken the rest of the family to the back yard, so it's quiet in a house where I'm used to noise. Irma follows them out, probably to give us some privacy.

"Hi, Amy." I keep my voice calm, like there's nothing strange about this conversation.

"You finally came back."

"Yeah." I eye up the food spread throughout the kitchen. "Ma's really outdone herself, like always."

Amy laughs softly. "You know Ma. She'll never change."

"Yeah. That's, uh, good to know. I mean, that some things never change."

"You've changed, Harry."

"Where are Jack and the kids?"

"Outside. I mean, you've changed for the better. Ma and Pa told me about your visit a few weeks ago. They said you've done well for yourself. I'm happy for you."

I smile in spite of myself. If only you knew the half of it, Amy. "I'd like to think I'm still the guy who can make you laugh."

"Stick around this time, Harry, and we'll find out." Amy hugs me.

We go outside to find the others, and I'm happy to see my kids playing with Amy's girls. I shake hands with Jack, who acts like it's only been a couple of weeks since we last saw each other. I meet Bethany, Amy's younger daughter. Jean's gotten so big. She was a baby the last time I saw her.

Eight years. That's how long it's been.

"I'm going back inside to check on the ham," Ma announces. "Gus, help the little ones find all the eggs, will you? It won't do for them to go bad and stink up the yard."

Pa laughs. "Okay, Lucy. Hey, Jack, Harry, help us out here."

Amy, Irma, and Kathy follow Ma soon after, leaving the guys and the kids to more or less play. It's a nice day, a little cool, but the daffodils are in full bloom in Ma's yard. After we're sure all the eggs have been found, I sit in one of the outdoor chairs with Pa and Jack on each side of me.

"When are the others gettin' here?" I ask. "I'm surprised Hannah's not here yet."

"Well, they know dinner's at 2:00," Pa says. "Can't be too much longer. And Hannah and Edward are visiting with his mother before coming here, I believe."

We talk about this and that for the next several minutes, but I start to feel antsy. I decide to go in and see how dinner's coming along. Ma and Amy chase me outta the kitchen. Another thing that hasn't changed. Kathy and Irma shoot me apologetic looks as I leave.

I debate on whether I should check out my old room or go back outside. Instead, I step out onto the front porch. Still no sign of Hannah. Moving to the bottom of the driveway by the rock, I look for Edward's car—not that I even know what to be on the lookout for. It was too dark that evening I came by the house for the first time to see much of anything.

I pull a pack of cigarettes outta my chest pocket and make to light one up when an Auburn sedan slows and turns into the driveway. I might as well be a yard decoration for how much like a statue I am as I watch my brother get out. Lily gets out on the other side, and before either of us guys can say anything, she shrieks and runs toward me, arms outstretched.

"Oh, my word! Harry, is that really you?" She hugs me with more strength than I expect from such a tiny thing.

I chuckle as I hug her back. "Hi, Lily, and yeah, it's me, in the flesh."

Lily releases me. "I didn't know you were coming today."

Erik stands just behind her, a look of concern on his handsome face. He seems like he wants to say something.

"I didn't know until a coupla weeks ago I'd be here." My eyes are on my brother as I talk to Lily.

"Lily, why don't you go inside and get a drink of water and put your feet up, eh, dear?" Erik says like he's talking to a child.

Lily giggles and waves him off. "Honestly, Erik, I'm not going to break. I'm not made of glass. I've just spent the last several hours sitting in a car. Sitting is the last thing I want to do right now, but I can see where I'm not wanted." She smiles at me and winks, then turns and leaves Erik and me standing there.

"So, uh—" I start to say, but I'm crushed in two strong arms.

Shocked, I hug Erik back.

He lets go and has the decency to blush.

I laugh. "Didn't know ya missed me that much, brother."

"Are you kidding? Harry, it's been... How long's it been?"

"Too long. So, Ma didn't tell you—"

"That you'd be here today?"

"Yeah. I stopped by the house not long ago. Quite the surprise. I thought poor Ma was gonna have a heart attack."

Erik claps me on the shoulder. "Your timing's always been awful, but here you are. Tell me what's going on with you."

"Well, I'm married to a great woman and have two kids, a boy and a girl."

"You mean, you're a dad? That's– that's great! Harry, what else have you been up to all these years?"

Where to start? There is a load of things I wanna tell you, Erik...one day. "Well, let's see. I got a job—nothing so fancy as an engineer, but I fix cars, mostly."

"That's great. You've really made a life for yourself."

"I guess, but it wasn't always easy. That's a story for another time." It would take hours to fill Erik in on Dawson and the years spent with Kathy's family. Someday I'll sit down with my whole family and share the less than pretty parts of my life with everyone at once, but not today. Seeing my family together again's a dream come true, and I ain't gonna ruin it. "But enough about me. What about you?"

"Pretty much the same daily grind—work and home."

"Nothing else?"

"Well, you know, we've, uh, done well for ourselves, I guess. We've traveled. Most people struggled financially where we didn't."

"But you had your own struggles." I remember our last conversation in jail like it was yesterday.

"True." Erik's voice holds a trace of hope. "Money and nice trips and things don't buy happiness. It's cliche, but it's a fact, Harry. I have to admit that I envy you—having your own family. You can't replace that with all the money in the world. And a job's just a job."

"Havin' kids and a wife who love me is more than I ever thought I'd have," I say quietly. I break outta my daze and smile. "But hey, enough of that serious talk. We're just waitin' on Hannah to get here, and then everyone'll be together again."

"Hannah's not here?"

"Didn't you hear that she's engaged?"

"No, I– I didn't know." Erik frowns. I can feel the shame pouring off him. "I guess I should've kept in touch better. I've got no excuse."

"Well, the only reason I know is 'cause she came to the house the same night I first visited. She's been dating a guy named Edward. Seems like a nice enough fella."

"So, is she with him right now?"

"Yeah, Pa said she'd be here soon. Visiting his mom or something."

Just then, Pa throws open the front door and yells, "Hey, you two! Come on inside! Dinner's nearly ready."

We exchange grins and join Pa and Jack in the living room. The women are still bustling about the kitchen. I can hear Ma exclaiming things like, "No, that goes over here!" and, "Wait, don't take that out of the oven yet!"

The kids are running around upstairs, their footsteps banging on the floorboards, the echoes going through the house like I remember from my childhood. The back door opens, and I hear more voices. Edward joins the men a moment later. Then Pa shares how he up and broke his leg with the new guy and Jack. The three of them block the way to the dining room and kitchen, so Erik and I light up and share some of Pa's ginger ale.

"You'll have to have kids of your own to add to the insanity." I grin at Erik, hoping to weasel something outta him.

Erik takes a sip of his drink. "Well, we might already be there."

My smile widens, my suspicions confirmed. I smack Erik on the back and chuckle. "You old dog! It's about time!"

Erik blushes. "Shh, we haven't even told Ma and Pa yet. Don't make a scene, Harry."

It takes me a while to stop laughing. "All right, I get it. I'm just happy for you, brother." I go serious. "I know you've been wantin' this for a long time. Congratulations."

Erik smiles, his eyes shining. "Thanks, Harry, truly."

"You weren't laid up that long," Hannah's voice cuts in. "You cursed more that night on the way to the hospital than I've ever heard, Pa!"

"You're ruining my story, Hannah," Pa says, smiling.

I try to catch Hannah's eye, but Ma announces dinner. We all manage to cram around the dining room table, and Pa leads grace. Hannah and I spot each other in the crowd and share a smile. The food's as delicious as ever. We talk ourselves stupid over the next hour around the table, and the fun continues until the sun starts to go down.

"I need to talk to you and Ma for a sec," I say to Pa that evening.

"All right, son." Pa motions me toward the kitchen, where Ma's cleaning up.

"I'm fine. I don't need any help," Ma says, her back to us. She turns. "Oh. I wasn't expecting you two. I already told Hannah and Amy a half a dozen times that I've got it."

"Harry's got something to say, Lucy."

Ma raises her eyebrows behind her glasses. "Oh?"

"Come outside with me for a minute."

My folks fall into silence as they follow me out the back door.

As we walk down the driveway, Pa asks, "What's going on, Harry?"

"I just wanna show you something."

We walk a bit farther until we reach the Caddy. In the semi-dark, it's hard to see much, but with the remaining sunlight hitting the hood just right, it's enough.

"I don't understand," Ma says.

"Does it look familiar?" I ask, running my hand along the side.

Pa steps closer and touches the hood, then the side door. He gasps. "It's just like our old Cadillac."

"That's right. I, uh, didn't really tell you the whole truth of what I do for a livin' when I came back. Guess I wanted you to think I was following in your footsteps and bein' a delivery man and all, Pa."

"Nonsense, Harry. You should do what you want. I gave up on making deliveries late last year. It was just too much anymore."

"Well, I do some deliveries, but that ain't what I came out here for. I fix cars, you see. I don't just do that on the side. I made you think it was the other way 'round. A great guy named Dawson taught me everything I know, and he's...he was Kathy's dad."

"Was?" Ma asks quietly.

"Yeah, he...he died last year." I don't need to go into the details of my conflicted feelings about Dawson and Pa, but still, this car's a mixture of everything I messed up for my own family and everything I fixed with Dawson's family.

"I'm sorry, son," Pa says. "He sounds like he was a great man."

"A shame we never got to meet him," Ma says.

"Yeah." Son. Pa's got every right to call me that. I blink the tears away. "Anyway, this car, it's for you. I– I fixed it."

"Oh, Harry." Ma cries and hugs me.

While I hold my mother close, I look into Pa's gleaming eyes and see nothing but pride.

"Thank you, Harry." Pa claps me on the shoulder.

"Sure thing, Pa. Uh, d'you mind if I just stay out here for a little while on my own? It's kinda been a long day. A great day, but long."

Pa chuckles. "I think Harry needs a break from all this, Lucy. Come now."

My parents retreat into the near darkness. I spend the next few minutes with only my thoughts for company, but unlike prison or those months right after Dawson's death, I feel free. I smoke another cigarette. The front door opens as I make my way back to my old yard, and I hear the voices of Edward and Hannah saying goodbye. Edward's car pulls away as Hannah turns toward the house. She stops and comes toward me as I step under the two sycamore trees by the street.

"Some day, huh?" she asks.

"Sure was."

"You're still smoking?"

"I've been smoking for years." I shrug. "So?"

"I didn't come here to talk about smoking. I just wanted to say...today was so great because you were back. Also your family and Erik and Lily. Having everyone together again was something I never thought I'd see."

I toss the cigarette aside and pull Hannah to me. "Good Lord, Hannah, I've missed you."

Hannah smiles up at me and returns the hug. "Silly brother, it's about time you figured out where you were meant to be."

Meant to be. Home. Family.

I can see Kathy and the kids through the front window. Ma and Pa are hugging them, like they're getting ready to leave. But we'll be back, very soon. My head spins. I can't understand it, but I love it. I love these people who are crazy enough to love me. After everything I've been through, here I am...right where I'm meant to be.

* * *

Later that evening, after we're home and the kids are in bed, Kathy and I step outside. The breeze is cool on my skin as we walk, hand in hand, deeper into the back yard. We sit in the damp grass. Silence passes between us, a stillness of understanding...the brush of her finger over my palm, the gentle weight of her head resting on my shoulder, the tickle of her hair on my cheek.

"Today was a great day, Harry," she says into the night.

I smile. "It was, wasn't it?"

"Your family is lovely. Hannah is every bit as sweet as I imagined, and your parents welcomed me and the kids with open arms."

A brief pang goes through my heart at the mention of parents. My eyes are on the stars. "It's a clear night."

Kathy shifts in my arms. "The stars, a million possibilities to discover."

"I have my star right here."

She pulls away from me and studies me in the near darkness, shaking her pretty head. "Harry, you are such a ham." Then she giggles and kisses me silly.

Each kiss is an undiscovered joy. I laugh like it's the first time. Like a baby who's just discovered he can laugh.

EPILOGUE

I could always find it in me to laugh after I learned the source of it—that true joy that only comes from knowing true love. The leaves are just poking out, the buds still on the trees. I walk, hunched over my cane. The ground should have a path carved in it, all the times I've walked these steps.

I stop, open the lawn chair, and ease my way into it.

"Hello, Kathy. It's been thirty-one years today since I said goodbye."

She is silent. Or is she? The leaves rustle above my silver head. I readjust my thick, square glasses on my nose. I smile.

"When will it be my day, Kath? I told Hannah to tell you I'd join you soon. That was ten years ago."

I could cry, but I don't. I've known tears too well, as much as I've known laughter. So many people—Pa, Ma, Dawson, Betty, Kathy, Erik, Hannah, Amy, yes...even Kat. All gone before me, but every one was part of me. Old Hank remains, as stubborn to go as I am, but an ever-steady friend. And sweet Irma, off living her life in California, is still my kid sister. I don't stand—well, sit—here today without knowing that I wouldn't be the man I am without them.

"Ah, it's okay, dear. You know, Heidi had another baby. Another great-grandkid. Beautiful girl named Addison. Addison, can you believe it? Never heard a name like that when I was a kid."

Sitting in a cemetery, some would say I'm a lonely old man. I'm old. I know that. Ninety-three ain't no walk in the park, but it is in the cemetery 'cause I figure I'll be joining these good folks before long.

I smile at the clouds. "Doc says it's only a matter of time. Six months at most. It's 2003 and no cure for cancer...what took you from me, what took Hannah and Erik. It's only fitting, ain't it? I say it's about time. Yeah, soon in God's eyes...thirty-one years. Ain't nothing." I take several seconds to stand as I lean on my cane. One step at a time, like everything in life. I stop in front of her tombstone and lay my hand on it. "See you soon, Kath."

ILLUSTRATIONS FROM A LAUGHING MATTER OF PAIN

Harry

By Cynthia Hilston

Dawson

Dawson and Harry in the garage

By Cynthia Hilston

Harry and Kat

Harry and Kathy

By Cynthia Hilston

A Laughing Matter of Pain

Distraught Harry

ABOUT THE AUTHOR

Cynthia Hilston is a thirty-something-year-old stay-at-home mom of three young kids, happily married. Writing has always been like another child to her. After twenty years of waltzing in the world of fan fiction, she has stepped away to do her debut dance with original works of fiction.

In her spare time—what spare time?—she devours books, watches *Doctor Who* and *Game of Thrones*, pets her orange kitty, looks at the stars, and dreams of what other stories she wishes to tell.

ALSO BY CYNTHIA HILSTON

Hannah's Rainbow: Every Color Beautiful

Lorna versus Laura: Lorna & Tristan Series #1

Mile Marker 139 (coming 2019)

Rocks and Flowers in a Box: Lorna & Tristan Series #2 (coming 2019)

Arianna: Lorna & Tristan Series #3 (coming 2020)

Murder: It's All in Your Head (coming 2021)

Short Stories:

Latent Infection (to be published in Horror13's anthology)

Flushed (to be published in A Writer's Path's anthology), third place winner:

[2018 Writing Contest Winners at A Writer's Path](#)

PRAISE FOR HANNAH'S RAINBOW: EVERY COLOR BEAUTIFUL:

"This is a beautiful story of how sometimes life can be cruel and unjust, but this can make you stronger and how not giving up goes a long way; after all, you can't have a rainbow without a little rain. " -Jessica Barbosa for Reader's Favorite

"It is a heartwarming story about family and relationships and will leave a lasting impression in the minds of readers." -Mamta Madhavan for Reader's Favorite

"Incredibly well-written and presented with tender emotions, Hannah's Rainbow is a fascinating saga that I would highly recommend, for it's not only interesting from c historical point of view but will certainly strike a chord with everyone." -Amazon Customer on Amazon

"A lovely story, loosely based on the author's grandmother. Cynthia Hilston's love of her grandmother shines through in this poignant story of family, relationships and life." -Kathleen Joyce on Amazon

"I've never cried when reading a story and this author managed to pull that emotion in her writing." -Amazon Customer on Amazon

"It is a beautiful story of love, loss, forgiveness, and family." -Paul Pater on Amazon

"It's a strong piece of fiction with strong characters with great development and a realness that hits home." -Kristina Losey on Amazon

"It does not read like a first novel. It shows a level of maturity and confidence far above many first books." -Paula on Amazon

PRAISE FOR LORNA VERSUS LAURA: LORNA & TRISTAN SERIES #1

"I think this book is a great read, and I think others will like this heartfelt story." -Daria White from Reader's Favorite

"This was a wonderful story of two people coping with the loss of loved ones. I enjoyed watching both Lorna and Tristan go on this journey of figuring out how to simply live again after going through so much pain." -K.B. on Amazon

"Lorna versus Laura is a twisting tale of grief and the lengths we will go to protect our own hearts." -Rebecca Charlton on Amazon

"The important messages it sends, such as the power of forgiveness and the necessity to move forward instead of living in the past, are dotted throughout the novel, making you root for the characters and hope for them to finally find their peace and a happy place despite all of the tragedies of the past." -Amazon Customer on Amazon

"This is a story of the redemptive power of forgiveness, both of oneself and others. The characters are full of life and complexity, and their love is like a roller coaster ride." -Kelly Griffiths on Amazon

"Thrilled to have taken a chance on such a new, yet detailed author!" -SuzieQute on Amazon

CONNECT WITH CYNTHIA HILSTON

Did you enjoy this book? Hate it? Whatever your thoughts, please leave a review on Amazon and/or Goodreads! I'd really appreciate it. Reviews help authors. Thank you!

Website: http://www.cynthiahilston.com

Facebook: http://www.facebook.com/cynthiahilstonauthor

Instagram: http://www.instagram.com/authorcynthiahilston

Twitter: http://twitter.com/cynthiahilston

Goodreads: http://www.goodreads.com/cynthiahilstonauthor

EXCERPT FROM MILE MARKER 139

(coming late 2019)

A woman with inch-long hair and large black sunglasses steps out of her car at 3:14 AM at the rest area at mile marker 139 on the Ohio Turnpike, just like she does every night. She glances left to right, right to left, and dashes across the parking lot to one of the picnic tables, the one farthest from the building. And sits as the sun comes up, her yellowed fingers shaking as she smokes one cigarette after another.

It's usually the really young and the really old who notice her, and today is no different.

"One thirty-nine. Three-fourteen. Eight-twenty," mutters the woman, repeating it like a mantra.

The words reach a curious little girl's ears mid-morning. She turns toward the odd woman, then runs away. Her mom calls her back. "Stay away from strangers, darling."

Later that day, as the last rays of the dying sun illuminate his wrinkled face, an elderly man hobbles with his walker, sadly shaking his head, for he knows something of death. This youngish woman is living death, more sorrowful than frightful.

Her name is Michelle, although her friends call her Shelley. Or they would, if she had any friends.

CHAPTER 1: MIKE POPKINS

November 22, 2017 – Wednesday

The wheels squeak as he pushes the mop bucket across the floor. A couple of surly truckers look up from their large coffees and glare. He's used to it. He hates the noise, too.

Mike Popkins eases the rickety bucket to the men's room and ropes off the entrance– "closed for cleaning."

His arthritic hands clutch the mop. He squeezes the extra water from it with the bucket's wringer and drops the floppy, disgusting thing onto the grimy floor. Back and forth. Side to side.

"Hey, can I use the bathroom?" someone asks.

"Bathroom's closed," Mike says. He sniffs, just getting over a cold, and pushes his thick glasses up his long nose.

The man outside the bathroom mutters. Probably a foul-mouthed trucker.

"The things I put up with," Mike murmurs to himself.

In five minutes, he finishes cleaning and leaves the bathroom. It's pitch dark beyond the doors to the rest area and about five in the morning. For as long as Mike can remember, he's worked third shift as the janitor. Few guys want the job or the hours, but he's never been a picky man. Still, age is catching up with him as he takes a break and eases into one of the chairs on the rim of the coffee area. Brewing Up Some Happiness is the name of the latest trendy coffee joint.

To Mike, the coffee is overpriced, but he pays the price because he doesn't even take the time to make his own coffee at home. Besides, in another hour, he'll be free to go.

Mike shifts in the seat, wondering if he'd be smart to diet. Poor Barb, bless her soul, would have nagged him for the extra thirty pounds he'd put on since her death five years ago.

"Excuse me?"

Mike snaps out of his thoughts and stares at the woman in front of him. He's seen her plenty of times before, although she's usually outside at that picnic table. Some lunatic, he figures. Homeless, maybe, although she drives a car. Still, maybe she lives out of her car.

"Yeah?" he grunts.

"You got a smoke?"

Mike scowls. "Do I look like a charity giver, darlin'?"

"Sorry. It's just I'm out. I've, uh, seen you smoke a cigarette or two here and there."

"Oh, fine. Here." Mike stands, digs in his pants pocket, pulls out a pack, and offers her one.

"Thanks." She snatches the cigarette from Mike's hand like it's already lit and might burn her.

"You need a light?" Mike steps back a bit, hesitant. This odd woman has the look of a deer about to dash away.

"No." She reaches into her coat pocket and pulls out a lighter.

"You can't smoke in here." And here he was offering her a light just a second ago. What's gotten into him?

She shrugs. "I'm going back out anyway."

Just as she turns to leave, Mike pursues her. "Wait. It's freezing out there."

The late November weather doesn't keep people from traveling for Thanksgiving. Mike realizes that's tomorrow and half-wonders if he should call his son and accept the invitation to dinner after all.

"I'm fine."

Her dull tone speaks of anything but fine. Mike's mind whirls. Normally, he wouldn't care what some stranger does with her life, but something about this woman pulls at him. All the feelings that plagued him for months after Barb's death return. Why should he care if a vagrant has somewhere to go for Thanksgiving? What does he need to know about her story? She's probably a drunk and a drug addict. Maybe she's walked out on her family. But...

"I've seen you." Mike's mouth is dry. He licks his lips and bites the inside of his cheek. He's unshaven, his salt and pepper hair a mess until his ball cap. He knows he's not the picture of empathy, but his blue eyes have seen hurt enough times in his sixty-two years to know a thing or two.

"What?" She hovers by the exit. Her eyes are usually hidden by sunglasses, but they stare, exposed. Mike doesn't know if he's ever seen such hollow, dark eyes.

Sitting out there at that picnic table. I work here, young lady, every damn night but Sunday. You think I wouldn't notice you out there? It's been at least a couple of months you've been coming here every night. Don't know how long you stay or if you ever really leave, but you turn up right about three o'clock every morning. I'm due to leave soon, and I'm betting you'll still be out there for hours after that."

She just stares. The crease between her eyebrows deepens, but then she turns and the doors close automatically behind her.

Mike sighs. "Why do I bother?" he mutters, shaking his head.

He's got a job to do, damn it. He can't waste his time worrying about the crazies when he's got trash to take out.

ACKNOWLEDGEMENTS

My most heartfelt thanks go out to members of the writers group from the North Ridgeville Library: Kathleen Joyce, Kelly Griffiths, Betty Wilson, Alexia Patrick, Nancy Beach, Paul Pater, John Arnold, Scott Heidrich, Larry Schroeder, Richard Mann, and Scot Allyn. It's been an immense pleasure to be part of this wonderful group of writers since 2016. Without their invaluable critique of my work, chapter by chapter, over the course of a year, the final product would not be what it is. I am extremely grateful for their insight, feedback, support, and most of all, friendship.

A big thank you to my mom, Gail Combs, and online friend and fellow writer, Rachelle Shaw, for reading an early draft of this work and giving their overall impressions.

I am grateful for the support of my husband, Erik Hilston, for encouraging my writing and for listening honestly to what I read him and his help to develop Harry better. His feedback was invaluable for getting into the head of a man and writing him (hopefully) convincingly.

Finally, I thank Cole Graham, who inspired me in the first place to create this story. When I wrote *Hannah's Rainbow*, that a story based on my grandma's life, a story I wanted to tell for years. Harry came alive in those pages and was loosely based on my grandma's real brother, Karl. Like Hannah and Harry, my grandma (Emma) and Karl were very close, Karl only two years older than her (like Harry is to Hannah). When Harry stepped out of Hannah's story for a long stretch, many readers wanted to know more about him. What was his story? Cole's interest in Harry, in liking the character, is what prompted this spinoff, which became more detailed than I ever imagined. I also thank Cole for years and years of supporting and reading my stories, even long before I wrote original stuff. He, like me, sees the beauty in those flawed underdog characters, and I love that. Those are the characters I love.

Made in the USA
Middletown, DE
09 June 2019